Praise for *More Lives Than One*:

'an idiosyncratic blend of her journalistic voice
. . . with the skills of a writer who understands
the proper balance in a novel between issue and
narrative. This is her best novel [and] will find an
answering echo in many readers' Elizabeth Buchan,
The Times

'the kind of book that you race to finish and then
think about for a long time afterwards'
Beverly Davies, *The Lady*

'all the compassion characteristic of her writing
in her previous novels and columns . . . This is
a humane and perceptive novel' *Woman & Home*

'done with a finesse which makes the words live on
in your memory long after the novel has been put
away' Gina Sykes, *The Examiner*

'As ever, Libby Purves draws you into the laughter
and tears in the life of her characters, in this case
teachers Kit and Anna . . . Like all her books, this
is a cracking story'
Woman's Weekly

'a brilliant dissection of troubled lives' *Prima*

'Purves's evocative descriptions of Venice intensify
an already gripping narrative' Poppy Davidson,
Books Gazette

'a good story, crisply and lightly told, that touches
on many of teaching's current preoccupation and
dilemmas and that grows in depth as it unfolds' *The
Times Educational Supplement*

Also by Libby Purves

Fiction

Casting Off (1995)
A Long Walk in Wintertime (1996)
Home Leave (1997)

Non-Fiction

The Happy Unicorns (ed) (1971)
Adventures Under Sail, H. W. Tilman (ed) (1982)
Britain at Play (1982)
All at Sea (ed) (1984)
Sailing Weekend Book (1985) (with Paul Heiney)
How Not to Be a Perfect Mother (1986)
Where Did You Leave the Admiral? (1987)
How to Find the Perfect Boat (1987)
The English and Their Horses (1988) (jointly with Paul Heiney)
How Not to Raise a Perfect Child (1991)
Working Times (1993)
How Not to Be a Perfect Family (1994)
One Summer's Grace (1989; new edition 1997)
Holy Smoke (1998)

Children's books

The Hurrican Tree (1988)
The Farming Young Puffin Fact Book (1992)
Getting the Story (1993)

More Lives Than One

Libby Purves

FLAME
Hodder & Stoughton

First published in 1998 by Hodder and Stoughton
A division of Hodder Headline PLC
First published in paperback in 1999 by Hodder and Stoughton
A Flame Paperback

A CIP catalogue record for this title is available
from the British Library

ISBN 0 340 68043 1

Typeset by Palimpsest Book Production Limited,
Polmont, Stirlingshire
Printed and bound in Great Britain by
Caledonian International Book Manufacturing Ltd, Glasgow

Hodder and Stoughton
A division of Hodder Headline PLC
338 Euston Road
London NW1 3BH

To Rose for all the good advice
on schools (and teachers)

1988

It began with Anna Melville, nineteen years old and defiantly
alone, clinging to the rusting roll-bar of a Bedouin jeep a hundred
miles down Sinai. The desert road was straight and featureless,
strewn with boulders and humped by the earth-cracking heat.
When the jeep hit a bump particularly hard she was flung against
the juddering frames of the front seats; bracing herself with a
damp hand, she would clutch at the yellow foam rubber which
snaked out through jagged tears in the upholstery.

Once, stricken with guilt at having done damage to the tool of
Ari and Muhammad's trade, she bent to try and stuff the padding
back in through the hole. As she did, the jeep hit another bump
and her head collided with the metal frame. Defeated, she sat
up again and concentrated on survival. The driver and his
aged, straight-backed father in the front seat exchanged staccato
remarks in their own language, oblivious of their passenger's
panting dismay. This unawareness did not bother Anna; for
one thing, in her present confusion one kind word might well
have made her cry. For another, after two weeks in Egypt she
had accepted the double lowliness of being a foreigner and a
young woman. Coming as she did from a nation, class and
generation where pretty young women had little doubt about
their own status, she found it interesting and even piquant to be
discounted thus. At last she was sharing the experience of most
of the world's women; slumming it for a while in the sisterhood
of ignored females. It would be something to remember, like the
pyramids.

And the driving. The jeep hit a particularly deep pothole,

bounced out of it and skidded before accelerating furiously onward with a force which flung her backwards until she could feel the sweat-slicked plastic of the seat through her cotton shirt. The old man in the front seat yawned and fell asleep. Perhaps, she thought, Bedouin phlegm in the face of this wild ride could be explained by early familiarity with the dreadful jolting paces of a trotting camel. She had ridden one with Rob and the others in Upper Egypt, clinging on as the creature jerked along the track on feet spongier than rubber tyres. Perhaps the dark men around her, cool as cats with their shamaghs wound carelessly round their heads, considered this horrible jeep a comparatively smooth and gentle way to travel.

Or perhaps – she looked out at the yellow mountains stretching immeasurably in the hot haze – it was simply that they were so grateful to be motorized that no discomfort could reach them. Speed must still seem wonderful to a race which had survived for centuries by crossing vast tracts of pitiless rock and rubble on long, slow camel journeys. There had been a camel train on the skyline an hour ago when the jeep stopped for the men to pray. Against the afternoon sun it was a line of black silhouettes, paper cut-outs from the set of a Nativity play. Anna, sore and tired and frightened by her own temerity in being here alone, had drawn obscure comfort from the sight of it and from the bowing, murmuring men. She was doing what she had meant to do: travelling in wild places, seeing immemorial sights, making her own way. Without Rob. For all she cared, Rob could stay forever on Al Daha beach, flirting with his stupid new friends and smoking himself silly. She, Anna, had not saved up for two years in order to sit around on kilims smoking hash and listening to bad guitarists. As she had forcefully told Rob, she could do those things back at college.

'There wouldn't be such good sunsets back in Keele, though, would there, babe?' he had said idly. She could see him now as he said it: cross-legged on the concrete porch of the squalid bungalow, his pale dirty hair glowing in the pink evening light, rolling a Rizla paper round its crumbly, gritty contents. As she finally left him, after a year of coupledom, he could hardly even be bothered to raise his eyes and watch her go.

Anna blinked, furious at her own tears. It was nearly sunset again now, and the light in the west took on miraculous colours as it filtered through the dust of the spiky mountains. Anna spoke, as steadily as she could through the juddering of her body, to the driver.

'Ari. How far now? To Manta Bay camp?'

'Very soon now, miss,' said the driver. 'See?'

Taking one hand off the wheel, he gestured to the left. Anna could see nothing but the distant blue prospect of the Gulf of Aqaba and a dusty yellow moonscape of rocks and sand. In a few moments, though, Ari pulled the wheel hard and left the main road for what she could now see was a faint but usable track towards the sea.

'Are you sure I will be able to get a room here? Without booking? Wouldn't it be better to go on with you to Sharm?'

'This very good place. It is my uncle. He is Sheikh Al Arak, this his camp. Very good room. Very beautiful coral reef. Very many rays. No bad shark.' Terrifyingly, Ari swivelled right round to grin at her, one hand resting on the wheel.

Anna saw no building between the road and the sea. A cold nervousness invaded her; she had been rash and petulant in taking a long lift into nowhere. She knew nothing of Ari. She had a flash of longing for Rob, for his sheer size and maleness. But what use would these things be, given that he did not care what became of her?

Tears pricked behind her eyes, not because she had been in love with Rob but because she had not. A new sense of shame overwhelmed her as she recognized that only convenient friendship had ever bound them, with sex as an occasional shared pastime. At college this had not seemed ignoble; against the desert and the sea it somehow did. It shamed her that she had made do with so little, so lightly. During the whole Rob year she had avoided the songs and poetry of passion because she knew that their idle mating had nothing to do with the vast incomprehensible feelings others sang of. She had left the party at Al Daha on a surge of bravado and romanticism; now the romance was jolted out of her and there was nobody to see the bravado, so two lonely tears cut rivulets through the desert dust on her cheeks.

*   *   *

Ari braked the jeep, throwing up a shower of sand and small stones, and said simply, 'Here. You speak to this man, he give you room.'

The man stood at a desk in a long, low, open-fronted stone building, the size of a seaside bungalow. It had the familiar Moorish arches and slapdash white paint and a handwritten sign saying 'RESEPTION'. Further along the stony shore was another building, this time with a palm thatch shelter in front of it, marked 'DIVE CENTER'. Racks of scuba tanks, their paint peeling, stood out in the sun, fins and masks lay on flat boulders and rubber suits swung on rope clotheslines between the pillars of the shelter. There were a number of thatched beach umbrellas, some with windbreaks, and a ragged cluster of red-and-white striped tents whose guy ropes were held down by rocks. A goat wandered among them, ripping occasionally at the ropes with big yellow teeth.

Anna, fighting back panic, went to RESEPTION where the man stood at the counter, studiously ignoring her, his cotton robe fluttering white in the sea breeze.

'Is it possible,' she began, 'to have a room? A single room?'

The man looked at her. Another crazy yellow-haired foreign woman, all alone with a great burden on her back.

'You with diving?' he asked abruptly. 'Coral Scuba? Or Oxforuniversity?'

'No,' said Anna. 'I'm on my own. Ari said you'd have a room.'

He sniffed. 'Oxforuniversity has got one hut, empty, no people. This is booked but not paid. They say they do not pay.' He looked as if he wanted to spit on the ground, but did not. 'You sleep there, you pay. One week, two?'

'Just a couple of nights. I'm taking the bus down the coast to Ras Muhammad on Wednesday,' said Anna.

'One week. Bus is not good,' said the man, still abruptly. 'One week, mi-ni-mum stay. You give me passport, Mustaf will show you.'

After some argument, Anna reluctantly gave up her passport and followed a lithe boy in cotton robes who showed no inclination to help with her rucksack. She had time to glance sideways and notice some young men lounging on rugs in a big tent, before the boy began to climb to the left away from it. Sweating, she followed as he bounded up uneven rocky steps to a higher level of the seafront cliff. At the top, on the red-brown plateau, she now saw that there were more beach umbrellas, this time with makeshift walls of bamboo sticks. Pushing aside a veil of palm leaves across the doorway of the nearest one, the guide ducked his head and jerked it towards the low, dim interior.

Anna bent and peered in. Most of the floor space was occupied by an ancient double divan mattress, its cover peeling at the corner to show rusted springs. On it was a folded sheet, surprisingly clean, and an old and felted blanket. The last of the light filtered in through the bamboo walls. Behind her, the guide said, 'Shower, toilet,' and when she turned she saw that he was pointing at another blockhouse a hundred yards away along the clifftop. Then he was gone, bounding down the slope, his headdress streaming in the wind from the sea. Anna eased off her rucksack, put it on the small patch of floor beside the mattress, took a long shuddering breath and flung herself face downward on the mattress, alone. It was her twentieth birthday.

It was an hour before she felt sufficiently composed to climb back down the steps and look for food. It was dark now, with a few stars over the jagged horizon. She moved towards the red glow of a fire and the yellow light of lanterns and found herself at the big tent. There were six young men there, lounging on rugs on the sand. They looked curiously at her, and one motioned towards a counter in the far corner, placed in front of a dark opening. Emerging from this, presumably from some kind of inner tent, was the wiry youth who had led her to the hut. He said abruptly, 'You eat now?'

'Yes please. Is there a menu? Do I sit, er . . .'

Behind her, one of the young men sniggered. She stiffened and swung round, her fit of misery turned suddenly into healing rage.

'Is something funny?'

'No,' said the boy hastily. 'Just the idea of Mustaf offering anybody a menu. Come and sit down.' He had a soft, Midwest twang.

Gingerly, Anna sat down on the rug, to find the surface

surprisingly soft. She leaned her back against a mound, equally soft.

The American boy said, 'More comfy 'n it looks, huh? Ten layers of rug under here. When it gets worn out, they whap another layer on. We call it home.' He stretched out a foot and kicked a piece of wood further onto the fire which burned, low and smoky, on a heap of stones in front of them.

'Are you on holiday?' asked Anna.

'Coral Scuba. One week at Sharm el Sheikh, one week in the desert. It's the last night here. We're going to some oasis tomorrow. All the other guys are German.' He gestured to the rest of the group who sat a little apart from him, smoking and talking quietly. 'I'm studying in Freibourg, so I came along. Name's Eddie. You here for the diving?'

'No,' said Anna. Mustaf appeared silently beside her, and put down a wooden dish with a pool of tahini on it, a salad, and a bowl of chips with a few strips of cold fried chicken on the top. She glanced up, smiling at the dark impassive face. 'Thanks. I'm sorry to be late. I see everybody else ate long ago.'

'No problem,' said the boy, and turned away, not smiling back.

The American grinned and said, 'It really is no problem, not tonight. You're lucky. The Oxford lot are night-diving, so they aren't in yet.'

'Oxford?' said Anna, then remembered. 'Oh, the man said Oxford University. It's one of their booked huts I've been put in.'

'Jeez, they'll be thrilled,' said the American. 'There's been a row going on for two days about that. They turned up one guy short, and the camp says they have to pay for the hut.'

'Well, so they should,' said Anna, dipping a chip in the tahini and finding, as she ate it, that the combination of flavours and textures worked strangely well. 'If they booked it.'

'That's what their boss Kit said. But his other guys didn't want to. They're all students, he's a bit older. He's their instructor. There was a row. Two rows. First the one between Kit and his guys, with him threatening to cut the dives if they didn't fall in line. Then another one, when he wasn't looking, with the young guys going on at the Bedus and calling them stupid towelheads.'

Anna frowned. 'That's terrible. They sound like a shower.'

'They're not so bad really,' said the American boy. 'They're just big kids. They've been pissed off ever since they found out Muslims don't sell beer.' He looked up at the sound of heavy footfalls on the coarse sand and rubble beyond the tent. 'You'll see. Here they come. The Empire strikes back.'

Anna followed his gaze and saw a shadowy group of young men, swaggering and laughing as they walked up from the dive shelter. A snatch of 'Food, glorious food!' was taken up by two or three of them in rough, ragged, adolescent voices and there was a cry of 'Feed us, Mustaf baby!' From behind them came a deeper, steadier voice, and Anna noticed a tall man following a few paces after the main group.

'Say please,' the voice said.

'Food pleeeese!' said the voices together.

'*And* say sorry,' said the voice from the darkness again.

'Aw, we're sorry, Mustaf.'

'Mr Mustaf.'

'Sorry we were rude foreign yobs.'

'Sorry we have no manners'

'And we'll pay for the hut.'

'And this is a superb camp. World class. The huts are palatial. Anything else I may have said, disregard it. That was nitrogen narcosis speaking. My veins are clear of toxic bubbles now, and I see it for the architectural triumph it is.'

'Cut it, Jeremy,' said the deep voice again. 'Enough's enough.'

'Sorry. Last toxic bubble now dispersed. Promise.'

The group were in sight now, under the paraffin lanterns which swung from the bamboo frame at the edge of the tent. Anna saw six young men, whose ragged shorts and T-shirts could not disguise the unmistakable loose-limbed loping arrogance of the British public schoolboy. She rose stiffly to her feet, and said awkwardly to the American, 'I'd better go and get some sleep.'

From the back of the group the older man said, 'I'm sorry. Don't let this rabble drive you away.'

'They're not. I'm tired.'

'We deserve this,' mourned one of the boys. 'No beer, no women, then the first girl all week turns out to be a mirage.'

'Hey, beautiful, you coming diving?'

'Need a buddy?'

'She doesn't need your heavy breathing. Don't go with him, ducky. He's so susceptible he'll use up all his air in ten minutes.'

She smiled down, less tensely, at the boys who had flopped with careless grace on the mats nearest to the fire. For all their noisy arrogance they struck her now as harmless, a litter of romping puppies.

The older man said, 'Have you got a torch for getting up the hill?'

'No,' said Anna. 'I hadn't realized quite what a camping sort of camp it was. Camp-hotel, it said. I suppose I read the hotel bit and censored out the camp.'

'You'll be glad it's a camp,' said the tall man, 'when you see the moonlight coming through the hut walls. No sodium lights to spoil it. Let me light you up there. We've got spare dive torches in the truck. I'll give you one tomorrow.'

'Thanks.'

Half embarrassed, half pleased to be the object of chivalry after days of disregard from Egyptians and months of egalitarian mateyness from Rob, Anna followed the man and his torch. There was a light, cool breeze on the hillside and the sharp mountains were black shapes carved out of a jewelling of cold white stars. The man moved surely, agilely over the stones and up the rough stairway, holding the torch back to light her more uncertain footsteps.

At the hut he politely inquired whether she had matches for the lantern, and produced some. When the wick flared into life, she saw his face: hard with fresh air and exercise, dark-browed, energetic, the mouth in a quirky, crooked half-smile. But his eyes were soft and wide, and looked at her in the lamplight with equal surprise.

'Kit Milcourt,' he said. He handed her the box of matches, smiling again.

And Anna knew, all of a sudden, what the poems had been about.

2

Kit, or so he always claimed, saw his future in the same moment of lamplight as Anna. Plenty of girls had thrown themselves at him but he had reached the age of twenty-eight uncaptured. He had a name for chill asceticism among his peers in the bank, and among the young men and women who followed him underwater and on the mountainsides.

In another milieu he might have been the subject of irreverent whispering, but when a man is an expert diver, daring free-climber and marathon finisher, some compensatory law of machismo makes his peers overlook the romantic shortfall of his life. To question Kit's credentials as a real man when he was fresh up from a fifty-metre blue hole or fresh down from an Alp would have been out of place.

'No time for girls,' the men would say, but with respect rather than curiosity. They had girlfriends and wives of their own, after all; they knew all too well how easy it is for women to prevent a man going for the highest peaks and deepest caverns. Not to mention the most expensive equipment. However essential women were to them personally, Kit's outdoor companions could see quite easily that if you could somehow learn to manage without them, life would be a lot simpler.

As for the girls Kit taught to dive and climb, it generally took them time to realize, as one crudely put it, that they were never going to undress this particular Action Man. But one by one they came to understand the hopelessness of sighing after him and gave up, some with their dignity intact and some without. All the same, Kit – who had a kind heart and hated to disappoint – preferred to lead all-male groups. So when his old college contacted him at short notice to replace the divemaster instructor on a Red Sea fortnight, he thankfully remembered that this particular citadel had not yet fallen to women, and rearranged his holiday dates at work.

'Another free holiday?' they said in the bank. 'Lucky for some.'

With his very heavy diving bag and very light backpack he duly met six undergraduates at Gatwick Airport, each armed with a club diving qualification and the kind of baseless confidence which helps young men believe that a brief immersion in a Midlands reservoir makes them natural-born kings of the coral. And that is how, worn down by four days of exercising steady, good-humoured discipline on his rubber-clad rabble, Kit Milcourt met Anna Melville and had his life transformed.

He escorted her up the hill that first night as a courtesy, a counterweight to the boys' teasing. In the flare of the lamp, though, he saw her face as he had never seen a woman's face before. As he turned away from her to walk down under the stars to his supper, Kit felt a pang of loss which made him gasp. It was as if he was down on the reef and his air bottle had run out. Shocked, staring into the smoky campfire, he ate hardly any of his food. When the boys had stolen his last few chips and dispersed to their messy huts, he sat for a long while, watching the glimmer of starlight on the calm black sea and thinking.

'You can come on the dive boat,' said the boy Jeremy coaxingly to Anna in the morning. She was at the dive shelter, hiring a mask and fins to snorkel the reef by the beach. The Oxford party had clustered round her. 'You can come down to the Ras Muhammad, the reserve. There'll be shallow bits. The coral's brilliant down there. You can snorkel while we dive. Oh, go on.'

'We need civilizing,' said another, seriously. 'Kit says we're a disgrace to Britain. If we had female influence—'

'You could be a mother to us, Wendy!' squeaked a third in Disneyesque tones. 'We're the Lost Boys. You could give us *thimbles*.'

'I'm not sure,' began Anna a little stiffly, but a third boy interrupted.

'Say yes, quick. Here comes Cap'n Hook. We'll tell him.'

Kit was approaching, dive bag in his hand, wearing nothing but a faded pair of blue denim shorts and some ancient leather sandals. He smiled tentatively at Anna.

'Are they pestering you?'

'No, no, I'm just going snorkelling.'

Kit hesitated. 'We have the dive boat on charter. You could come down to the Ras with it, if you like.'

'That's what we keep *telling* her!' howled the boys.

'They cook us lunch on board,' said Kit. 'Fish stew. There's always too much. And the patch we're diving today has got a high reef table. You could snorkel there. Ahmed will keep an eye on you from the boat. You're really welcome. It's cooler out on the water.' He heard himself rattling on, sounding so unlike his normal self that he fell abruptly silent.

'Come on,' said the boys, severally and together.

So Anna, still tired, went along with the tide of goodwill and soon found herself moving steadily southward across the waves on a battered, workmanlike converted fishing boat. She sat for a while on the lower rail, fending off boisterous flirtation from the boys and admiring the golden desert coast. After a time, a heated discussion about equipment broke out among her admirers, and she took advantage of the distraction to climb the ladder to the upper deck.

The skipper Ahmed stood barefoot at the wheel, looking ahead at the horizon. The wind was from the south, dead on the bow, so that his long white robe was blown flat against his thin chest and legs and streamed raggedly behind him. Anna saw rolled mattresses and blankets under the benches beside the helm, and realized that he and the boy Aziz who was chopping fish down in the galley must sleep permanently aboard the boat. Walking down that morning from the hut she had seen them on the upper deck praying towards Mecca.

Ahmed turned slightly when he heard her and inclined his head with dignity. Anna bowed her head back, glad that she was wearing a modest cotton sarong and shirt. She had given up shorts and bare midriffs in Al Taba, after dressing on the first day as the other tourist girls did and noticing a look in the desert men's eyes which was neither lust nor contempt, but a kind of shocked sorrow. After that, pleading her pale skin, she made a point of covering her body almost as thoroughly as an Egyptian woman.

Away from the lower deck, far from the engine noise and the boys' commotion and the clanking of dive tanks and the swaying of the rubber suits on hangers, this small high platform moved across the face of the waters with the timeless quiet of a sailing ship. Anna looked ahead and thought about the point where the two horns of the Red Sea would meet: the Gulfs of Aqaba and Suez, merging in the rocky coralline chaos of the Ras Muhammad reefs. She took a deep breath and smiled. She was travelling. Travelling on, alone, with Rob and the others fading into the banality of beach life far behind her.

She tilted her chin to the wind, and felt her hair lift and flutter like a banner. Kit Milcourt, his long legs sprawled on the deck and his back against a reel of cable, sat reading a few feet away from her. He glanced up, amused at her Valkyrie pose, and said, 'Glad you came?'

'Yes.' She could not look away. The silence grew. She had to say something. 'What are you reading?' His book was old, and thin, in dark-green cloth binding stained with much travelling.

'Hassan. James Elroy Flecker.'

'I don't know it.'

'Sit down, then. I'll read to you.' The command came so naturally from him that Anna, without thinking it odd, sank down next to him on the hot wood. Kit did not look at her again but picked up the book and began to read.

> *Away, for we are ready to a man!*
> *Our camels sniff the evening and are glad.*
> *Lead on, O Master of the Caravan,*
> *Lead on the Merchant-Princes of Bagdad . . .*

She leaned inward to look over his shoulder as he read, and saw that it was a play. Kit, however, read it on as poetry, not naming separate speakers and ignoring any illogicality this might produce in the verse. Anna decided not to try and make sense of who was persuading who, and who was going where, but leaned back with her eyes closed, letting the images flow past her: rose-candy and spikenard, Indian carpets dark as wine, terebinth and oil and spice, swords engraved with storks and apes and crocodiles, ragged dirty-bearded pilgrims walking through it all into wilderness. She abandoned herself to the swooning exoticism of the verse.

> *We are the Pilgrims, master; we shall go*
> *Always a little further: it may be*
> *Beyond that last blue mountain barred with snow*
> *Across that angry or that glimmering sea.*

Anna shivered suddenly. Kit paused, and glanced at her.

'I half know it,' she said. 'So many lines borrowed. Like bits of music you recognize and don't know why, but you want to cry. Who was he?'

'A late Victorian,' said Kit. 'Killed off by overseas service in Beirut, died at thirty-one. Never even had the play published in his lifetime.' He looked down at Anna, his eyes narrowed with amusement at her emotion, and dropped his voice to a soupy, comic reverence. 'But his moosic still lives on.'

'Oh, don't!' said Anna, in real distress. 'You've spoilt it.'

'I won't,' he said. 'I don't think so. It's not that easy to spoil.' And they stared into one another's eyes, mooncalves for a moment.

Then Kit picked up the shabby green book again and said briskly, 'It isn't very feminist, you know. The women get dumped. They keep calling "O, Turn your eyes to where your children stand. O Stay!" and the men still go off, and never mind the children.' He read:

> *What would ye, ladies? It was ever thus.*
> *Men are unwise and curiously planned*
> *They have their dreams and do not think of us*
> *But take the Golden Road to Samarkand.*

Anna said nothing. Rob had had no dreams.

Kit continued lightly, 'Poor women, left behind while the men walk off to find a prophet who might not even be there. Bet they don't pay child maintenance.'

Anna looked at his profile and said steadily, 'It isn't only men who can walk off into the desert. I did. Yesterday. I did exactly that. It was my boyfriend who decided to stay put and sit around smoking dope on the beach.'

'Then I dedicate it to you,' said Kit, and read:

> *Sweet to ride forth at evening from the wells,*
> *When shadows pass gigantic on the sand*
> *And softly through the silence beat the bells*
> *Along the Golden Road to Samarkand.*

He looked towards her and for a crazy moment, her heart hammering, Anna thought he would kiss her. Involuntarily she closed her eyes. She breathed the exhalation of his breath and her chest constricted, painfully, as it never had in all her twenty years. But in a moment his voice read on, measured as before:

> *We travel not for trafficking alone;*
> *By hotter winds our fiery hearts are fanned;*
> *For lust of knowing what should not be known*
> *We take the Golden Road to Samarkand.*

The next days passed in a haze of heightened feeling. Kit and Anna sat together undisturbed for long hours on the upper deck as the boat ploughed along the coast to each new diving site. Sometimes he read aloud but mostly they talked, laying their lives and hopes out before one another like precious carpets.

'I've got a sister who's just married,' Anna would say. 'Mary. She's sweet, she's really funny, she's my favourite person. And I've got a brother who's terribly noisy and boisterous and lives for cars, you'd hate him. My parents live in Richmond, which was a pretty good reason to go to college in Staffordshire.'

'I've just got my parents.' Kit frowned, fiddling with the book which, as always, lay on his lap. 'My dad used to be a prep school headmaster in a windswept barracks called Priory Shore. Right down in Cornwall. They still live there, but Ma is very frail. I live in a horrible chi-chi flat in Docklands. Handy for work.'

The banalities of what they told one another were belied by

the looks they gave; Keele and Richmond, Docklands and Cert. Ed exams and the Institute of Bankers became words as glittering as spikenard and terebinth, caliph and scimitar.

Other hours were spent with the boat bobbing quietly in coves and under headlands while Kit led his party to the dive sites. Anna put on a mask and snorkel, and as the diving party submerged in the glittering water she would fly above them on the surface, looking down at the towers and gardens of bright coral as the dark slow-moving figures vanished into the depths. While they were away she would swim gently around, stretching her hands through skeins of bright fish, and often treading water for a long time with her mask half-submerged. That way she could see two worlds at once: the pale, arid, mountainous desert coast of Sinai above the waterline, and below it the moving kaleidoscope of colour in the living sea.

When she climbed back alone onto the boat to wait for the divers, Aziz would bring her a mug of hot sweet black tea, and she would sit huddled in her towel until the first pair broke surface with loud hissing breaths, then the next pair and the next and finally Kit himself with his distinctive sharp-green snorkel tube, glancing keenly round to check his charges. Only when he had counted them and seen each grasp the boat's ladder safely would he look up from the water, see Anna silhouetted against the sunshine, and smile beneath his mask.

She loved more than anything to swim above him when he first sank into the darkness of each dive. Great wobbling, glittering bubbles came up from each diver's mouthpiece like bright jellyfish, rising with a stream of smaller bubbles to burst on the surface or against her body. Sometimes, as Kit led the group from a short distance ahead, she would dive a little way down as if to follow them, and swim deliberately through the shining stream of his bubbles, stretching her limbs as they burst around her, his life's breath tickling and fizzing on her bare skin like champagne.

Each evening after the communal meal Kit and Anna would move aside to the corner of the big carpet, away from the lanterns and the fire. There they sat with their backs against the padded rock, side by side. Sometimes they were quiet for a whole hour together, regarding the dark sky and darker sea, their fingers just touching as the starry universe tilted around them and the white moon rose. Sometimes they would talk, for the keen pleasure of having their ordinary lives transformed by the loving attentiveness of such a listener.

'I don't want to be in the bank forever,' Kit said once. 'I went in after university because my uncle pulled some string or other. I was more interested in climbing and diving than in whatever my job was. My parents were just relieved I had a job at all. And now it's been nine years, and I'm nearly thirty. A thirty-year-old banker. Christ, how do these things happen?'

'I suppose I'm lucky. I always knew I wanted to be a teacher,' said Anna thoughtfully. 'Since I was ten. I really liked school. My sister and brother hated it, but I thought it was magic to be somewhere where people were learning new things every day. My parents' world never changes. Year after year they say exactly the same things. If you told my dad or my brother you were taking the golden road to Samarkand, they'd pull out the road atlas and start telling you how to avoid the M3 interchange on the way.'

'Useful, though,' said Kit. 'My father can hardly find his way round the house now Mum's ill. God knows how he managed when he was a headmaster.'

'Did you go to the school he ran?'

'Yes,' said Kit shortly. Then, changing the subject, 'What will you teach?'

'Modern languages. French and Italian. Then if I have children I can do it part-time, for adults.'

'All sorted out, aren't you?' said Kit teasingly. 'Everything planned and labelled.'

Anna turned to him. 'I was,' she said. 'I was. Now . . .'

Again, she thought he would bend and kiss her. It was dark enough away from the fire, and cold enough now for her to long for closer contact. Instead, he lifted her hand and gravely kissed it, then held it and looked into her face.

'I know. Now, everything's up for review.'

The Oxford boys caught their flight home at the end of the week, but Kit missed it, pledging himself to go north on the bus with Anna. They spent their last days swimming and talking in companionable peace. When it grew too hot for activity they would lie side by side on Anna's mattress in her hut, to read and doze in the filtered sunlight through the bamboo.

They did not make love. Anna was glad; she felt too much, and feared too much. On the final afternoon they went down to the beach and swam out with snorkels and fins to the Manta reef. After a few moments Kit jacknifed down and stretched his hand out underneath the overhang of rock and coral, as if he was feeling for something on the sand. Anna, on the surface above him, hung idly gazing at a school of small, brightly-coloured parrotfish which were feeding on a purple cauliflower cluster. Kit swam to the surface and, turning to see him, she knocked her hand against a razor-sharp protuberance of fan coral. Dismayed, spitting out her snorkel tube, Anna looked at the blood on her knuckles, sucked them and swore.

'Bugger! That's going to be sore. My first coral cut.'

She expected sympathy and chivalry and an escort to the shore. Instead Kit cut short her sucking and swearing and said abruptly, 'Ssh. It's coming up, near the surface. Look. It's an old one. It must have known people. Some of the local boys dive with them.'

Anna pulled her stung knuckles from her mouth, bit down on her tube again and dipped her mask into the water to follow his pointing hand. Shock ran through her. An enormous turtle was approaching upward from the sea bed, moving towards them, its comic flippers graceful and purposeful as it swam. Kit took her arm and pulled her towards it, stretching out his other hand to touch the creature's neck.

It did not pull its head in, but stretched it with apparent pleasure to his hand, letting him scratch the soft wrinkled skin near the edge of its shell and chuck it familiarly under the chin. After a moment Kit left off tickling it to pull the hovering Anna closer. Firmly, he placed her hand on its great neck. As she touched it, Anna forgot Kit for a moment in a rush of new feeling; an indescribable, almost mystical sense of connection. It was, she said to him later, 'Like meeting a dinosaur and being – forgiven. It felt as if everything in the world was all right.'

'As if we'd never left Eden,' said Kit. 'That's just it.'

At the time she made no attempt to express the fullness of

the moment's feeling. When the turtle finally turned and swam majestically away, she raised her head from the water, shook her soaking hair and turned to Kit, who was treading water beside her. All she said then was, 'Why aren't you a teacher?'

Kit began finning back towards the shore, his head twisted to see her behind him.

'Why do you say that?'

'Because,' less fit than he was, she puffed slightly, 'because you were so determined I should meet the turtle and touch it. You were so set on it that you didn't care about being nice to me over my poor hand.'

'Is that how teachers are?'

'I think they should be,' said Anna seriously. 'I think good teachers should be very like you.'

Later, obscurely cured of their mutual terror by the turtle, they did at last make love.

Anna wept, moved by his gentleness and by an aching dread of losing it. Kit wept too. Into the warm darkness of the hut he said, 'Will you marry me? Please?'

Much later, when that was agreed between them, he said something else.

'I think you might be right. Perhaps we'll both be teachers together.'

3

1997

'Saint Agnes Eve,' said Mr Milcourt to Year 7. 'Ah, bitter chill it was! The owl, for all his feathers, was a-cold!'

He paused, the book loose in his hand, and dropped his chin to glare at them from beneath dark eyebrows. Then, half reading, half remembering the lines, he went on, his strong voice cutting through the stuffy sleepy air of the classroom.

To one boy in the front row it seemed that the voice blew away the shoddy room: the thin, shabby, kick-marked walls, the curling maps, the plate glass windows and the warped plywood doors in primary colours which should have been cheerful but which, some years away from their last repaint, merely added to the general dispiriting look of the place. The boy leaned forward on his elbows, fixing the teacher with big brown eyes. Kit read:

> The hare limp'd trembling through the frozen grass
> And silent was the flock in woolly fold:
> Numb were the Beadsman's fingers, while he told
> His rosary, and while his frosted breath
> Like pious incense from a censer old,
> Seem'd taking flight for heaven, without a death,
> Past the sweet Virgin's picture, while his prayer he saith—

A stifled, bubbling giggle travelled along the further rows of the classroom. It had its origin and epicentre among the seats near the big blank windows, seats which were generally favoured by those Year 7s who preferred to ignore the succession of jaded individuals who stood, peddling their knowledge, in front of the smeared whiteboard. Kit sighed. 'Virgin' had been too much for Josh and Darren, as he might have guessed it would be. Now Leanne and Kara, Kylie and Sara were joining in and shaking with silent embarrassed mirth. He passed the back of his hand across his brow, theatrically, then put the book down.

'How cold? Darren? How cold was it?'

'Who, sir?'

'How cold was it, on the eve of Saint Agnes?'

'Was she the virgin, like?'

Leanne and Josh exploded, louder this time. Kit ignored them and looked down at the big-eyed child in the front row, the only one he could be entirely sure had been listening. 'How cold was it, Andrew?'

'He said it was so cold that even the owl was cold. In spite of his fevvers.'

'Right. Excellent. What else?'

'An' the beadman's breath got frozen, an' the grass. An' the hare was trembling. That's sad, that bit.'

'How did the verse make you feel?'

The child shrugged, and grinned. 'Cold.' The teacher grinned back. 'Good. What else? Let's hear from Josh. How did it make you feel?'

The lumpen mass of the class, the uncommitted whose attitude to English lessons fell somewhere between the keen wimpish sensitivity of Andrew and the rump of hopeless philistines led by Josh, waited expectantly for entertainment.

'I dunno,' said Josh slowly. 'How do I feel? Bored. Yeah. Bored.' A wide smirk split his face, the expression of one well-accustomed to experimenting on the fringes of permissible insolence. But it faded under Kit Milcourt's cool, steady look until he found himself adding, to temper the impertinence, 'I s'pose it's because I don't understand those old words.'

'Which words?' said Kit, silkily. 'Frozen? Grass? Trembling? Numb? Death? Frosted? Surely you know frosted. Like your breakfast cereal.'

'He dun't eat breakfast,' volunteered Leanne. 'His mum says that's why his brain don't work till after lunch'.

'Far more likely,' said the teacher, 'to be overheating. The curse of modern education, overheated schools.' The children tittered dully. He looked at them for a moment, part exasperated, part speculative, as if they were an interesting and not unwelcome problem to be solved. They were new to him since September, but he knew which primary schools this group had emerged from; in fact, the same two local schools fed in most of each year's new intake for Sandmarsh High. One, on the grey outskirts of the dead little town, abutted onto an estate long used for housing the depressed overspill of the East End of London thirty miles away. If parents on the Meadowbrook estate got their children to school at all the system considered itself to be winning.

The other familiar feeder primary school served a tangle of older, more established streets to the north of the town; but it was still an area where parents lacked the determination or the desire to wangle and nag until their children got places at schools higher up the examination league table. Anna had worked at both primary schools as a supply teacher before she got the Sandmarsh job, and reported on them to her husband with her usual frankness.

Kit, as a connoisseur of first-year pupils, knew only that on the rare occasions when he got a child who was not formed by either of those two schools, it was as if a peacock had suddenly appeared in a hen coop. Little Andrew, in the front row, had just moved down from Suffolk, and when term began he had plainly been the only one who knew what a poem was. Certainly the only one who cared. Never mind, thought Kit. He would wake them up. Shake them awake, if necessary.

'Start again. Saint Agnes's feast day is in January. Imagine how cold. "*Saint Agnes Eve – ah, bitter chill it was. The owl—*"' he strode to the window and, without pausing, unclipped the latch and slid it open, '"*—for all his feathers, was a-cold. The hare limp'd trembling through the frozen grass . . .*"'

An icy north-easter was blowing in across the grey marshes, a deathly blast straight from the Steppes, presaging winter. The children were suddenly awake, indignant, shuddering exaggeratedly.

'Oh, sir, s'freezing.'

'I got a bad chest, sir.'

'Gor, s'cold, Mis'Milcourt, s'horrible . . .'

Implacably, Kit read on. In the front row Andrew listened
wide-eyed, accepting the raw fingers of cold around the neck of
his shirt as part of the poem. Once or twice Kit glanced directly
at him, a look of unreadable amusement warming his eyes. The
rest of the class, with the usual exceptions, was slowly kindling
to the poem. The temperature in the room dropped until even
the teacher in his thick, navy, cable-knit sweater began to feel
threatened by the darts and squalls of icy air. After seven verses
he paused, went to the window and closed it to a chorus of
groaning relief. He began reading again as he crossed the room,
mincing slightly, making the children laugh: '"*She danc'd along
with vague, regardless eyes . . .*"' Reaching the end of the stanza,
he paused again to fling questions into the corners of the room.
'What's going on? Mick? Josh? Marianne? What's happening?'

'What's "amort" mean, sir?' asked a dough-faced, earnest
girl.

'Don't worry about it. We'll do a word list later. Just get the
story. Tell me the story.'

'She's gonna have a vision,' said a mop-headed boy with bright
black eyes. 'Girls do that sort of thing. Like, my Nan gets my
sister to put wedding cake under the pillow to dream about her
husband.'

'Or orange peel,' said his neighbour. 'My sister throws orange
peel over her shoulder to see the initial. Of her beloved. It's
always S.'

'Apple peel,' chimed in a red-haired boy scornfully. 'You use
apple peel.'

'Orange!'

'Apple!'

'Banana?' said the teacher. 'All right, on we go. Will she
dream? Or will something better happen?'

The class settled to listen, not discontentedly, to the charged
and sensual poem. At least Mr Milcourt read it well. More like
an actor than a teacher really. He sounded so keen, thought

Leanne McDougall, that anyone would think he read that sort of stuff for fun, even when he wasn't at work being a teacher.

When the old crone Angela hobbled into the story, Andrew, in the front row, shivered in pleasure, his eyes enormous. 'S'a *witch*,' he murmured to his neighbour.

There were still hurdles: when Porphyro promised the old woman he would not harm Madeline 'or look with ruffian passion in her face', Leanne and Kara broke into muffled salacious giggles. Kit paused, only for a second but enough to make them subside. Then, verse after ornate verse, he read on through the feast, the wooing and the escape.

The College of Education had advised him to take long narrative poems in short sections, preferably on successive days. It was one of the many axioms of his training that he regularly ignored.

Once, a couple of boys began to yawn and fidget, and Kit glanced at them and moved, still reading, towards the window catch. Outside, wet grey sleet was blowing sideways on the wind, spattering the pane. They stopped. At last he reached the final stanza: ' "*And they are gone; Aye, ages long ago, those lovers fled away into the storm . . .*" '

His voice grew quieter with each line, and when he had finished, a deep silence held within the grimy walls of Room 46T.

Andrew broke it, blinking his eyes, wriggling in emphasis. 'They done a runner!' he said wonderingly. 'They got away!'

Then Leanne spoke. She had stopped playing with her hair at the point where Porphyro spoke to his lover (in tones, Kit would privately have admitted, somewhat over-theatrically tremulous). All she said was, 'Yeah,' but the teacher smiled.

'Good,' he said. 'Something Has Landed. Ten minutes left. Spend five minutes writing down, as fast as you can, whatever comes into your mind about this poem. A string of words will do. For homework read the poem off these sheets,' he skittered round the room, distributing photocopied sheets with dizzying, athletic speed, 'then look back at what you've written now, your first impressions, and write two sides about it. If you only write one side, it had better be very, very good stuff. Yes, Sally, we'll do a word list on Thursday. There really aren't that many difficult words, not when you stop and think. Meanwhile, I propose to let you out five minutes early to prevent any more fights with 7Z at the Coke machine.'

'I have had complaints,' said the deputy head, raising his reedy, nasal voice, 'of windows being opened and consequent *disruption*—' He had been unable to stop himself eating a chocolate biscuit from the staff-room tray, and on the word 'disruption' a discreet spray of crumbs could be observed leaving his mouth. Aware of this, Mr Merck stopped speaking quite abruptly to gulp at the mug of coffee he had brought in with him from his own study. 'Disruption to the heating system.' He glared round at his indifferent audience and concluded, 'I've been asked by the Head to see it doesn't happen again.' He left, unregretted, as the eyes of the handful of men and women in the room turned back to their own break-time preoccupations.

'All schools are overheated,' said Kit, with the superior tranquillity of a man who never ate biscuits and had therefore managed to get to the best of the staff room armchairs with his coffee. 'Nasty, fuggy, stultifying dead air everywhere. I did them a favour, opening that window. Sharpened up their brains. Do you know what Leanne McDougall wrote in her rough book?'

'Leanne – fancies – Josh?' said a lank-haired woman from the corner where she was swiftly, ruthlessly, marking maths homework. 'Or School Sucks?'

'No,' said Kit triumphantly. 'She wrote "dream, shuddering, ghosts in storms, escape". The only word spelt entirely right was "in", mind you, but it's a start. Ghosts came out rather close to gussets.'

'Ghost gussets. Phantom panties. I like it,' said the mathematician. 'She could say it was a poetic conceit, spelt wrong on purpose as a creative rebellion against the underwear taboo. How wonderful to teach a subject where there are no right answers.' Her dark oily hair swung forward as she bent anew to her marking.

'There's spelling,' said another English teacher irritably from the corner, 'and grammar.'

'Was Andrew Murray sick this time?' asked a voice from behind the *Guardian*. 'It was your class he was sick in, wasn't it?'

'Yup,' said Kit lightly. '*Lycidas*. Kept it in right to the last line, then ran into the corridor and honked. Said he felt seasick.'

'*Lycidas*? Milton?' asked a pale eager boy out of college for his teaching practice. 'I didn't think we did that until GCSE, if then.'

'*We* may not,' said Kit carelessly. '*I* sometimes do. I did an hour at the beginning of term on the poetry of mourning. Because of the Princess Diana funeral. They were all wrapped up in it that week.'

'Merck didn't approve, did he?' The first man put down the newspaper, showing a round, pink face and a bald crown ringed with blond hair. Were it not for an incongruously sharp nose, Ian Atkins would have looked cherubic. As it was, the children to whom he taught science called him Vulture. 'I seem to remember quite a fuss about that.'

'That's right,' said Kit. His voice, the student noticed, sometimes had a hint of upper-class drawl to it. 'Would you believe it? The school contingency fund shells out four hundred quid to bring in those poxy grief counsellors in tracksuits because someone told Merck the children might be in post-traumatic whatsit after the funeral. At the same time he starts grumbling when I do the job for free, with *Lycidas* and *Cymbeline* and Cowper.'

'I thought Andrew's parents complained,' said Ian Atkins. 'He was sick, then he had nightmares about drowning.'

'That's my boy!' agreed Kit dreamily. 'When he came back into the room, reeking slightly, we were doing Cowper: "*I, beneath a rougher sea am whelm'd in deeper gulphs than he . . .*" I thought he was going to be sick again, but he didn't want to miss one minute of it. It was a good session.'

'Mr Merck's concern had nothing to do with the grief counsellors,' said the woman who had mentioned spelling and grammar. Unlike the others who sprawled in wooden-armed but reasonably comfortable armchairs, she was sitting on a hard plastic chair with her elbows on a cold Formica-topped table, painstakingly writing in the margins of exercise books. 'Mr Merck was concerned that you were wasting teaching time, departing from the agreed curriculum and distressing the children unnecessarily.'

'Rubbish,' said Kit. The drawl was gone now, his voice full

of energy. 'What should we have done? The kids came back to school full of mopey sentimentality and cheap cellophane-wrapped emotion about Diana. The whole country had gone maudlin and convinced itself that what Elton John sang at the funeral was poetry. It was what our political masters would call a window of opportunity. The children were hungry for a proper expression of grief. It was only one period, and I call it time well spent. We did Auden, too. "*Stop all the clocks.*"'

'None of it was material from the teaching structure which we had agreed as a department,' reiterated the woman stubbornly. She was small and rounded and choleric of complexion, and her name was Molly Miles.

'I didn't agree it,' said Kit. 'You and Roger cooked it up with Merck.'

'You were invited,' said Molly. 'It's all very well your playing games with Year 7, but I have to pick up the pieces next year and get them on the way to their SATs. Key Stage 3 doesn't teach itself, you know. If you knew the extra time I have to put in on Information Retrieval Procedures . . .'

Kit Milcourt looked with disfavour at his departmental colleague, and stood up, uncurling his long body to tower over her.

'*SATs*,' he said with loathing. 'Government yardsticks. Pen-pushers ticking boxes, while the hungry sheep look up and are not fed.' He turned aside to drain the last coffee out of the Cona machine into his mug. Molly Miles looked at him as if she was braced for more, and indeed rather relished the idea of a fight, but his broad back remained resolutely averted. She fired a shot at it.

'I don't know why you became a teacher, if you have no intention of preparing children for important qualifications.'

'I don't know why anybody becomes one,' said Kit to the Cona machine, 'if they have no interest in preparing children for life.'

Ian Atkins threw down his newspaper. 'Oh, stop bitching, you two. Kit, you shouldn't be let out without Anna to keep you in order. When's she back?'

'Tonight. Thank God.' Kit sipped his bitter coffee, and made a face.

Atkins turned to the red-faced little woman next, as if taking pains to be even-handed between his fractious colleagues. 'Do admit, though, Molly, there's something to be said for Tinkerbell here. Do you know what Tracey Button's brother told me on the field trip last week? He said that after that Diana class Tracey copied out the whole of "Fear no more the heat o' the sun" and drew borders of flowers round it with felt pens, and six weeks later it's still Sellotaped up in her mum's kitchen.'

Miss Miles sniffed, and did not respond. The science teacher persisted, 'Come on, old duck, getting *Cymbeline* into the Meadowbrook estate, that has to be an educational milestone.'

'Yes,' said Molly Miles, with a hiss. 'But we're not here to—'

'Not here to educate them?' Kit felt his better judgement implode and collapse, and spilt lukewarm coffee on his cuff as he turned round abruptly. 'Just shelf-stackers in the national curriculum factory, are we? "Information Retrieval" exercises deconstructing crappy semi-literate texts about safety standards in processed cheese factories? The art of filling in forms? Children—'

'Ah, Graham!' said Atkins, in loud warning, looking past Kit to the door. 'Back again, ever busy!'

And, indeed, Merck was back, peevish, heading for the noticeboard with a memo and some tin-tacks in his hand. At the same moment the bell shrilled for the end of break. Molly Miles, hissing to herself as Merck passed, clamped the lid defensively back on the staff-room biscuit tin. Kit gulped down the unpleasant dregs of his coffee, gathered up his books and left without another word. Ian, a beaky cherub, looked after him with pursed lips and back to Molly Miles.

'Saved by the bell,' he said with jovial malice. 'What do you think our friend was going to say? Do you think it was going to be the full mission statement, or the convenient abridged pocket version?'

The small woman glared at him. 'He does it on purpose. Him and his moral high horse! Traps me into feeling . . . into feeling . . .' She was almost in tears. Ian Atkins did not like women in tears.

'Same here,' he said hastily. 'Oxbridge blue. I know. Very snooty. They always know best, and to hell with the system and the way that ordinary joes have to get through life. There was one in my last school, Gonville and Caius, taught history, rabid Jacobite, ended up throwing a bottle through the head's window when he was drunk. They'd had a row about Charles Edward Stuart.'

'Kit Milcourt will get his comeuppance,' said Miss Miles bitterly. 'In any other school he would have been brought up short long ago. If it wasn't that Mr Harding's so *gullible* about his self-indulgent, exhibitionist theories . . .'

Graham Merck had his back to her as he stood pinning up his strictures against reckless opening of windows, but something attentive about that back prevented her from continuing too explicitly. Merck the Nark was what Caroline Chang called him, and not without reason.

Atkins waited a moment to see whether the explosion was over, then shrugged and left for the science block where 10U Biology awaited him. The dark mathematician in the corner, who had been studiously ignoring the row conducted well within her hearing, gathered up her books and made her way unhurriedly to the door, turning finally to Molly Miles with a pale, placatory smile.

'Don't let the two of them wind you up, Moll,' she said. 'Kit's a good teacher. In his way.'

Molly made a noise which would have explained, to anyone hitherto mystified, exactly why her Year 9s called her 'grunter' behind her back.

4

On that same afternoon, Anna Milcourt was buying a magazine at Charing Cross Station. 'Thank you,' she said when the newsvendor took her money, 'Thanks' when he gave her the few pence change, and 'Thank you very much' in return to his own crisp 'I-thenk-you'. Nice girl, thought the newsvendor, cutting the string on a new bundle of *Evening Standards*. Hell of a looker, too. Not like all those sour scrawny bints in black jackets; this one was dead cuddly. Not fat, but sort of fluffy. Like they used to be when he was young. Nice smile, too, and said a proper thank you.

Anna walked on down the station platform, feeling anything but fluffy. As it happened, she was a woman who always said 'Thank you' a lot when she was inwardly angry and upset. It was as if, behind a cloak of punctilious good manners, her inner self could more safely shriek and bawl and beat its fists. In the last few hours her mood had come to need all the disguises she could muster. An unselfconsciously healthy young woman, she always felt ill at ease with doctors, and the last hour in Harley Street had dismayed and depressed her very much. She had not yet recovered her equilibrium after the chilly probing of the consultant and, almost worse, the unsmiling chaperonage of his nurse. Nor had all the tests and examinations produced any useful conclusion.

'There is no apparent reason you should not conceive,' the stately silver-haired oracle had pronounced. 'Everything seems to be well in order. Your weight's fine, which is more than I can say for most of the fashionable young women who come to me. Did you know that excessive thinness has become one of the prime causes of patients presenting with infertility? But you're healthily covered, plenty of reserves there.'

Anna had tolerated this humiliation and listened carefully to the rest. The doctor spoke of cycles and fertile windows and avoiding stress while maintaining a positive and welcoming attitude to life. How do you do both? wondered Anna, huddling her clothes around her and staring balefully at him beneath her ruffled hair. Surely you needed a good healthy dash of cynicism and negative expectation in order to identify the source of stress before it got to you, and duck. For instance, if she went through her day at school maintaining a positive and welcoming attitude to Graham Merck, she would end up being the one who listened politely to him and thereby undergo pronounced stress.

Finally the consultant had said, 'And to come to the most obvious thing last, you and your husband *are* giving nature a chance, aren't you? It's surprising how many of my patients don't think of that. You working women are always busy and tired. Sometimes I find my girls conceive the week after they give up working. And buy a frilly new nightie to celebrate, perhaps!'

Anna had a vision, gloomy and complete, of the domestic life of Mr Consultant: a bright, plump little wife at home raising his nicely spaced children, ironing his palest pink shirts, supporting his Rotarian charities and making sure he never left home without a spare pair of reading glasses with gold-wire rims. No wonder her mother had recommended him so excitedly! Probably met the dutiful wife at one of her PP sessions. Suddenly Anna decided that this man had nothing whatsoever to tell her, and that she – or rather, her insistently benevolent mother – had paid eighty pounds for very little.

Well, fine. All she had wanted to know was a negative: that there was no reason – no physiological reason – why she and Kit had no child at their fireside.

Returning to the moment, she looked up at the doctor and found that he was waiting for some kind of answer. He repeated the question, 'How often do you and your husband have intercourse, would you say?'

The answer to that – the real one, not the evasive version she gave the consultant – was another reason for Anna's depression.

The smug silver-feathered old vulture could well be right, she thought now as she strode down the platform towards the train home. There could be a pretty simple solution to this particular fertility conundrum. *Not often enough*. Despite all the love there was between them, not often enough.

And if it wasn't happening often enough, then the odds were that they repeatedly missed those windows of fertility the doctor was so keen on. Perhaps, month after month, they were inadvertently practising the rhythm method. The thought cheered Anna up. The rhythm method was notorious for failing, wasn't it? Well, then. She glanced down at the magazine she had bought a moment ago, with a grinning tot on the cover and the bold line *'Know your body's secret baby clock'*. She would read it on the train and talk to Kit tonight.

He had come straight from school to the station to meet her. It was a mark of their devotion that after nearly ten years together neither Kit nor Anna easily tolerated anything that lengthened their separations even by half an hour. For her, to spend a night away from him even in her childhood bedroom in Richmond meant chilly, broken sleep; she would keep waking and missing the heat of his body and the solidity of his shoulders, and long to lie as she usually did with her face flattened against his broad back like a puppy sleeping on its mother. She broke into a run when she saw him standing by the car, and flopped into his arms with a sigh of pure relief.

'How was it?' Kit asked solicitously, propping her upright again with his hands on her shoulders.

'Gruesome.' Anna flopped back onto his chest. 'I don't care if he does do all the crowned fannies of Europe, he's creepy. And the nurse was Morticia Addams in person.'

'Did he find anything?' Kit opened the car door for her and threw her holdall onto the back seat, on top of a heap of exercise books.

'No. He was most admiring of my insides, and the tests the GP sent in were all fine. All hormones present and correct. And he asked a lot of questions about abortions and VD and PID and stuff, none of which I've ever had. So he doesn't think it's a tube or an oviduct or anything.'

'God,' said Kit, starting the car. 'What a lot of plumbing. Anyway, at least we've drawn level in the personal humiliation stakes. I might even forgive you for Dr Mattheson.'

Anna giggled, and put her hand on Kit's thigh. 'Oh, I'm sorry!'

Kit pressed his lips together, but his eyes danced in merriment. 'It wasn't your fault. I'm just over-educated. Not primitive enough for the NHS. If I'd gone private they might have given me a Rubens reproduction to spur me on. Or something by Augustus John, instead of *Mayfair Mandy*.'

The two of them, happier now that they were together, shook with laughter as the little car crawled through the rush-hour traffic along the dock road. Three months before Anna's appointment, Kit had volunteered to take a fertility test himself. It had taken four visits to the hospital clinic and the increasingly embarrassed young Dr Mattheson before Kit was able to provide a sample to be tested. Anna had been afraid he would feel humiliated by his inability to do what all the younger men seemed to manage in that clinic: to go behind a screen with a pile of erotic magazines and perform to order. But Kit seemed immune to embarrassment on this score, apparently regarding the whole exercise as no worse than ridiculous. After each appointment he would get home laughing, pull her onto his knee in the armchair, and reduce her to hysterical giggles with his spirited description of Dr Mattheson's hesitant, embarrassed instructions, the apparatus, and the cheerless little side room with its curling magazines and – he particularly enjoyed this detail – an ecclesiastical-looking lectern on which to prop them.

'I did love that lectern,' he said now. 'It only needed a carved eagle and a Bible. Actually, come to think of it, after spending most of my puberty in a public school chapel I might actually have done better with the Book of Leviticus than *Playboy*.'

Anna laughed, happier than she had been all day, as Kit swung the car into the narrow driveway of their house. It was an odd-looking house: tall Victorian Gothic, with pointed windows and a castellated brick turret and a lion's head over the front door. By the time Kit first qualified as a teacher, they had got through most of his savings from his palmy years on a big bank salary, but there was enough to put down a £20,000 deposit, nearly half the value of this monstrous edifice. Anna loved the turret, and the stained-glass knight in armour who stood amid flowers in the tall window that dominated the stairs. It reminded her, in romantic moments, of her husband.

Kit liked the creaking floors and the stone scullery and wild lawn, and particularly appreciated the way that a certain grand randomness in the design of the building gave it enough peculiarly shaped stair cupboards to accommodate all his climbing and diving kit, including air bottles, and Anna's kit too when he finally persuaded her to join him underwater.

Moving from London to the small dull town was made easier by the house's space and eccentricity, and by its distant view over the industrial wasteland and marshes to the river beyond. All through their first year in Sandmarsh, friends had come down for weekends to shriek with mirth at its sinister personality. Kit's cousin Elinor had painted an enormous mural pastiche of the Boyhood of Raleigh across the dining-room ceiling, putting Kit's face on the old sailor. 'To launch your teaching career,' she said. 'Though why you have to do it here is anybody's guess.' Elinor rarely left North London.

'It's a job,' said Kit. 'I'm an NQT. Newly qualified teacher. Junior to Anna, you know. It's not like Dad, lording it over the brats of the gentry at Priory Shore.'

He had stubbornly rejected the idea of independent schools, where his background would have been an asset, and meekly suffered rejections from two London comprehensives who informed him that it was a liability. His accent and bearing, they explained, would make it hard for him ever to be 'relevant' to the children they taught. When he was offered the job at Sandmarsh High, he was, Anna thought, rather touchingly pleased and proud. He clearly liked its head, the diffident, weary-looking Ronald Harding. Equally importantly, Ron Harding had intimated to him that one of their modern languages staff was retiring at the end of the year, and that this could mean a job for Anna.

So Anna left her own first job – at a top-rated West London comprehensive – and spent the intervening year doing supply work in the primary schools which fed Sandmarsh.

'Well,' she said to the incredulous colleagues she left in London, 'it *was* me who told Kit to become a teacher, after all.' When she did join the Sandmarsh staff room, it was just in time for her easy, friendly popularity to counterbalance some of the upheavals Kit caused in the school. Particularly where Molly Miles was concerned. Molly often said, rather too loudly, that Anna was A Saint. In less discreet moments she would add that anybody who put up with That Man would have to be. Among the other teachers and young professionals in the small, dull dormitory town, the Milcourts made friends. The London friends came down less and less, as each couple in turn had babies.

Coming home now, Anna put her bag down on the scrubbed kitchen table and said, 'About the baby. There is a way we could give ourselves a better chance. I read it in this magazine . . .'

Kit was not listening. He had chucked the armful of exercise books down on the table and become distracted by the newspaper left over from the morning.

'Do you fancy a cinema? Film Club's got *The Third Man* tonight.'

'Don't know,' said Anna. 'I'm tired. I'm trying to tell you something important, about the baby.'

Kit pushed the paper aside, and sat down, facing her. He looked tired too, thought Anna. Her night away made her notice it. His slight pallor prevented her from pursuing her own line, so when he said 'What?' she shook her head.

'No. Sorry. It's all right. Don't worry.'

'It's bound to happen,' said Kit, conciliatory. 'If there's nothing physically wrong.'

'Yes,' said Anna. 'Of course.' And she leaned to nuzzle the top of his head. 'Nice to be home.'

Beyond him, as she rested her cheek on his hair, she could see the magazine, rolled in the top of her bag, and the words 'secret clock'. She smiled.

Some miles to the north and west of them, in a neater house by a less forbidding river, Pamela 'Poppet' Melville was giving a final polish to the cutlery and glasses for her own husband's imminent return. Derek Melville had standards. When he came home from the office he liked to find the house tidy, the table laid with silver from the wedding-present canteen, and a wife prepared to greet him with the proper amount of affectionate ceremony. On the rare occasions that this did not happen, Derek sulked.

On the other hand, it was not a bad bargain he offered in return for this small effort. For a bit of coddling and the pleasure of her chubby golden prettiness around the house, he had long since devolved every family and domestic decision to his wife. Known at the office as something of a tartar, at home he meekly acquiesced in his wife's choice of furnishings, appliances and holidays, deferred entirely to her judgement over their three children's education, and since the day they married had paid his entire salary into their joint account. He was confident that Poppet would never overspend or mismanage, and Poppet never did. She even made her own money now, with the PP club. Wonderful woman.

'Darling!' he called from the hallway. 'Home again!'

Dutifully, Pamela called back, 'Lovely! Supper's nearly ready!' and appeared, broad, blonde and smiling, to hang his coat up for him. When she stood on tiptoe to kiss him on the cheek, he could smell her light perfume and feel the pressure of her rounded breast; then she stepped back and handed him a glass of gin and vermouth. As usual, it stood on the polished hall table, ready mixed and protected from dust by a small white circlet of linen weighted with jingling glass beads round its scalloped edge. Derek smiled as he sipped it, relaxing. All was well, as usual. He roamed through into the dining area of the long living room.

'Did Anna get on her way all right?' he asked, as a matter of form.

'Yes!' said Anna's mother with emphasis. 'Rushing off as usual, no time for breakfast because she lay in. She went to see that doctor, Maureen Harpenton's husband. About you-know-what.'

Derek grunted. He knew that modern young men discussed these things freely. Sometimes they discussed them in the office, a trend which he heartily abhorred.

'Well,' he ventured after another sip, 'wouldn't mind another grandchild, would we?'

As he spoke, an unwelcome vision arose of the six he already had. There were Mary's four – Janie and Martin and Maggie and Lee, all with fringes through which, at an assortment of different heights, stared piercing blue eyes which made Derek uncomfortable when he muddled up their names. He usually did muddle up their names; in fact, he couldn't even tell which were the girls, in those terrible flashy neon sports clothes they all seemed to wear. Pamela used to put his little girls in skirts, and quite right too.

But Mary's brood were easy company compared to Mike's fourteen-year-olds, Dirk and Deelya. The twins were less frequent visitors to their grandparents; for all the rapport Derek had with them they might have been aliens beamed down from another galaxy: dangerous, blank-eyed, spiky-headed creatures with enormous black boots and headphones which went *chitter-chitter*, sometimes even during meals.

'Keeps 'em quiet, know wha'I mean?' Mike's brassy Barbara would say, chewing with her mouth open and ripping up pieces of Pamela's tidily cut bread. 'What I say is, for the price of a disc player, you get peace perfect peace. Nice pattay, Pam.' And Mike, as appreciatively uxorious as his father, would smile fondly at his wife and affect not to notice how much his children alarmed their grandfather. Pamela was less awed and would sometimes try, with brisk, steely kindness, to 'draw them out', but with little success.

Thinking of Dirk and Deelya, Derek shuddered, but continued hopefully, 'Little baby for little Anna. Be a good thing. Reckon she and Kit might make a good job of a child.'

'It's *what they need*!' said Pamela firmly. 'All that gadding about like a Royal Marines training course, up mountains and in the ocean, it's all very well when you're a young thing doing your Duke of Edinburgh's. But Anna's thirty. High time she had babies to look after.'

'Well, it sounds as if she's trying,' said Derek heartily, and then, because it rounded off the sentiment nicely, 'Nothing venture, nothing win.'

'I might just ring Maureen Harpenton after dinner,' said Pamela reflectively. 'I need to talk to her about moving the PP session. She might know something.'

And, shamelessly, so she did. When Derek had been duly fed and settled in front of *Inspector Morse* on television, Pamela stood by her tidy kitchen noticeboard and dialled, taking the number from one of the many lists on the cork board headed, in an exuberantly curly font, *'PP – Positively Plump – with Poppet Melville!'*

This organization, founded by herself some ten years earlier as a modest exercise class for the larger woman, had the motto, 'Nothing wrong with fat as long as you keep it *moving*!' It had grown beyond anybody's expectations – except, of course, those of Pamela herself, who had always had faith in it. Fighting off offended, alarmed opposition from several local slimming clubs, she had preached the gospel of abundant but healthy flesh to kindred spirits in her keep-fit classes, which were conducted not to a rock or rave beat but to the jovial oompah of brass band tapes. Then she made the national press by leading a thundering mass jog of large, laughing women across Richmond Park on a Saturday morning. She caused several minor traffic accidents as motorists, awestruck, stamped on their brakes. On arrival at their 'teddy bears' picnic', her followers had openly, despite their generous curves, eaten doughnuts in front of the nation's press. One or two had even got carried away, offered cream cakes to policemen and pointed shrieking, contemptuous fingers at the skinny, intense girl reporters sent to cover the event.

As the years went on, her followers, some of them very large indeed but most merely what their husbands called 'comfortable', had told their friends about the health and hilarity of the exercise classes, and gradually Pamela Melville had recruited fifty teachers and spread the PP groups from Oxfordshire to Essex.

Poppet had her eye on the North next, and was only disappointed that her daughter Mary, who lived just outside Sheffield, had grown up not only comparatively thin but comparatively reserved as well. She shrank with horror from her mother's suggestion that she take the PP gospel North. Anna – whose adult weight had always lain halfway between her buxom mother and skinny sister, and who had never given her a moment's worry – was amused by it all, admiring of Pamela's drive but adamant that she would not get involved. This led to some arguments. Only last night they had been through it all again while they loaded the washing machine.

'But you're a *teacher*, darling,' her mother would wail. 'All those girls who go anorexic and bulimic and think they have to look like twigs, it's just the age we should catch them and *get that message home* – that Fat can be Fit!'

'Mum,' Anna said, scraping plates into the kitchen bin, 'I think it's great what you do, and I'm sure it helps some women. And you're right about the stick-insect thing, and the heroin-chic models, and all that. I'm with you. But I don't think PP indoctrination is any more suitable for school than any other indoctrination. Anyway, what about the thin girls? You're terribly rude about thin people, and that's not nice either.'

'Nice!' Pamela retorted with massive scorn. 'Nice! You're just too nice, dear. Thin women have always oppressed fat women. I'll lend you this really interesting book from America.'

'What about poor Mary?' Anna, still laughing, refused to be provoked. 'Thin as a rake, doesn't oppress anyone.'

'She was quite rude when I asked her to make me a list of northern local newspapers for the "Fat is Funky" press release,' said Pamela. 'Said I could look them up in the library. It's lucky I've got that Harman woman to act as northern franchise manager.'

'Mum, we all just get on with our lives, OK?' said Anna crisply. 'Give it a hundred years and all our bodies will look much the same. Skeletons.'

'Don't be disgusting, dear,' said Pamela.

But Anna had looked drawn and preoccupied, and to a mother's eye far thinner than she should be. As she dialled the number of the consultant's wife, Pamela reflected that a couple of babies would go a long way to bringing back her daughter's bloom and enhancing a healthy plumpness. A *positive* plumpness.

'Maureen? Is that you, dear?'

A tinny, affirmative voice chattered at the far end of the line. It ended, '. . . suppose you must be relieved, marvellous news, nothing to stop them.'

'She hasn't rung me yet,' said Pamela guiltily. 'But you reckon all's well?'

'Oh *dear*, I shouldn't have said anything,' said Mrs Harpenton. 'Geoffrey didn't, really. He's very discreet. But he just said he'd seen your Anna, looking bonny, and then went on for a bit about all these modern young women who think they're infertile and don't give nature a chance.'

'Ah!' said Pamela, with the satisfied sigh of one who well understood how information could be extracted from spouses without their ever realizing it. 'Well, that *is* good news.'

When she had put the phone down, her hand hovered over the receiver. How nice to ring Anna for a mother-and-daughter celebratory chat. She reached for the dial and then, gripped by an unaccustomed moment of insight, realized that it might not be nice at all if Anna were to realize the efficiency of her mother's spy system. With a small sigh, Pamela left the telephone and put the kettle on for Derek's coffee.

Miles away, with the October wind blowing hard from the grey Thames Estuary and rattling the loose sash windows, Kit and Anna lay in their marriage bed under a scattering of exercise books and photocopied worksheets. Anna had decided to go straight to bed after supper and read her magazine article again, and Kit, after working desultorily downstairs on his own, had missed her and opted to bring his marking up to bed. After a while, bored with ticking grammatical exercises, he leaned over with his chin on her soft bare shoulder and read the headline aloud: '*Miracle Microchip which showed me the way to Motherhood*'.

'You're not having a microchip fitted, are you? For a baby robot?'

'No-oh!' said Anna, faintly annoyed. 'I'll explain, if you like. It's a thing they market for contraception, but it works the other way. A sort of computer. It tracks your fertile period of the month and shows you a red light when you're ovulating.'

'Ugh,' said Kit.

'Why, ugh?'

'Dunno. A bit clinical.' He nuzzled her shoulder, and stretched himself luxuriously the length of her soft body. Unheeded, a shower of 7X's homework books slithered off the bed and scattered on the rug and the floorboards. 'Does the red light shine out of your navel?'

'Fool!' said Anna, lovingly, throwing the magazine on the floor and turning to him. 'It's on the computer. Miles away. In the bathroom, or wherever you keep it.'

'Yum!' said Kit, biting her shoulder gently; and together, amicably, they made love. Afterwards he turned away and slept but Anna, who had been studying the article very carefully, lay awake for a while reflecting with a tinge of bitterness what bad luck it was that according to her calculations this could not possibly have been a red-light night. No life kindled within her yet.

Turning over, carefully so as not to wake Kit, she caught sight of their wedding photograph on the scuffed pine chest of drawers. Around the two of them the generations gathered: Anna's mother, broad and buxom under a mass of springing blonde perm, and her grandmother in the wheelchair, a shrunken, white-haired version of Pamela with the same keen eye and obstinate jaw. Behind them her father, thin-haired and slightly stooping, eclipsed as usual by his womenfolk. There was Mary, markedly standing at the opposite end of the row from her parents. She was pregnant and holding baby Jane in front of her as if for defence. Don looked away from them, out of the picture, his face blurred as if he had been distracted at the moment of the flash. Staring at the camera like police suspects were Mike and Barbara, each with a twin held firmly by the hand. Incongruously next to Barbara's flashiness stood Kit's father Eamon, distinguished and senatorial, his face like a more forbidding, secretive version of his son's. Next to him Kit's mother Marion, sweet-faced and tired, already showing signs of the final onslaught of illness which would kill her a year later. Then there was some uncle of Kit's – Alan? Alec? – who had stood in as best man at the last minute.

Anna stared at them for a moment, and her eyes filled with tears. Family. Ah, family! It went on down the generations, faces and quirks and tones of voice and talents passing on, sometimes in straight lines and sometimes skipping, darting, zigzagging from aunt to nephew, uncle to niece, weaving the tapestry of the generations. Would the thread run out with her and for Kit? Were they a dead end?

She shivered, and turned away from the picture again to move closer to the warm radiance of her husband.

5

The antipathy between Kit Milcourt and Molly Miles, twin pillars of the English department, was a thing which worried the headmaster a great deal. Ronald Harding was not a strong leader; two years off retirement and all ambition spent, he would have preferred a school which ran peacefully along the tracks. Even if they were not very elevated tracks; he was reconciled to a certain mediocrity. While Sandmarsh pupils did not actually reach the leaving age illiterate or innumerate, neither did they tend to reach it with any distinction. A few went on to the sixth forms of bigger local schools, or to the FE college at Gravesend; most did not. Where Sandmarsh stopped, at the age of sixteen, they stopped too. In the government's examination league tables the school usually came second last in the county.

On the other hand it was not unduly disorderly, nor any more rife with drugs and alcohol than any other school of the late 1990s. The shrill disciplinary regime of Graham Merck, its deputy head, ensured decent minimum standards of attendance and behaviour, even though there were often clashes between the two men over the matter of expulsion. To Merck, 'exclusion' was a weapon of vengeance and terrible example, to be wielded with frequency and brio *pour encourager les autres*. To Ronald Harding, a gentler spirit, it was an admission of failure. Graham Merck thought the school would be a better place without children like Josh Bannerman. Harding, chewing fretfully at a Biro in his study, knew in his deepest conscience that it would be a better place if, somehow, it could contain and change Josh Bannerman.

Indeed Ronald Harding, despite the lassitude which marked

the closing years of his career, was still at heart an idealist. In his top desk drawer, typed out thirty years before, was a yellowing and much folded sheet of A4 paper bearing the words of Sherlock Holmes haranguing Watson in 'The Adventure of the Naval Treaty'.

'Look at those big, isolated clumps of buildings rising up above the slates, like brick islands in a lead-coloured sea.'
'The board-schools?'
'Lighthouses, my boy! Beacons of the future! Capsules with hundreds of bright little seeds in each, out of which will spring the wiser, better England of the future!'

He rarely looked at it these days. His generation of teachers had begun with high hopes, then mired itself in ineffective theory and simultaneously been overwhelmed by a dead weight of young men and women who had no vocation, let alone a teaching vocation, but no other ideas on what to do either. This faltering army had run up against increasingly disorderly generations, then undergone insult and blame from successive governments and physical assault at the hands of pupils and even parents. Harding himself had taken the deputy headship at Sandmarsh after losing the use of one ear while breaking up a playground fight at his previous school in Birmingham.

'It wasn't even a fight between kids,' he would say, telling the story with morose pride. 'It was between two mothers.' His wife Eileen had wanted him to claim industrial injury and retire early to a cottage in the Cotswolds, but even at that late stage he did not want to separate himself from his profession. So Ron Harding had come to this bleak outpost of north Kent, and Eileen, angry and hurt, had left him and set up home with her widowed sister near Burford.

Within a year he was headteacher of Sandmarsh. His predecessor had retired early – on 'health grounds', although the main symptom was an uncontrollable tic and fits of stuttering whenever governors or inspectors were due to visit the school. At first the new head had felt reborn and reinvigorated. In charge at last, Ron Harding had nourished high ambitions for his first command. He would turn the place round, make it an example to the county, and – his dearest wish – transform it into a full secondary school with a sixth form of its own.

But after five years in the job, without a warm Eileen to go home to, he in turn found himself settling into an attitude of glum endurance. He would serve out his time for pride's sake, then attempt a reconciliation with his distant wife. Conan Doyle's words about the beacons remained folded dustily in the drawer, and few things disturbed this particular lighthouse-keeper's gloomy equanimity.

Until Kit Milcourt came. He had turned up for interview five years previously, a newly qualified teacher at the surprisingly advanced age of thirty-three. The English department had just lost two veterans to early retirement, so that only faithful Molly Miles remained, assisted part-time by a choleric retired head of department called Roger Randing. With a falling school roll – it fell in gloomy harmony with the school's reputation – Harding knew that he could only afford to replace one of them. English, as the chairman of governors rather cavalierly put it, was the subject most easily 'filled in' by students on teaching practice, or agency temps. There was no call to overload the department with experienced, expensive staff. The other post must be given to an information technology specialist, it was decided, and any cheap NQT would pass muster for English.

Kit Milcourt, so Harding saw in the first incredulous minutes of the interview, would more than pass muster. Listening to the younger man, with his easy establishment confidence, talking about the uses of literacy and the vitality of language and the unexplored capacity of children, the head felt for the first time in several years a stirring of his own old longings and ambitions. He looked at this unusual applicant with a kind of dawning hope which was mistaken for doubt.

'I know that I've come to it late,' Kit had said, defensively. 'I'll be frank with you. I resisted the idea of teaching for a long time because my father was a prep school headmaster, and I've got – well, rather equivocal – memories and feelings about prep school. So I just qualified as a diving and climbing instructor, as a spare time thing. You could say I was getting teaching experience there, I suppose. Some of the characters I taught in the university clubs were about twelve years old emotionally.'

'You have a very good degree.' Harding was looking down at the CV in front of him in amazed wonder that anybody with first class honours from Oxford should be sitting in his office, petitioning for a low-paid job teaching children with nose studs and attitude problems.

Kit nodded in brief acknowledgement, and went on, 'It was something my wife said before we were married that crystallized it in my mind that I was meant to teach. That was why I was hating the bank.'

'And has your experience of the profession so far justified your change of direction?' asked Harding.

'No,' said Kit, and the room seemed to light up with his sudden, crookedly mischievous smile. 'Absolutely not. The training was largely meretricious crap and half-digested pop psychology, with a few rather desperate last-minute modules on how to "deliver" the National Curriculum as if it were a bottle of semi-skimmed milk.'

Harding was silent, but it was the silence of hope not the silence of disapproval.

Kit continued, after a pause, 'OK, there were some useful things. Mainly organizational. Some of the psychology was almost credible. The teaching practice was best. You learn more in half an hour with a roomful of children than you do in six months at college. I enjoyed that a lot. But I didn't always get the best of reports.'

'So I see,' said Harding, looking down again. 'But with your qualifications and background, and the sort of lively style to which these department heads took exception,' he gestured at the tight-lipped reports in front of him, 'I can't see why you aren't interested in the independent sector. They'd snap you up. You could be down at King's School Canterbury at this very moment. There's an English post advertised there. You'd probably get it, and earn more, and have more rewarding children to work with.'

'No chance,' said Kit, smiling. 'Beacons. Lighthouses. The wiser, better, England of the future. Conan Doyle, if you recall.'

And the head had thought, for an insane moment, that he was going to cry.

*   *   *

Chewing his pen now in his office, staring at the memo in front of him, Ronald Harding reflected that he should have foreseen a clash between this glittering, maverick new staff member and the solid reliable Molly Miles. Where Kit was imaginative and dramatic, Molly was steady and plodding; he was sweeping, inspired insouciance and she was prudent carefulness. Kit was a performer who could hold a classroom spellbound, even a Sandmarsh classroom, whether or not they understood what he was reading in his beautiful voice. Molly, with her corncrake tone and estuary vowels, could make Keats' *Ode to Autumn* sound like the North Kent telephone directory.

Their aims were different. Kit considered that his prime duty to the children was to drag them above the swamp of mass-produced cultural mediocrity, of formula movies and formula thinking, and startle them by any means in his power into a sharper perception of language, beauty, and a sense of transcendence. Molly considered that her job was to leave the children with a sound grasp of grammar, spelling, and the type and range of authors specified in the National Curriculum and necessary for passing the General Certificate of Secondary Education. Kit worried about their souls, Molly about their employability behind counters. Kit's methods were chaotic, Molly's impeccably organized. Molly was earth and Kit was fire.

And they were both right, thought Ronald Harding savagely. His hands snapped the plastic Biro in two, so that clear jagged splinters fell on the desk and left him twisting the soft clear tube of ink between his fingers. If Kit and Molly had decided five years ago to respect one another and work together, each throwing their own particular talents into the pot and complementing one another, his English department, even short-staffed, could have been an educational paradise. If Kit had been more respectful of Molly, and Molly less resentful of Kit . . . if he, perhaps, had been enough of a leader to bring them forcibly together and reconcile them early on . . . they could have been a formidable team.

Instead, they had tormented one another and him for five years, and sent a succession of supply teachers and students on their way battered and bewildered. There had been rows over lost books, over students' portfolios, over coursework and haikus, Oscar Wilde and Roger McGough, multiculturalism and *Macbeth*.

Their antipathy crackled with such electrical violence that other members of staff would be drawn in and make things worse by siding with one or other of them from time to time. The history department backed Molly in the battle about textual analysis in Year 9, the drama department stood up for Kit over the Dracula business, and Ian Atkins – blast him! – had quite unjustifiably put his oar into their row about the library computer and made things much, much worse. So, inevitably, did Graham Merck. His particular bent was physical education and he took an early grudge against Kit for teaching that Kipling poem – was it? – about 'flannelled fools at the wicket and muddied oafs at the goal'.

All the same, thought Harding gloomily, if you had a Kit Milcourt, you needed a Graham Merck to curb him. Once, in a fit of fury at his Year 8 group's failure to respond to the opening chapter of *Great Expectations*, Kit had led thirty-two children across the playing field and out onto the marsh, without their coats, on a misty February afternoon. He had made each one stand alone for a moment behind a rusty wrecked car and imagine how it would be to hear the rattling of a desperate convict's chain coming closer through the fog. The children had come back wide-eyed, elated and scared. One of the girls had cried. Two of the parents had complained.

'It was improper. Indefensibly irresponsible,' said Merck, carpeting the teacher.

'It worked,' said Kit. 'You should see the essays.'

Ronald Harding would have liked to take Kit's side more often against Molly, but knew he must not. Kit, in some ways, was less trouble; in their thousand small feuds he was never the one to complain, preferring simply to take his own line in defiance of Molly. And he did work hard; worked himself white sometimes, never coasting, spending explosive concentrated energy on every single class.

Yet in the rows between the two teachers, the Head knew perfectly well that Kit was often to blame. He deliberately lost textbooks bought out of Molly's budget if he considered them dull; he illegally photocopied text from books without registering it if he thought it would help his classes; he refused to do 'Daffodils' from Molly's neatly made Year 9 worksheets and instead scoured second-hand bookshops with his own money to bring in piles of ancient, filthy, dog-eared anthologies and teach unfashionable poets like Flecker and Dowson. He embarked on projects of his own – many of them extremely popular with the children, who clustered to his unpaid extra sessions in the lunch hour and outside school. But he did not even try to co-operate with Molly's ideas.

Two years ago things had come to a head when Molly, newly confirmed as head of the English department, had declared a Year 7–10 project called 'Mysterious Planet'. All creative writing exercises throughout the school, from eleven- to fourteen-year-old groups, were to be subordinated throughout the Christmas term to the service of a science fiction saga.

She produced big charts with chapter headings: in Week 1 every class would write 'First Clues to the Mysterious Planet'. In Week 2, 'Flying to the Mysterious Planet', in Week 3, 'The Landing', and so forth. By the time everybody reached Week 12, 'Home at Last', the idea was that the best material would be ready for illustration by the art department and submission to a county inter-schools prize for something called 'Co-operative Creativity'.

It was not such a bad idea. It could have worked. But Kit, after two weeks, had quietly rebelled. He thought his groups were getting bored, and gave them licence, even encouragement, to leave the rails. Under 'The Landing' several of his better pupils wrote lively descriptions of their own domestic interiors ('The landing is ware you colide with yore Dad, crash! comming out of the bog in the deep nigt hours,' began one). Others briefly described a spaceship landing then veered off: 'Having landed, we looked around and desided it was dull, so we flew back and found ourselves in a medeeval castle where King John . . .' As the weeks progressed and this insubordination became the fashion throughout the school, the project crumbled. By Week 9 (scheduled as 'Animals of the Mysterious Planet') even Molly's own groups had begun turning in work with openings like 'Annie Mals worked as a stripper in a ragga club in Chicago calld The Mysterious Planet'.

Molly never saw the joke and blamed Kit bitterly. It was after this that Ronald Harding called them both in, administered a gently desperate reprimand, and drew up a scheme which he thought would enable Kit to pursue his idiosyncratic, inspirational teaching without unduly troubling Molly. Kit would do all the Year 7 teaching and half of Year 8; Molly would carry the burden of the GCSE course in the older years, assisted by old Roger Randing and the temporary staffer of the moment. It meant considerable upheavals in the timetable, but would keep their zones of responsibility as separate as possible. Kit, oddly enough, was the one to protest privately after that meeting.

'I'm not sure I'm best with the younger children,' he said. 'Wouldn't it be better the other way round?'

'No, surely not. The Year 7s and 8s adore you. You don't want to get bogged down in GCSE syllabuses. If you stick to the young ones you can have far more scope to wake them up and get them going, and be far more free about texts and projects.'

Kit was not, for some reason, happy at this, but co-operated. Harding suspected that his very, very nice wife – dear little Anna, sweetest, most easygoing girl on the staff! – had talked him out of protesting further. So the system worked.

Its only flaw, he thought, picking up the memo again, was that nowadays poor Molly was confronted with a steady stream of children who had experienced two years of Kit's verbal fireworks, eccentric texts and bouts of off-the-wall humour. Sometimes when they encountered her methodical, reliable pedagogy they were frankly and openly bored. The Head, a sensitive man, could understand that to Molly Miles it must be a torment at the beginning of each year to see, refracted three dozen times in the children before her, glittering shards of the one personality she most disliked.

Hence the present problem. Kit, among other things, was meant to teach his year groups how to write a letter of complaint to a company or government department. The three letters attached to Molly's crisp memo on his desk must have been unspeakably irritating to her. One began:

Dear Sir, I wish to complain about my washing machin. After six months it has broken and your repareman refuses to come. The whoreson dog! God rot his gallygaskins . . .

'The inappropriateness of language in these examples,' began Molly's accompanying memo, 'is only one out of many dozens of examples of the sloppy, self-indulgent foolery encouraged by . . .'

Harding sighed. Maybe it was time for another talk with Kit. Only ten minutes ago Graham Merck had been in with some whining complaint about Mr Milcourt having opened a window and compromised the integrity of the thermostat. On the other hand, the OFSTED inspectors had been dazzled by Kit's classes. And at the governors' last meeting, Anita Cox, a local GP and mother of a boy with a severely crippled leg in 7Z, had spoken glowingly of the poems her son was reading and writing since Kit had taken him for English. 'It's the first time since he was five years old and the car hit him that he's expressed what he feels about the disability. He's visibly happier. I don't know how it happened, but everything's falling into place at last.' No, thought Harding, he couldn't give up Kit. Even if it were possible. The two teachers would just have to make some compromises. But why, he thought, *why* – and here he stabbed the point of the ruined Biro savagely into the worn leather of his desk – why was it so much easier for a teacher to get reprimanded for being interesting than for being bloody dull?

He did not like calling staff to his office, so as the bell went he set out along the wintry, neon-lit corridors to catch Kit casually between classes. On the way he first met Kit's wife, dismissing a group which had been sticking French words on bits of blue card to features of the architecture. *Porte* fell off the door as he brushed against it to let her escaping class through, and he noticed *Couloir* being trampled under their feet.

'Anna! I'm glad you're back. Better?'

'It wasn't an *illness* sort of visit to the doctor, Ron. It was a *tests* sort of visit. Women's stuff.' Anna smiled up at him, pushing a lock of fair hair back from her bright face. Whenever Harding was with Anna, he missed his own Eileen. Which was daft, really; Eileen was thirty years older, grey and stout. But there was a womanly softness, he thought with a sad pang, a whole dimension of life . . . He pulled himself together.

'Ah. Sorry. Yes, you did say. Everything all right here?'

'As ever.' She grinned. 'You're out looking for Kit, aren't you?'

'Yes, yes. Oh dear. Is it obvious?'

'I just met Molly. She's just had one of 9X begin a specimen letter of complaint to British Gas with "Howl, howl, howl, howl, howl! O, ye are men of stones!"'

'Oh God.' Harding was comforted by Anna's grin; awful though the dilemma was, her bright face reminded him that it was also a very good joke. 'Do you think the kids do it on purpose? To wind her up?'

'Yes. Obviously. If Molly would just deal with it as a bit of naughtiness, and a springboard to teach from, it'd be fine. If the same thing happened to Kit he'd have a rousing time doing a session on appropriate words, formality and informality, and it'd be a riot. But Molly, poor love, just gets furious with Kit and takes it personally. She thinks he sets them against her.'

'Did you talk to her?'

'I told her to think of it as a natural progession, like baking bread. Kit yeasts the kids up till they're all puffy and above themselves, then she's got to knock and knead them down again. But in the end they turn into perfect loaves, thanks to both processes.'

Harding was struck with admiration. 'That is absolutely wonderful, Anna! I wish I'd thought of that.'

'Kit did,' said Anna, ruefully. 'Not that he believes it. He said that what he really thinks is that he's the caffeine and Molly's the Mogadon, and that the most he can ever achieve once he passes them on to her is to make sure they kick about a bit in their sleep. But I'm trying to teach him diplomacy, so the bread idea was his contribution. Just call him Metaphor Man.'

'Metaphor Man,' said Harding wonderingly. He put a fatherly hand on Anna's shoulder. 'Without you, where would we be?'

'Since I'm clearly basking in your favour, *sir*,' said Anna, looking up at him from under her lashes. 'Can we talk about the Dewar?'

Kit saw his wife and the headmaster deep in conversation as he passed the end of the long corridor. He smiled to himself. Anna would crack it. A long-held ambition, a plot between the two of them, was about to be realized.

*   *   *

Later, Anna was happy too as she walked home. She had been to the chemist at lunchtime and bought the little white plastic computer with its set of chastely wrapped 'test sticks'. Within the next day or at most two, her period would come and she could begin to use it. She had read the instruction book surreptitiously in the corner of the staff room and knew how it would work: green lights for useless days, red lights when she might conceive.

At the back of her mind was a faint, niggling worry about Kit. He was staying on to take the junior Latin club – Latin for Louts, he called it – which he had inaugurated in the previous summer term. The sessions, alternately flippant and raucous, mainly involved racing around the assembly hall hurling Latin jokes and insults between two teams named for Romulus and Remus. Shouts of *'Tua culpa, stultissima!'* and *'Noli te macerare, sceleris!'* rang through the hall every Wednesday afternoon, to the amusement of some staff and the tight-lipped irritation of others.

Anna had encouraged Kit in the idea on the grounds that it would help her to instil French and Italian into her GCSE groups in the following years. Today, however, for the first time she had looked at him and wished he did not do so many after-school clubs. Now that his summer tan had faded he looked paler than usual and tired. In all their ten years' adventures together at home and abroad, she had rarely known Kit look tired.

Anna frowned, but the small worry could not quell the great and swelling hope within her, the hope brought by the little white computer. Kit was fine, strong as an ox. Always had been. She would make him something very good for supper and tell him what she planned.

6

In the event, she never mentioned the computer at all. Kit came home that evening looking pale, but apparently in high spirits. His interest was not, she saw with rueful affection, likely to be gripped for very long by a discussion of her reproductive rhythms. So she stirred the onion soup, and listened to his plans, and reflected privately that maybe her mother's generation were right when they insisted that some things were 'women's talk', best kept ring-fenced against male curiosity and male indifference.

Another comforting thought came to her as well, and made up for many moments when she had been puzzled and a little wounded that Kit seemed less desperate for a child than she was. Maybe, she reflected, men did not become obsessed as women did with the longing for children. Maybe there was something admirable and practical about the way men failed to pine and swoon for love of imaginary babies. It could be that they only grew loving and protective feelings towards real babies: babies that were firmly in the world, warm and solid in their arms. She played happily with the idea. Men were not unfeeling. Of course not. They were just practical and manly and down-to-earth. They liked reality more than dreams. Anna smiled. For all her competence and independence, she was as feminine at heart as her mother.

At all events, once her husband had dumped his work upstairs in the study and poured them both a drink, the only thing he wanted was to pump her about her conversation with the head.

'Did he say we could have it? Did you crack it?'

'He almost promised. Wanted to talk to Merck.'

'Oh hell, hell, hell! Merck will want it for geography!'

'No, he doesn't. Apparently he said it was a bad time of year. Too cold, and interferes with mock GCSEs. The usual stuff.'

Kit paced up and down the kitchen, brandishing the heel of a French loaf and intermittently tearing bits off it with his strong white teeth.

'Well, someone else then. Atkins. Nellie Armstrong.'

'Calm down. I really think we've got it.' Anna smiled at him, and Kit punched the air, bringing his fist down and turning it round to show her the crossed fingers.

'Keep them crossed,' she said. 'But the signs are good.'

The Dewar Expedition was almost the only mark of distinction held by Sandmarsh High. Decades earlier, before the education reforms of the 1960s, the school had been a secondary modern, taking in children who failed the 11-plus exam for the grammar school at the far side of town. Sandmarsh in those days was good of its kind; a respectable proportion of its pupils clawed their way out of the low status implied by being there, and achieved enough to carry on into sixth forms elsewhere. A few even made it to that ultimate goal, rare and distinguished at the time, of a university place. One such child had been Eddie Dewar, only grandson of George Hamilton Dewar, who ran the first TV hire shop in the town.

Dewar senior, a widower and a strict Catholic moralist from Dundee, was inordinately proud of his grandson's entry to St Andrew's University. He became a governor of the school in his gratitude, and boasted about how wee Eddie had 'shown up the system' and 'taught a lesson to those that called him a failure'. The headmaster of that period, hearing this boast, challenged George Dewar to do something in return. 'Give us a sports cup, or a prize. Put your son's name on it.'

The tradesman had been much struck with this idea, and toyed with it for days. During those days, by coincidence, he was riled at a Chamber of Commerce dinner by a rival electrical retailer who had a granddaughter at the grammar school. This rival had been bragging about the trip abroad her class had taken to improve their Italian. 'They went to Florence. Firenzy, she calls it. You should hear her jabber on in Italian.'

Sandmarsh at that time did not do any language but French, and nor did it have school trips. This comparison rankled in George Dewar's soul until he came up with a solution.

'I won't give you a cup,' he said heavily at a later meeting. 'I'll leave ye a bit money. For a good purpose.' The head thought no more of it, until in February 1981 George Dewar died, leaving the bulk of his money to his son and grandson but a startlingly solid amount bound up in a trust for the use of the school.

There was a snag. It was for one use only: the will stipulated that funds from the trust must be drawn annually to support, in full, a cultural trip to Europe for fifteen able children. The trip was to be taken in whichever month of the year George Dewar died so as to further his memory. Moreover the children, said the will, should light a candle in a Catholic church abroad and pray for his soul.

The local education authority of the time was not best pleased. Such eccentric bequests might be all very well for private schools, but its restrictive conditions – particularly the one about the candles – were gall and wormwood to their modern sensibilities. Besides, February was a terrible month for school trips, what with the weather and the disruption to mock exams if two teachers had to be away at once. Representations were made to the trustees, asking to lift the conditions and allow the legacy to be used for more routine field trips and sporting tours. The trustees were adamant. If Sandmarsh wanted the money, Sandmarsh must take fifteen children to a European country every February for educational and cultural purposes. And light the candle to old George Dewar. They also pointed out that although the length of the trip was not stipulated, there was a clause saying that if the school failed to take up the option in any one year, the Trust would automatically be wound up and the money given to the local children's home. George Dewar had always said that the trouble with teachers was that they kept putting things off while they looked for reasons to do nothing. 'It would never do in business,' he used to say. So his will, cruelly, forced them to instant action on pain of ignominious loss.

Since then, every February, the school had managed some-thing. At times 'the Dewar' was no more than a coach down to Dover and an afternoon in Boulogne or Calais. Once Ian Atkins took a group of his best scientists to the *Cité des Sciences* in Paris; once Caroline Chang took Year 10 to Bruges. Molly Miles and Doreen Nixon the French specialist had taken a party from Ashford station to Lille aboard the Eurostar, and made them walk around in a crocodile, composing one French sentence about every shop window. This was fairly dull until the boys spotted *Le Video Sexy-Sex* in the Rue de Roubaix.

Anna had led a disastrous two-day excursion to Holland on the ferry three years earlier, when her colleague suffered food poisoning and had to be left in a Dutch hospital, and then the ferry had run aground and stranded her at the docks with fifteen snivelling thirteen-year-olds through a long, cold night on hard plastic chairs. Since then there had been only bad-tempered, unenthusiastic day trips to Calais. The word 'Dewar', spoken in the weeks before the Christmas holiday, now had the power to throw the headmaster into the deepest of glooms.

But Kit, quite accidentally, had found something out. He played squash on Tuesday evenings with a cheerful and indiscreet young local solicitor, and while they were drying themselves off in the shower room one night in the previous February, the conversation turned to interest rates.

'We're still seeing the effect of those enormous rates in the eighties,' said Henry Parker, rubbing his wet hair. 'Some of these trust funds we look after virtually doubled.'

'God, I'm glad I got out of banking,' said Kit. 'I used to hate watching rich bastards get richer by doing bog all.'

'No,' persisted Henry, throwing the towel down and reaching for his trousers, 'it's quite uplifting, when it's a trust for a good cause. Look at your Dewar thing at Sandmarsh. *Pots* of money. You haven't used up half what you could have done, year on year. So it's grown *enormous*. You could take the fourth form for a month on the Costa now and hardly know the differencee-oh.'

'Isn't there a limit? For any one trip?' said Kit, intrigued.

'Nope. Very basic conditions. Just fifteen children, Europe, culture, light the candle for old Dewar, and if you don't use it, you lose it. I was reading the deed the other day because it's a bit of a curiosity.'

'Hmmm,' said Kit noncommittally. But his eyes were alight.

Now, in the kitchen, Anna served the soup, tossed in the

toasted cheese and said, 'Ron Harding's not against your Venice idea. He's confirmed with the lawyers that there's plenty of money. But he says it's so far to go that the trip has to fall at least partly inside half-term.'

Kit got up from the table, pulled open an untidy drawer in the corner of the kitchen, and consulted the 1998 calendar for a moment. Coming back, he said, 'Fine. Perfect. I was going to suggest that anyway. The dates fit.'

Anna, blowing on her soup, did not ask him what dates. After a moment, she said, 'You still want to do it as a double act? You wouldn't rather go with someone from the art department? Nellie would love to go.'

'We need another Italian speaker,' said Kit. 'And *I* need *you*.'

Anna smiled at him through the steam of her onion soup.

A few days later, it was common knowledge in the school that a more adventurous Dewar than ever before was in prospect.

'Crafty devil,' said Eileen McCafferty, a dark, vivid woman who taught history and geography. 'Venice! Why should Venice fall to the English department, I would like to know?'

'It's more of a language trip,' said Molly Miles, whose outrage was so extreme that she prudently hid every vestige of it. 'Anna, of course, is a linguist.'

'But they're taking Year 7s,' said Ian Atkins tactlessly, blowing out his pink cheeks. 'None of them do Italian, do they?'

'It's an Eng. Lit. trip. Kit says the point is that Venice has inspired generations of English-language writers, and that physically it has hardly changed. So the kids can get inspired too, and understand the vision of Ruskin. See?' Caroline Chang spoke with her usual calm. 'I think it's a good idea. It's pretty rare for our sort of children to see virtually what their ancestors saw. No cars. Rich, dense, beautiful decay. It'll be a cultural jolt.'

'Ruskin!' said Nellie Armstrong. 'Oh well, I suppose it's an experiment worth doing. Show the same city to Ruskin, Byron, Wordsworth, Goethe and Leanne Mc Dougall and see who comes up with the best line.'

'That's right,' said Kit, coming into the room. 'They all think that Continental Europe consists of Disneyland Paris, the Calais hypermarket, a couple of Costas and the European Cup terraces.'

'Venice,' said Ian Atkins, 'from what I remember, consists of a hell of a lot of corners and dark alleys. You must be batty. You'll lose the lot of them in five minutes.'

'Oh, it's ever so quiet out of season,' said Eileen McCafferty. 'Dave and I went on our honeymoon just after Christmas. They'll be all right. We're all just jealous, Kit. We never had the brains to think of the Dewar as anything more inspiring than a day of hell in Calais. I'd come with you if Anna wasn't. And if it wasn't half-term.'

Eileen had two young children; she and Anna had been close friends for some time, although there was some recent strain on the friendship because Anna could not help envying her colleague's effortless fertility. Now Eileen asked, 'Why *is* it in half-term, anyway?'

'Because of the distance,' said Kit quickly. Anna, who had followed him into the staff room, gave her husband a sharp, puzzled glance. Why, uttering a banal enough truth, had he suddenly sounded as if he was lying?

In late November, Anna's sister Mary drove south to see her. The two were close, although they saw one another no more than three or four times a year. Ironically, they were far more closely in touch than Anna and her brother Mike, who lived only fifty miles away. But then, Mike travelled from his home territory only when he heard a rumour of a good new pub, generally with a name like the Ferret and Fishtank or Mucky Magee's. His weekends were spent banger-racing or watching races at Brand's Hatch. And Barbara did not much like Anna. Teachers, she would say to Mike whenever the families had briefly met, gave her the creeps. To compound this distaste, she could never get Kit to flirt with her. Every other man she knew did so, and she took it as a grave discourtesy.

Usually Anna went up to Sheffield to visit, on her own and by train. She was a fond aunt to Mary's four children, particularly the elder two, Janie and Martin, because they had been born before she herself had wanted children. Little Maggie and Lee were dear things, of course, but their very existence always seemed a reproach to her own failure. She should have given them cousins of their own age. She had tried hard enough. In a way, she thought as she made up Mary's bed, that would be an extra dimension of pleasure when – if – she had her own baby. She might find a new capacity to be genuinely, warmly, unenviously fond of her small nephew and niece. Already she glowed at the thought.

Mary's visit was not entirely for Anna's sake. She had left the four children with Don's sister and come south because Pamela Melville had declared in her masterful way that it was 'time Mary had some pampering'. Anna knew the meaning of this maternal summons: an expensive hairdo, a morning at the Sanctuary in Covent Garden attended by masseuses and make-up artists and waxers and exfoliators, and a trek to Knightsbridge for two or three pieces of 'good' clothing. Before her marriage, when she was a penniless student saving hard for Egypt and hardly able to afford face cream, Anna had played along with this. After she was with Kit she accepted three more of Pamela's summonses, but felt more and more awkward about it. Finally, two years into their marriage, she had said to her husband, 'My mother treats me and Mary like dolls.'

And Kit had said lightly, 'I wondered when you'd notice.'

After that, Anna had gently refused the invitations, with the same steadiness that she used when refusing her mother's nagging about 'Positively Plump' fitness classes.

'Mum, I'm sorry. It's not me. Any of it.'

'You've got a *very attractive* man there,' Pamela would say. 'A woman has to *work* to keep her husband. You're still young and pretty, dear, but once the babies come you'll be glad of some help to stay gorgeous.'

Anna squirmed, but did not contradict her. Mary, five years and four children older, certainly seemed to respond to Pamela's summonses with alacrity. Don did not earn much working for the council, and Mary's part-time earnings as a librarian were more likely to go on children's clothes than beauty treatments. She teased Anna for her stand against the pampering days. 'If Mum wants me to be Barbie and pays for me to be Barbified,' she said, 'that's what I'll be. I am pink plastic putty in her hands.'

So she arrived on Saturday evening, laden with carrier bags and smelling overpoweringly of beauticians' oils and creams.

Anna hugged her sister, then pushed her to arm's length and wrinkled her nose.

'Phwoo! The full monty, was it?'

'Totally,' said Mary. 'Well, I drew the line at the bikini wax.'

'Colonic?'

'No, she's decided they're bad news.'

'They are. Mine was hell. It was a *perfumed* colonic. Imagine!'

'I've got pots of fibre pills and vitamins, though,' said Mary, 'and she had my toes pulled all over the place by a Chinese man. And then we went to some patronizing crone in jet-black Kenzo to have my colours done. I'm Bird of Paradise: cerise and lime green. Ma, so it transpires, is Arctic Sunset.'

Anna giggled, happy to share the humour and the horror of their mother.

Mary looked her up and down and said, 'You look pretty OK, even without having your toes pulled. You're not . . . ?'

'No,' said Anna. 'But the specialist said everything was OK.'

'I know. Mum told me.'

'I never told her!'

'No, but it was *her* specialist, wasn't it?' Mary grimaced. 'And she is a person who thinks the "my" in "my doctor" means roughly the same as it does in "my shoes" or "my cat". She'll have wormed it out of him. Or his wife.'

'Yes,' said Anna with a sigh. 'Anyway, she did pay the eighty quid for the appointment. I'm accepting it as my pampering for the year. Why do we do it? We're grown women. These aren't presents, you know. They're acts of domination.'

'I don't care,' said Mary. 'Mum means well. And the fact that she doesn't listen means she never knows about the really important things. Which is good. Some mothers try and change you from inside. All she does is clamp clothes and stuff on the outside of us. I think we get away lightly.' She eyed Anna up and down again, expertly. 'So anyway, the doc says you can get pregnant?'

'Yup. Kit's fine too. So we will, I suppose. I've got this brilliant new thing . . .'

And, at last, she had somebody to tell about her white fertility computer. She told her sister every detail of its working, expatiating on the miraculous technological union of chemistry and the silicon chip. Mary sat across the kitchen table, listening and watching Anna's face.

'You wee on a stick whenever it shows you a yellow light,' explained Anna earnestly. 'And slot it into a hole, and the light winks, and when it stops winking the test's over and you pull the stick out and throw it away, and then it shows a light. Green means you can't be fertile. Red means you might be. Last month I got heaps of red, but it doesn't mean anything because they stay on the safe side. It's meant for people who are trying not to get pregnant. But I thought, how perfect for if you *do* want to! You know the exact fertile days!'

'Does Kit like the idea?' asked Mary, privately thinking how unlikely Don would be to respond to any such system of traffic lights.

Anna blushed. 'He doesn't know. It just felt better not to go on at him about cycles and things.'

'So you get your red day, and slink around in your best silk knickers?' said Mary. 'Is that the idea?'

This time it was Anna who privately reviewed her married life, and realized how little silk underwear had ever meant to Kit.

'Well . . .' she said. 'But there is something I want to show you. It happened today. I did know it would, in theory, but – oh, come on, Mary, come and look. It's so exciting I could die.' Scraping her chair, she rose from the table and put her hand out to her sister. 'Come on.'

The two went upstairs, and Anna dived to the back of the bathroom cupboard, a matchboarded Victorian cavern under the basin. Reaching behind the waste pipe (Mary's eyes widened at this concealment, but she said nothing) Anna pulled out a flat, white plastic case half the size of a paperback book. She flipped it open and pointed to the little LCD display screen. The number 18 was shown, and above it a red light. Beside the number, to the right, was an oval lying on its side, with a small dot just off centre.

'Look!' said Anna. 'You know what that is?'

'It's an egg.' Mary giggled. 'You've laid an egg! A happy hen!'

Anna smiled, and sniffed, and dashed her sleeve across her

eyes. 'You don't know what it means. It's the first time I've known, really known, that I'm normal. I have eggs. That's proof. Chemical, computer proof. I could conceive. Mary, I cried for half an hour this morning when I saw it. Luckily Kit had gone out for a run.'

'How long will the egg be there?' asked Mary.

'I rang up the helpline to ask. Perhaps two or three days. It's the absolute peak fertile time.'

'So, go for it. Are you going to tell Kit?'

Anna closed the display after one more loving look, thrust it back into the depths of the cupboard, and while her face was still hidden under the basin said, 'No. It feels a bit tacky. But I know, and that's the main thing.'

Kit came home at six thirty, yawning and muddy, having driven the last of the under-thirteen football team home.

'How'd they do in the match?' asked Anna.

'Lost, seventeen to two. Mick Harris had a cold, and Darren let every goal through. I wish Graham Merck would stop buggering off on courses. It's his rotten bloody team.'

'It was good of you to stand in,' said Mary. 'I tell Don he doesn't know he's born, working office hours.'

'I bet I know what he says right back.' Kit was stripping off his shorts and sweater in the shower room by the kitchen, entirely careless of modesty in front of his sister-in-law. 'I bet he says teachers get long holidays.' The blast of hot water almost drowned his words.

'He does,' said Mary. She was drinking beer, and quite unfazed by Kit's reappearance in a skimpy towel a few moments later. He bent and kissed the top of her head, for he was fond of Mary.

'Everything all right with Don and the children?'

'Oh yes,' said Mary. 'Only Lee says he wants to be a deep sea diver, and he knows Unca Kit is one, because you showed him your tank and mouth thing once. He says will you teach him? One day? And can he come and stay in the holidays and try breathing through your mouth thing?'

'Regulator,' said Kit. 'Tell him it's called a regulator. And yes, of course he can.' He pulled the towel together where it threatened to fall off, and vanished upstairs. Anna picked up his sports kit and threw it into the gaping maw of the washing machine.

Mary was silent for a moment, then said, 'Seriously, though, Anna. Silk underwear. Dance of the Seven Veils, every egg night. He'd be a brilliant dad.'

7

The egg symbol on the little screen came and went in November, but was met by no more than sleepy hugs and long drowsy bedtime conversations. Anna, aware in honesty that the relative scarcity of their lovemaking had never bothered her before, tried not to allow herself to be resentful. She loved him. He loved her. They touched and hugged constantly and joyfully. They were as they were. The sexual act was not all that bound them together, nor was it even the centre of their marriage. It was hard for Anna, who some nights could see nothing but the shape of the egg, floating before her as if the air in the room was a computer screen; but a sense of integrity upheld her. This was her marriage, and it had its own rules.

One image at least helped her to be patient: whenever she was tempted to storm, smoulder, weep, vamp or manipulate this man who was her husband and best friend, a vision of her mother at her most kittenish came unbidden as an awful warning.

But during the long cold days of December, Kit seemed to grow tired and nervous and – paradoxically – more amorous. He had nightmares but would never tell them in the morning. Moaning and thrashing, he would often turn to embrace her in the small hours, muttering 'Anna, Anna, Anna' as if her name could be a charm to efface some horror. In the morning after these encounters she would wake early, kiss his sleeping shoulder and go in the darkness to the cold bathroom. Usually, the light on the little console glowed a mocking goblin green.

On the day after Boxing Day, though, they drove back in the evening from a long, difficult lunch with his father at the retirement home in Cornwall. Kit, who had been silent for most of the long drive, had a wild, fretful night of bad dreams. In the morning a warm red light dazzled Anna as she opened the case in the dark bathroom. By its glow she saw something else: the brave little egg symbol with its black dot. This time the dot looked to her like a curled tadpole, a life in waiting. Two hours before, Kit had turned to her with passion in the dawn, kicking off shreds of nightmare as he mumbled her name and holding her so tight that she was breathless. The egg, thought Anna with a sudden deep happiness, had finally had its chance.

In an agony of self-control, she waited a whole fortnight before buying a test at the chemist's, and carried the box around in her bag for a further week before she used it. One grey January day she could wait no longer. It was mid-morning break at Sandmarsh High, and a certainty was growing in her heart. For days she had been unable to bear the smell of fried food, and a hopeful queasiness overcame her sometimes in the morning.

All her life, she never forgot the moment. While she did the test in the bland white cubicle Molly Miles was running taps outside, walking heavy-footed to yank and clank the roller towel, and talking contemptuously to Doreen Nixon about the new maths syllabus. Anna sat on the edge of the seat, looking at the ceiling, counting up to twenty before she dared look down at the white tab on the testing stick. Molly was saying, in her customary tone of severe irritation: 'I don't know how they get away with it!' and Doreen Nixon, quieter, was apologetically murmuring something about free-choice modules.

As Anna let her eyes drop to the stick held tightly in her hand, it seemed to her as if the blood pounding in her ears drowned all voices, all noises, in a great joyful roaring flood of happiness. The double blue stripe was unmistakable. She was pregnant.

She sat alone there for a few moments, then put the stick into the side pocket of her bag and emerged, walking with self-conscious care, terrified of shaking the baby loose.

Kit, looking round the staff room at break, missed her. Disconsolately he wandered over to where Ian Atkins was pinning a scrap of newsprint to the board.

'What's that?'

'Look.'

Kit read it, and laughed. A jolt of high spirits went through him. 'Told Molly yet?'

'You tell her, sweetie. With a gentle, sweeping arm movement.' Ian Atkins stepped back, a cherubic vulture, laughing at his work.

The cutting was from a teachers' magazine, advising the profession on how to defuse anger and aggression in the classroom by body language. 'Wide, sweeping, gentle arm movements with upturned palms,' wrote the psychologist author, 'and a mellow but resolute calmness of tone are important. Body language can convey stillness, concentration, a sense of communality. Smiles should be wide, tranquil, and not show too many teeth.'

'What are you giggling about?' asked Caroline Chang, with an armful of maths books. She read it with some indignation. 'Why does every stupid shrink and every wally journalist think they can tell teachers what to do? Do I go around telling them how to do their jobs?'

Kit had turned aside and was writing, in his beautiful prepschool boy's italic hand, an addendum to the advice. He dug out drawing pins to fix it under the original, not minding that in order to do so he left Graham Merck's latest memo about cloakroom hooks to hang forlornly by one corner. Kit's notice said: 'Should this tactic work too well and the class become comatose, experts recommend punching the air, stamping the feet, rotating the pelvis, jutting out the jaw and uttering robust cries of "*Caramba!*"'

So it was that Anna found him – and would always remember him, on the first day she knew him as a father – laughing in the centre of a knot of colleagues.

He came over to her, stomping like a flamenco dancer and clapping his hands above his head. 'Body language – the new teaching aid. You want them to learn French? Make your whole body a Moulin Rouge!' He grabbed her to join his impromptu tango, but she stiffened and shook her head. She felt too fragile, too tremblingly full of precious cargo to be swung around by his strength. Kit let her go and looked at her, puzzled.

It was several minutes, and the other side of the 10.50 bell, before she could separate him from the group for long enough to whisper, 'I'm going to have a baby. We're going to have a baby. I'm pregnant. Really, I am. I just did the test.'

Kit looked down at her, astonished. He felt too much, and was too confused by the feelings, to speak. For him there was always a poem to hand. A voice in his head began quoting Louis MacNeice:

I am not yet born; O hear me!
Let not the bloodsucking bat or the rat or the stoat or the club-footed
  ghoul come near me . . .

The poem brought the child suddenly, shockingly to life: a thin insistent voice from deep within Anna, asking and accusing and hoping and dreading. A child. Kit shuddered, and his eyes widened, unseeing, in a kind of horror. How hard to be a child!

Then he saw Anna again, wholesome and untroubled, her shining happiness a miracle in itself. A small frown was beginning to crease her eyes as she saw that she had startled him and feared that he was not pleased. Kit took back control of himself; gently, he stroked her hair away from her face and bent to kiss the tear in the corner of her eye. It was typical of him that he did not care that Ian Atkins and Graham Merck were both watching him, one with sardonic affection and the other with no affection at all.

'Well done,' he said. 'Well done, my love. Are you all right? Do you want to go home and lie down?'

'No. Yes. No, of course not. I'm not ill,' said Anna. 'Only I do feel frightened all the time that it'll just suddenly go. Fall out or something.'

'They don't, very often, do they?' said Kit. 'Don't worry.'

Anna did worry, although a little less as the weeks went by. Her GP Dr Ransom, a chubby young man her own age with two bouncing babies at home, confirmed that her health was excellent and the portents good. He gave her a buff-coloured card to record her blood and urine tests. The dates on the card stretched ahead, nearly nine months, to the second half of September. EDD. Expected Date of Delivery.

'It's a nice time to have a new baby,' he said. 'Not too hot, not too cold. And you can finish the school year without worrying, and have the last two and a half months without too much stress. Very nice timing. Are you planning to go back?'

'I haven't planned anything,' said Anna. 'It seemed like tempting fate. But I suppose I could take two terms off as maternity leave while I think about it.'

'Can you afford to go part-time?' asked Dr Ransom, twirling his pencil.

'Yes. I think so. We don't have a big mortgage.'

'Everything else all right? At home?'

'Wonderful,' said Anna. 'But meanwhile, please tell me, what can I do? Should I travel? I just don't know. I'm out of touch. I've sort of avoided pregnant women for the last few years.'

The doctor, whose own wife had undergone a similar few years of looking away from bumps and pushchairs, regarded his patient with sympathy. 'You can do everything you normally do. Lay off the scuba diving in summer, obviously, and try to have a more relaxed time than you and your husband usually seem to do. No mountains, perhaps. Or hundred-mile hikes. Or bicycling up the Pyrenees.'

Anna hesitated. 'Isn't it the first three months that are most risky?'

'Y-yes.' He frowned, not seeing what she was driving at. 'Though a lot of women don't know they're pregnant until they're past that stage, astonishingly enough. So the statistics aren't clear. But you live close to work, and should be able to keep the stress down, with your experience. Not going ski-ing, or anything? I advise against it, though plenty of girls get away with it.'

'Not ski-ing. It's just that I'm supposed to be going with a school trip to Italy. To Venice. It's in less than a month. I don't . . .' She could not go on. Immense guilt overcame her, for she knew that she was trying to make innocent Dr Ransom forbid her to go on the Dewar journey at half-term. If he forbade it, it would be easier to tell Kit. She could stay home instead, and lie down a lot, and nurture the seed of new life without which, she suddenly thought, she would die of grief. A sob rose in her throat, and the doctor leaned forward and looked carefully at her.

'You don't want to go? You do know there isn't any reason you can't fly? Not at this stage?'

'We aren't flying.'

Kit had vetoed the idea, saying that a vital part of the educational impact of the trip would be for the children to appreciate the real size of Europe, the barrier of the Channel, and the existence of land borders. 'I don't want them just fork-lifted up into the clouds and dumped down three countries further on,' he said. 'Travel education matters too. We'll take the ferry, and the train to Paris, and then the Venice sleeper, and go over the causeway to Venice in the dawn. I've found a little *pensione* on a back canal near the station that will let us have all six rooms. We can walk there with the luggage.'

Anna agreed with his thinking, but now the prospect of an eighteen-hour journey with a shrill pack of children filled her with dismay. And there would be all the walking in Venice, the climbing of San Marco to see the four stone horses, and the queueing for *vaporetti*. As she sat in the doctor's surgery, she became convinced with a rising sense of panic that some time during those five days of travelling and trudging she would lose the baby. The sob was followed by others as she buried her face in her hands, speechless.

The doctor, too innocent to worry about being misinterpreted, reached an awkward hand out to pat her shoulder.

'The one thing I say to pregnant women,' he said when her sobs had subsided, 'is that of all times in your whole life this is the moment to follow your instinct. Please yourself. If you don't want mother-in-law to stay, don't have her. If you don't want to leave the country, stay home. Tell your school your doctor advises against chaperoning this trip, and let them send someone else.'

He was puzzled, as Anna left, that although she accepted this dictat and seemed grateful for it, there was still a visible shadow of worry and unhappiness over her. He did not, of course, know that it was Kit's trip.

Kit was waiting for her at home, making cauliflower cheese with frowning concentration. As usual, he dropped the spoon in the pan to turn and hug her. She stood close to him, head bowed, resting on his chest. As he picked up the spoon again to stir the cheese sauce, she stayed close, within the circle of his arm.

'Kit,' she began, 'this baby. It's really important to us, isn't it? The most important thing?'

He stopped stirring. *The bloodsucking bat or the rat or the club-footed ghoul* ... 'Something's wrong? With the baby? Did the doctor say?'

Perversely reassured by his fear, Anna calmed it and continued, haltingly, to explain her fear of going on the Dewar trip within the first fragile months. 'I won't be such a wimp once it's established. But I am so constantly scared of losing it. Kit. I'm sorry. I just am.' At this point she burst into tears, and slumped on a chair with her head on the kitchen table.

Kit looked down at his wife with a mixture of amusement and dismay. For nearly ten years, ever since he had first seen her in the lamplight at the desert camp, Anna had been the anchor and focus of his life. She had given him the confidence to leave his career, to forget his cold childhood at Priory Shore School and admit that his vocation was to be a teacher. She had come on his restless travels and adventures, climbed with him, walked with him, dived the seas with him. She had made him strong by trusting him, and safe by loving him. She was his home, his friend, his shelter. He had been struck one day by some words in a rock song, played at killer volume on the Bannerman boy's ghetto-blaster in the playground:

> *Baby you're the only thing in this whole world*
> *That's pure and good and right;*
> *An' wherever you are and wherever you go*
> *There's always gonna be some light.*

Anna was the light. Without her he would, Kit thought with a rare pang of self-pity, have been a lonely man. Marion, his mother, who loved but never understood him, died in the year after his wedding; he had no siblings, and his father was – well, never mind his father.

He knew Anna, every inch of her and every quirk of her mind. But not a pregnant Anna. Seeing her thus, collapsed and sobbing, Kit felt that he was entering uncharted ground. Nothing in his masculine education had prepared him for this perilous swamp of hormones. As a romantic and avid reader he was quite at home with high emotion, but this kind of small half-physical hysteria was strange to him.

Nor had Anna ever before let him down over an adventure. He did not want to think of her as letting him down now, but with a pang of unease he felt it. To take fifteen Year 7 children, utterly inexperienced travellers and cultural blank slates, for three days at large in Venice was challenging enough. To do it the way he planned was even more so. It had been good to know that he would have Anna at his side to collude in the excitements and dramas he had secretly resolved on. Now he would not have her assistance. Nor was it fair to ask for it; he could not be a bloodsucking bat or a ghoul to threaten his own child.

Trained by his pastimes to think clearly, act resolutely, and control his breathing in times of panic, Kit gently put his hands on Anna's heaving shoulders and said, 'Don't cry, sweet one. Of course you mustn't come if you're worried. You stay here, put your feet up. I wish I could stay with you.'

Anna raised her face to his, tears smudging the mascara she always wore to darken her long, pale lashes. 'Are you sure? It'll mean you have to get someone else from the staff. And it'll have to be a woman. What about the rooms?'

'They originally offered to put four kids in a room, not three. If we cram the kids in a bit there'll be a spare room. The *pensione* won't mind: they can charge more. I'll find some-one.'

As Anna blew her nose and returned to her normal state of calm, they discussed who to ask.

'I'd prefer Eileen McCafferty,' said Kit. 'She did say she fan-cied it.'

'Yes, but half-term – even though you're back on the Tuesday night. What about her kids? Her husband's at work.'

'Hmm. Or Caroline Chang? Maths teachers never get to go on trips. Do you think she'd come? Or Nellie Armstrong?'

'Sweetheart, you'd go mad with Nellie Armstrong. You'd lose them all. She can't find her way to the door without dropping half a dozen things.'

'I wish Doreen Nixon could come,' Kit said glumly. Doreen

Nixon, nearing retirement, was in a wheelchair with a degenerative spinal disease. He and she had an affectionate sparring relationship: Doreen slapped him down without malice and supported him without sentimentality. It was the kind of rapport, Kit often thought, that he would have liked to have with a mother. But his own mother had been sad and vague and passive, and near the end of her life had hardly spoken from one day to the next.

'Yes,' said Anna, sighing. 'I'd feel happy if you had someone like Doreen to keep the show on the road. But Caroline would be terrific too.'

Together, they ate their cauliflower cheese and discussed the problem of Kit's travelling companion.

Neither of them, for a moment, entertained the ridiculous thought that it might be Molly Miles.

8

The tableau was timeless: on one side of the big desk, authority triumphant and on the other its victim, stunned with disbelief. Authority was represented by Ronald Harding (although he spoiled the picture rather with a nervous and hunched mien) and by Graham Merck, who stood at his side in more upright and commanding pose. On the other side stood Kit Milcourt. He had always put his hands behind his back when he was trying to disguise discomfiture, and now, biting his lip, he looked as if a Roundhead tribunal had just asked him when he last saw his father.

It was Friday morning, the beginning of February half-term. At noon the coach was set to depart for Dover and the ferry. Kit had arrived in school bearing his usual briefcase and in addition a large and ancient leather suitcase with his father's initials stamped on it. He had gone up to the staff room with these, raided a certain cupboard and made himself a cup of coffee while he waited for Caroline Chang, his travelling partner. She always arrived early; her soft grey woollen coat was hanging on a peg, with her squashy briefcase beneath it, but there was no sign of her.

Ahead of schedule as usual, thought Kit, with brotherly affection. He had always enjoyed Caroline's dry intellectual wit and spinsterly precision, and had come to like her even more during the weeks they had conferred about the coming trip. He told her almost everything he planned for the children – the night walks through the city, the relentless diary-keeping, and the expenditure of the Dewar contingency fund on specially briefed gondoliers so that the group could scatter into twos and threes on the dark water, to feel for a while the ancient melancholy and terror of the city, instead of being herded around in a group.

He had run through his schedule of readings, and of visits, and even finally told her why his suitcase was so cumbersome. She had said, unprompted and approving, 'I like it. Very different. It should fan a few sparks.'

She must have gone straight down to L71, thought Kit, to start checking the labels and solidity of the children's bags. It was a necessary job. Sandmarsh children, except for the few who had experience of aeroplanes to Spain, were often unaccustomed to travelling anywhere except in the family car or van, and their holdalls were notorious for falling open or falling apart in the course of school trips. Designer labels and football club logos were, it seemed, no guarantee of the integrity of zips. Before her trips, Molly Miles always brought two empty cases of her own to school on the day of departure and insisted on decanting the contents of suspect nylon rucksacks into these. Many children bore well into adulthood the psychological scars of having gone on a field trip carrying one of Miss Miles's stout, practical, green tartan suitcases.

Kit proceeded unworried to Room L71, and found fourteen of his fifteen charges there, but no Miss Chang. Kit asked after the fifteenth child, Sarah Midali. There had been some trouble with her parents over the dangers of her 'catching things' off foreign food. But that, surely, had been resolved by the intervention of her grandmother? Kit frowned irritably as he asked where she was. In the past weeks several of the original members of the group had dropped out and been replaced, causing him endless paperwork.

'Yes, sir, Sarah's here,' volunteered little Andrew Murray, looking up at his teacher with huge brown eyes, and struggling a little with a lisp. 'She just went with a message for Mr Atkins. About the doctor.' Kit sighed with relief, and ticked her name on the list he had pulled out of his pocket. Full house. Except—

'S'rotten about Miss Chang, innit, sir?' said Darren Oxtey, a bright-eyed boy whose father was in Pentonville Prison but whose spelling was quite the best in the class. 'I s'pose she can't come now.'

'What? What's happened to Miss Chang?' Kit looked up from his list, startled. Several voices chorused:

'Broken leg, sir.'

'Nah, it's 'er ankle.'

'Din't you know, sir? Fell down the steps helping Mrs Nixon with her chair.'

'Is Mrs Nixon all right?' said Kit wildly. He needed to ask a question, any question, rather than face the horrible fact.

'Yessir. Mrs Nixon fell half out the chair, but she's fine. Pulled back in, says she's got ever so strong arms, 'cos of not having legs that work. Miss Chang got *her* leg caught in the wheel.'

'Nah, it was the brake thing.'

'Was not, so. Was the wheel.'

'Right,' said Kit. 'I want you all to stay right here. No question of anybody leaving the room. Except to the toilets. Marianne and Mick, I'm putting you in charge of everybody staying put. When Sarah gets back, tell her not to wander off. Even for Mr Atkins.' He took a deep breath and exhaled with careful control, like a diver testing his regulator. When he reached the door he paused and turned back.

'Hang on a minute.' He opened his briefcase and handed the two eldest children wads of notebooks and a bundle of pens. 'These have each got names on. Give them out. They're your diaries, and they're the most important thing about this whole trip. You hand them back to me every lunchtime and evening. If you lose them you have nothing but bread and water for the next three meals. *Stale*, *mouldy* bread. Start them now. We've all had a shock, with Miss Chang's accident, and that's part of travelling too. I want you all to write one page about it. It's all right, Josh, they're very small pages.'

'Can it be a poem, sir?' asked Mick Harris.

'Yes. Anything but a drawing.'

'Are we still going to go, then, sir?' asked Andrew.

'Of course we are,' said Kit. And he went straight to the headmaster's office.

He found the head and the deputy waiting for him. The first thing Kit did, to Merck's irritation, was to ask Ronald Harding whether he, perhaps, could come instead.

'The rules are quite clear. You are perfectly aware of that. You have to have a *female* adult,' said Graham Merck. 'The headmaster is not female. Mrs McCafferty is not free. Mrs Milcourt we know about. Mrs Nixon is unable to travel. Miss Armstrong—'

'Look, forget the ones who can't come. Tell me who can,' said Kit, desperately. The last few female members of staff were flashing before his inner eye, and with a moment's hopefulness he blurted, 'The new girl – bright girl – CDT – the one who does the welding. What's her name?'

Merck smiled, not pleasantly. 'Miss Dinsdale is hardly experienced.'

Harding, looking across the desk at Kit, raised a hand to silence his deputy. Merck was, so the headmaster thought, enjoying the occasion far more than was decent.

'Kit,' he said gently, 'there is a staff member who says she will come. She has a valid passport and plenty of experience, and I for one think it is very sporting of her to give up her weekend plans.'

'Miss Miles,' said Kit. 'You mean Molly Miles.'

'I do,' said the headmaster. 'She's gone home, to pack.' He turned to Graham Merck. 'Graham, that reminds me, would you mind going down to X37 and telling Miss Miles's Year 11 group to get on with some work?'

When Merck had gone, Harding motioned to Kit to sit down. Kit sank onto a chair.

'We're all professionals,' he said. 'I'm sure you'll work together splendidly. It might be the making of your professional relationship.'

'Um,' said Kit. 'Er, um. Yes. So it might, Ron, so it might. Why can't I have Miss Whatsit the welder?'

Harding raised both hands, as if a gun were being pointed at him. Placatingly, he said, 'We've had no rows for a couple of weeks, have we? Between you two?'

'No,' said Kit. 'There has been a lull in hostilities from Miss Miles. That is true. But it's only because she knows I've been ripping through the dull stuff so we can work on Venice before Easter.'

Harding looked slyly down at the table, avoiding Kit's eye.

He ventured a joke. 'I suppose you aren't planning to do much parsing in Venice? Even a little bit of grammar, at the end of each day – ask her advice a bit, perhaps?'

Kit remained silent, but a smile twitched the corner of his mouth.

Snuffling, affecting a benevolent academic vagueness, Harding continued, 'And Wordsworth did write a very fine Venetian sonnet, "Once she did hold the gorgeous East in fee". That's his, isn't it? It's not "Daffodils", of course, but maybe it's included in your programme . . . Miss Miles is very fond of Wordsworth, I believe.'

Kit, as if abruptly deciding to cast off a cloak of gloom, threw his head back and laughed. 'OK, I give in. We'll be friends. A miracle will happen. It'll be like an American film. I'll say, "Gee, Molly, we've had our bad times, but I'd like you to know I really respect what you do," and she'll say, "Kit, put it there, buddy." Oh yes, I'll be good. *Ecco la commedia*.'

'Please, Kit,' said the headmaster, serious now. 'Be nice to Molly.'

In her tidy flat Molly Miles packed her little wheeled suitcase with speed and efficiency, folding drab skirts and flicking the sleeves of rayon blouses neatly into position as she laid them on the heap. She had planned to drive to Dorset over half-term and see her mother, but duty was more important. Her mother, on the phone, had entirely agreed. 'You do your duty, dear. If this is the man you've told me about, it would be criminal to let him loose alone in foreign places with those poor children and only some silly little floozy to help.'

Grimly, she laid a pink nightdress case on top of the clothes and zipped up the top of the case, locking the two ends of the zip together with a little brass padlock that gave a satisfying, spiteful snap! It was her duty indeed. The Dewar trip could not be cancelled or else the school would lose it; the only other potential volunteer to assist Mr Milcourt was Maria Dinsdale from the CDT department, who was only twenty-three years old and had never taken charge of a school trip, let alone abroad.

Moreover, this was not, in Molly Miles's opinion, likely to be a well-regulated trip. Travel and accommodation had not been organized through a recognized educational agency, so she had heard, but directly by Kit Milcourt. So *heaven knows* what the hotel would be like. A brothel, quite likely, and if it was, the man would just laugh.

She pulled her suitcase upright onto its wheels, glanced around the flat, and moved towards the door. Thank goodness, she thought briskly, that Tibbins had died, so there was no cat-feeding to organize. It was a blessing, really.

She did not like to admit to herself that she had wept for Tibbins all through Christmas Eve, alone. Molly Miles abhorred sentimentality.

When she got to school, the coach for Dover was already there, its steel flank gaping as children passed their bags to the driver for stowage. A little apart from the bus, Kit Milcourt stood deep in conversation with his wife.

Molly softened, as always, on seeing Anna. It was Anna who came over to her first, both arms outstretched in a gesture which in anybody else she would have dismissed as self-indulgently theatrical. But Anna grasped Molly's rough hands in her smooth ones and said, 'I am so grateful it's you. Kit's terribly grateful, too. To have someone with your experience step in at the very last minute! He says it's a real providence. You're a heroine. Thanks.'

Anna had decided on this tactic as soon as she heard the terrible news, and the substance of her conversation with Kit had been a rapid, desperate lecture from wife to husband on how grateful, how humble, how accommodating he must be.

'It's the only way!' she said. 'Don't play it the hard way, sweetheart, I just beg you. Don't tease her. Don't provoke her. Don't let her think you're colluding with the kids to mock her. She's human, she's got feelings.'

'I'll take your word for that,' Kit had said gloomily. 'But I am not going to let her make this trip boring for the kids. We are not going to write one sentence on each shop window. I mean it, Anna. I've spent ages planning this.' Longer than even you know, he thought guiltily. Even Anna did not know that months before the head's agreement – the very week, indeed, that Henry Parker had indiscreetly revealed the scale of funds lying unused in the Dewar – Kit had provisionally booked the whole of the Pensione Encaro for this particular weekend in 1998. Just in case he got his way.

Now Molly Miles was coming. Hell! Hell! But Anna, suddenly not soft and tearful and hormonal but quite her old strong self, was taking a firm line with him and insisting that he co-operate and behave. There was a kind of comfort in that.

'You sound like our old Matron,' he said fondly. 'Psyching us up in the infirmary for an injection with a blunt needle in the bum.'

Anna smiled, and kissed him. 'I'm going to start the ball rolling,' she said, and moved towards Molly to deliver her speech.

'Oh hell,' said Kit under his breath, and then he, too, moved across the tarmac towards his squat, implacable little enemy. He smiled, showing rather too many teeth. 'Molly. Thanks. What a business, eh? Poor Caroline. We are grateful.' It was as much as he could manage.

It was not enough to soften Molly. She gave him a tight smile, and climbed onto the bus to sit down heavily next to dreadlocked Kara Brindley, who was wrapped in moody isolation because Leanne had gone off to sit with Josh Bannerman. When Miss Miles plumped down beside her, Kara, startled, swallowed her illicit chewing gum and huddled further into the corner.

With a heavy heart Kit lifted the wheeled suitcase into the coach, placing it at the far end from his own big battered case. As the driver clanged the compartment shut like a prison door he had a sudden absurd conviction that once the steel door was shut, Molly Miles's suitcase would wheel itself over and attack his case with tooth and claw, spilling its guilty contents onto the bus floor.

Looking round in hope of comfort, he saw Anna raising a hand to him in grave benediction as she walked back alone towards the dining hall.

At Dover, all went smoothly. Kit had regained sufficient control of himself to ask Molly meekly whether she would be so kind as to take charge of all the passports and train tickets. This trapping of authority pleased her, as he had intended it should, and she went so far as to say, 'Of course, this is your trip. But I'll be happy to take any *practical* matters off your hands. I do have experience of Continental travel, and there are things people don't expect, like Compostage des Billets.'

Kit, who had in his time travelled from Africa to Iceland, rowed Lake Titicaca and walked through Eastern Europe with a mule, made deferential, humble noises of gratitude. For the sake of the children, for the sake of the spark, for the sake of sowing fifteen lifetimes of memories, he had to make it work.

Anna went round to the hospital to see Caroline Chang, whose leg was in traction. The maths teacher, her thick Chinese hair spread on the pillow, looked at Anna with rueful dark eyes.

'Of all the wheelchairs on all the stone steps in the world, I had to tangle with Doreen's today. Oh, Anna, I am sorry. I heard what happened.'

'About Molly?'

'Yes, Ian Atkins told me. I told him to suggest little Maria Dinsdale, but it was too late.'

'Merck! I bet he kyboshed that perfectly sensible suggestion.'

'Yes. For some reason he really likes stirring the feud. He's not that struck on your dear husband himself, and I suppose Molly makes a good attack dog. But Kit won't rise to it. Will he? He won't be so stupid?'

Anna sighed, and patted her colleague's arm. 'To be honest,' she said, 'I never really have the faintest idea what Kit will do.'

The sea was glassy and calm, the ferry half empty. In a corner of the big saloon Molly sat alone with a cup of tea, solicitously bought for her by Kit. She had thought that he and the group would stay here too, out of the drizzling rain, but no sooner was her tea placed in front of her than they had all disappeared. Slowly she drank the hot brew, then felt the call of duty and supervision too strong to resist.

They were nowhere inside the ship; not in the central hall, not in any of the lounges nor in the open area, barbarically named the Plaza, which surrounded the reception and Bureau de Change. As it happened, she had never been out on the deck of a cross-Channel ferry before. It had never seemed worthwhile. The door to the deck seemed very heavy and thick, an uncomfortable reminder that the ship was not quite the bland shopping mall it pretended to be but a robust machine for confronting alien, dangerous elements. She pushed it with her shoulder and hip, irritated by the need to do so.

Outside was as disagreeable as she had suspected. Calm as it was, the ship was travelling fast so that the wind from ahead was strong enough to blow her hair untidily around her face, whipping the black ends of it into her eyes. There were steep, ladder-like steps between the decks, and the slight, surreal motion of the ferry on the smooth swell bothered her.

Eventually she found them, high above the sea on the boat deck, looking astern towards the marbled, foaming wash. Kit was at the centre of the group, pointing back with one hand and gesturing with the other at each child in turn. Molly moved a little closer, unnoticed, her hair fluttering and stinging uncomfortably round her face, until she could hear.

'OK, now adverbs. The ship moved . . .' began Kit, and pointed at Josh Bannerman.

'Er, the ship moved foamingly?'

Kit pointed at the children, one after another, taking up the sentence himself if they hesitated: 'The ship moved – come on, come on – the ship moved . . .'

'Oh – ow – I dunno. Proudly?'

'Happily!'

'Superbly!'

'Oh, I dunno, sir . . .'

'Kylie! The ship moved . . . ?'

'Bouncily?'

'Fine, good. Mick?'

'The ship moved wetly.'

'Hmm. Statement of the obvious, I should say. Marianne?'

'The ship moved *dauntlessly*,' said Marianne Denver, with breathy emphasis. She was a tall, darkly tousled, well-developed child who regarded Kit with what Molly felt was rather too much devotion. '*Dauntlessly* and *deftly*.'

'Ve-ry nice,' said Kit, smiling at her. 'Now, more! Look at that wash! Adverbs to describe that broken water.' He made a swift, vivid motion with his hand, as if he was whisking air into a bowl of cream.

'The ship moved washily?' said Kylie, and giggled. The giggle spread.

'Wearily!'

'Wildwateringly!'

'Boundingly!'

'Joyfully!'

'Beerily!' shouted Darren Oxtey, suddenly. A high shriek of mirth rose from the group, but the boy turned pink and held his ground. 'Look at it, sir, it looks jus' like beer! It does!'

'He's right,' said Kit, looking at the wash. 'I declare "beerily" the adverb of the day. Darren wins.'

He turned, laughing, to see Molly close at hand. He composed his face to a mask of courteous greeting.

'We were just doing some adjective and adverb work,' he said politely. 'Our best adjective was "translucent", from Andrew. We seem to have descended to the saloon bar rather abruptly with the adverbs.'

For a moment Molly hesitated, almost letting herself approve. But then she saw the children's faces change as they turned to see her. One by one, they dropped their animation and took on a familiar sullen wariness. A stab of pure, vicious envy went through her, taking her breath away. She did not show it. It was rare for anybody to read Molly Miles's emotions correctly.

'Very good,' she said, in a high, amiably commanding, teacherly voice. 'But it's a little cold, don't you think? Maybe everybody needs some time indoors.'

Dutifully, the sixteen of them trooped down the deck behind her towards the stiff, heavy doors.

9

Mary came to stay with Anna for the weekend, bringing Lee and Maggie with her. The children barged into the house and clattered up and down the stairs to slide on the broad banister. Mary dumped their bags carelessly in the hall and hugged her sister.

'Sorry about the racket. At least the big ones have gone off to watch United play at home, with Don and his mate. It's wonderful. Janie's as keen on football as Martin, so the three of them have these great orgies of fandom.'

'Do *you* like football, squidge?' Anna picked up Lee, who had paused briefly to catch his breath, and cuddled the child's solid, four-year-old rotundity. He was small for his age, with a thatch of yellow hair and pink cheeks. To his mother's relief, Lee still liked being the huggable baby of the family. His aunt nuzzled the softness of his cheek with a new, heady pleasure, conscious of the tiny thing growing within her that would soon be Lee's cousin.

'No. *Don't* like it. Football is smelly,' said Lee with confidence. 'I like racing cars, vroom, vroom.' With a violent wriggle, he freed himself and began tearing up and down the hall with loud automotive noises.

'Just like his uncle Mike,' said Mary, making a face. 'Which reminds me. I'm sorry, but I'm afraid I did promise to go down and see Mike and Barbara so they can take Lee to a banger meeting after lunch. It's replaced scuba diving as the current big fantasy. I'll go in the morning, if that's all right, and come back for Saturday night.'

'Would Maggie like to stay here with me tomorrow?' asked

Anna. Suddenly she could not get her fill of small children. 'We could make a cake.'

'I want to see racing cars,' said the little girl stubbornly. 'I want to go with Lee and see racing cars go BANG!'

'I want to make a cake *now*,' said Lee. So, while Mary made the children's supper, Anna and Lee and Maggie got in her way with clouds of flour and smears of butter and much dipping of small fat fingers in the eggy, sugary mixture.

Anna was so happily preoccupied that it was seven o'clock before she clapped her hand to her cheek and said, 'Oh goodness, they'll be in Paris by now, changing trains!'

The two women had just settled the children with books and drinks of water, and were coming down the broad dusty stairway. Mary, who had been told of Kit's predicament briefly when she arrived, easily picked up the subtext of Anna's dismay.

'Don't blame yourself. School trips must be really strenuous. If you aren't up to it, you aren't and that's that. You're quite right to be thinking of the baby. I put my feet up like mad before Janie. Mum said I might as well, because frankly after the first, you never get any mercy.'

They crossed the draughty tiled hall and pushed open the kitchen door, grateful for the warmth inside. Anna leaned back against the worktop and expelled a long, shuddering breath.

'Look, I'm crippled with guilt. I was meant to be there. It was a joint project. Now poor darling Kit is at this very moment trying to cross Paris on the Metro with fifteen Sandmarsh Year 7s and Molly Miles. I'm allowed to feel guilty. It would be a disgrace if I didn't.'

'Are they a particularly difficult lot of children?' asked Mary, nibbling at a leftover fish finger from Lee's plastic plate. 'Toughies?'

'Not too bad. By Sandmarsh standards. Josh Bannerman is the worst, because he's pretty big for twelve and a year behind everyone else and knows it. And Mick Harris needs watching. But Kit never gives a second thought to discipline: it just comes naturally. Anyway, once you get them off their home territory they're easier. It's not the kids that'll be his big problem. It's Miss Miles.'

'Oh, come on,' said Mary. 'What is so awful about this woman?'

'Nothing,' said Anna gloomily. 'Nothing at all. Not really. She's a good teacher. A bit prissy and spinsterish, I suppose, but I quite like her usually. It's just that she takes Kit so hard. She takes him personally.'

'But he charms the birds off the trees when he wants to. He'll do the boyishly wholesome public-school smarm, won't he, and it'll be all right?'

'N-no.' said Anna slowly. 'He only does that when he doesn't care at all. Sort of reflex politeness. But I've been thinking a lot about it, and I honestly think that over the last year, the feud at school has got worse and worse. Kit's fairly civil, but he can't bring himself to placate Molly or butter her up.'

'Why not?'

'Because he really thinks that what she does is bad. Not just ineffective, truly bad.'

'What *does* she do?'

Anna sighed, twisting strands of her gold hair between her fingers. She looked, Mary thought with sisterly affection, particularly beautiful since her pregnancy.

'He says you can just about be forgiven for being a boring science teacher, or history, or languages. But he thinks it's wicked to teach English badly.'

'Why?'

'He says that language and story and poetry are essential foods of the human soul, and that the most destructive thing you can do to a child is to make them dull and embarrassing. He says if there's any risk that you're going to spoil those things, and cut the child off from them, you should leave it alone.'

'Not teach English at all, you mean?' Mary asked sceptically.

'No. He says you could just drill kids in grammar and spelling like an old Dame School, and let them find their own books and lyrics and stories. In the library or on a Walkman or on telly, anywhere. Then at least they've got a chance of connecting, and getting pleasure and nourishment out of things when they do find them. But he reckons teachers like Molly make children grow up actually *hating* poetry, and good plays and books and resonant words. So they avoid them for ever.'

'He's a bit fanatical about his job, isn't he?'

'Yes. Well, you have to be.'

'*You're* not,' said Mary.

'I am sometimes. I feel the same way Kit does about exams, for instance. He says they aren't that important, and they don't matter nearly as much as getting ideas into their heads and making them start thinking. In a way, that's why we both like teaching at a despised sort of school like Sandmarsh. Nobody expects too much in the way of results, so we can get on with actually concentrating on the children's minds, and doing whatever works.'

'Jeepers,' said Mary. 'Don't say that to Don. He's obsessed with getting Janie into a top league table school. Ob-sessed. He goes on about Qualifications all the time. Says his whole life would have been blighted if he hadn't got his O levels. He'd have been down the steelworks.'

'Well, they do matter, I suppose,' said Anna, wretchedly, for her mind was not on Mary's Don and the steelworks but on Kit, trapped in the Venice sleeper with his adversary. 'But Kit's kind of teaching sometimes does both. Another thing Molly can't forgive is that when he did that two years of teaching GCSE, she gave him the worst set, the absolute pits, and still their grades were a good bit better than anybody expected. Even though he had ignored all her systems and kept veering off onto different books, and doing his famous adverb-shouts and the fresh air thing.'

'What's that?' asked Mary, intrigued.

'He suddenly takes them all out of the classroom and starts tearing around the playground with a basketball, playing stuff like rhyme tag and games about tenses. You know: yelling "was – is – shall be – would be – would have been" while they hurl the ball around.'

'So what's the problem?' Mary thought ruefully of the dour grammar-school sobriety awaiting her bright little Janie.

'There shouldn't be a problem. There are lots of different ways of teaching. But he doesn't make any effort to defer to Molly and she hates that. And he genuinely does do stupid things that get up her nose, like losing her precious audio tapes – which he despises – the ones that come with the teacher's copy of the grammar textbooks. He doesn't answer memos, ever, or submit teaching plans. Sometimes I write dummy ones to keep him out of trouble.'

'But he loves teaching, right? He likes the kids? They like him?'

'Yes,' said Kit's wife, with some fervour. 'He's focused on them and they like that. It's as if every kid in his classes was a puzzle box, and he has to work against time to find the right panel to spring it open before they move away.'

Mary, who had unobtrusively taken over cooking the supper while Anna twisted her hair and rattled on about her husband, pushed the onions around in the hot fat for a moment and then mildly said, 'Well, I think you're worrying far too much. He's competent. He's not a fool. He'll get through it. There's not a lot she can do on a school trip, is there?'

'I suppose not,' said Anna. 'Here, let me do the salad.' But a cold, formless fear lay on her stomach all evening, so that she could barely eat.

In fact, the transfer of fifteen children from the Gare du Nord to the Gare de Lyon had diverted the two teachers' energies sufficiently to prevent any hostility. At the top of the first Metro escalator Kit turned to Molly and said, 'If I lead, will you be sweeper-up at the rear?' and she nodded assent.

Kit plunged down into the tunnels with his huge suitcase, setting a breakneck pace. Once the children were safely counted aboard the train – Molly leaning solidly on the open doors for safety as they all went through – he wound his arm round a post in the corner of the carriage and began fishing out the diaries he had made the children update on the journey from Calais.

'Into a dark foreign land I go,' began Andrew Murray, 'afraid and excited on a strange smelling train.'

Josh Bannerman was less lyrical: 'French train toilets smell of poo and you can see the tracks.' But then Kit saw that Josh had embarked on some gratifying scansion and a bold stab at a rhyme: 'I did not have the nurve to look, and so I turned my back.'

Kit glanced up, and saw Leanne McDougall sitting close to Josh, giggling at him.

'You've been helping,' he said, over the train's rattle. 'Josh? Leanne helped you, didn't she? I recognize her knack with iambics.'

Leanne, to the outward eye a gape-mouthed, eye-blacked,

mini-skirted copy of her sullen thirty-year-old mother, had revealed in one of Kit's poetry classes that she had written lyrics for her elder brother's rock group since she was ten. They were remarkably good, despite the spelling, but she had not hitherto revealed their existence to any teacher.

'I wrote a bit in hers,' said Josh.

Kit shuffled through the pile. Leanne had not been inspired to use her talent in her own notebook so far, and had written only a dull 'We left Calais on the traine to Paris'. He was pleased to see that an 'i' had at last introduced itself into her spelling of 'train', although its arrival had not been enough to dislodge the final 'e'. Next to her uninspired sentence another hand had added the sprawling endorsement: 'Josh BANNERMAN woz HERE and woz DED SEXXY.'

'Sorry, sir,' said Josh, grinning all over his big, daft face.

'Bastille! Next stop Bastille!' said Molly Miles. In the packed carriage, French heads turned in wonder at her commanding English tones. 'We change to line one for just one stop. Everybody, get your bags ready.'

The children scuffled.

'Natalie!' said Molly sharply. 'I have told you before *not* to fiddle about and get things out of your bag on short trips like this. You'll end up leaving your zip undone and losing things.' Guiltily, just out of her line of sight, Kit stuffed the diaries back in his briefcase, zipped its top, and avoided the satirical eyes of his pupils.

So they changed, and rattled on, and ceremonially composted their seventeen tickets at the Gare de Lyon and bought drinks and sandwiches at the kiosk ('Look, sir! *Psscht!*'). All in all, they reached the Venice sleeper with far less disruption than Anna, drooping far away in her cavernous kitchen, had feared.

The sleepers were of the cheapest: randomly mixed as to gender, six to a compartment, a head-banging, knee-bumping business of cramped shelves and awkward ladders. Most of the children found this an entirely happy, if not positively hilarious, state of affairs. The party of seventeen had to spread over three compartments; it was decided that Kit and five boys should share one, six girls the second, and that Molly should chaperone the third compartment with a mixed group consisting of the three smallest and best behaved boys, and Sally Addams, who said she might be sick.

However, two minutes before departure, the guard appeared, whistling insouciantly, and showed an embarrassed businessman from Liège into the sixth bunk in Molly's compartment. Seething with rage, she squeezed out into the corridor and hammered on Kit's door.

'Surely this can't be right,' she snapped. 'Our compartments are reserved—'

'Our *bunks* are reserved,' said Kit. 'There's a spare bunk, they're allowed to fill it. It's OK. Nobody undresses much on these things.'

'Have you even *begun to consider* the legal implications? The Children Act?' said Molly furiously.

'They're chaperoned,' said Kit. 'You're there. And the guard's outside, in case of trouble.' Unwisely, he allowed himself a huff of mirth. 'I mean, poor bloke, he'll be more scared than you are. But I'll change with you if you want, and we'll move some boys across and re-jig it.'

'That won't be necessary. But I will be making a full report,' said Molly darkly.

In the compartment, to deafening giggles from the children, the Belgian salesman had stacked his bag at the foot of a bottom bunk, hung up his jacket, painstakingly attached a line of bulldog clips down the front of each trouser leg to preserve the sharpness of his creases, and lain down fully dressed on his back, eyes closed. When Molly Miles came back she found him there in the bunk opposite her own, with four children hanging out of their bunks giggling. Gently, remorselessly, the stranger began to snore.

Molly said later, to her friend Louise Chorton from St Jude's, that she did not sleep a wink all through that night. There on her narrow bed she heard every snore, every chink of the Belgian's trouser-borne bulldog clips, every wheel-banging, shouting, shunting stop. She felt every jolt and sway of the train go 'right through her body', so she told Louise, until at last the pale rays of dawn glimmered round the edge of the blind. Some of the children snored too, on higher notes than the salesman; once, little Morrey Hart asked for the toilet. Swaying with fatigue, Molly dutifully accompanied him the short way along the chilly corridor and waited, silent, until he came out and lurched back to his warm bunk. Once Sally Addams had some kind of nightmare and squealed quite loudly from the top layer. Once Molly thought she heard talking and giggling from the girls' compartment which adjoined hers, and got up to glare round the door into the suddenly silent, innocent darkness. Once in some dim station two deep, infuriatingly masculine French voices laughed together loudly just outside her window.

Kit at first slept deeply, as he always did on trains, waking only when Darren Oxtey tried to tiptoe past to the toilet. He did not get up to chaperone the excursion, just said 'OK?' then lay awake for a few moments until the boy's safe return.

His second sleep, however, was more turbulent. He was back at Priory Shore and his father was angry. He stood before the big, ugly marble fireplace in the headmaster's study and held up a small tube, asking Kit, 'What is the meaning of this?'

'It's Anna's baby,' said Kit, small in the dream, bare-kneed in the grey shorts of school uniform. 'It's our baby. We had to go to a clinic, because of the lectern.'

'How dare you!' said his father. 'You know what the punishment is for this sort of behaviour. The dog returneth to his vomit!'

Small Kit saw him reach for the worn bamboo cane which hung by the mantel; thirty years on, big Kit woke sweating in the dim red light. He hunched his shoulders in the thin blanket and stretched his long legs; a shudder wracked him, and he felt for a nightmare moment as if his own perspiration was a thin, oily, rotting film of some unspeakable filth. *The dog returneth to his vomit*. He could smell it. His whole body grew suddenly cold, appalled at its own vital warm greasiness, repelled at the weight of flesh on flesh where his limbs touched one another.

Closing his eyes again he searched for other images, with an urgent efficiency born of long practice. He found glittering seas of bright fish, clean bare golden desert, St Catherine's monastery at dawn with Anna huddled, entranced, beside him in a rough blanket. He found ragged Irish coastline and the beehive huts of

Skellig Michael, minarets and towers and the dome of St Sofia, a long Scottish glen glowing purple and gold in an autumn dusk. At last he found Venice, and his mind's eye conjured the lion of St Mark triumphant on its pillar, the Canaletto sweep of the lagoon and the gentle holy curves of mosaic gold inside the Basilica.

He smiled. His body grew warmer and relaxed into itself again. The dream faded. Around him in the compartment he could hear the breathing of the boys: slight, sensitive little Andrew, big, dim Josh, sharp Darren, Mick Harris with his mop of bright blond hair, and Joe Baldwin, who limped a little because his stepfather had thrown him on the sofa as a baby and missed. Kit smiled again into the darkness. He knew with strong certainty that what he was doing was right. These children's lives, although not on the face of it particularly deprived, were nonetheless awful to contemplate. They needed somebody – him – to cut them a porthole through the grey walls and offer them other ways of seeing and believing and yearning. Even though these might be, as all great yearnings are, incapable of fulfilment.

Poor children! he thought drowsily. They were fed and clothed and minded well enough, but it was their misfortune to be born to an age which saw no need to clothe them in one single rag of noble thought, Christian or pagan. Neither high tradition nor peasant practicality was offered to them. They saw no stars above their neon streets, dug no soil, sang no hymns. Instead they pushed buttons and looked at screens and were taught to call these things 'skills'; they ate food of whose origin they had no notion, and were driven across tarmac to exercise their bodies, if at all, in artificial environments of chlorine and carbon fibre, in the beat of mindless music and the smell of hot nylon.

Their local history was buried under car parks, their ancestral religion forgotten, their emotions formed by video and their values by the shopping mall. None of this group's parents even went to church, and music tuition had been stopped entirely the last time the money ran out (if you played an instrument, however badly, you could generally bend the system to get into a better school than Sandmarsh High). The only transcendent experience which most of Year 7 could expect to meet on their way to Year 70 was that they would fall in love. Even that, Kit reflected, would be defined for them by mass market standards of beauty, interpreted by slickly marketed media expertise on sexual behaviour, and eventually turned sour by the failure of messy reality to match an airbrushed ideal.

The girls might find a spiritual depth in loving their babies – for a while at least, until the babies grew as rebellious and unprepossessing as they themselves were now. Of the boys, a few would learn passion and loyalty through following a football team or developing a fetishistic interest in cars. But it would not be enough.

None of it, thought Kit to himself in the darkness, would ever be enough. They would grow resentful and discontented and prone to talk a great deal, angrily and emptily, about their 'rights'. Little of the life mapped out for these unregarded children had any chance of rising above a banal, monotonous prairie. But they were human and they needed more. Life was more. The least they should be given was a glimpse into greater hearts, and a look at beauty through other eyes in other centuries. If they were given that, they could begin to forge their own nobility. Their own armour.

He knew that there was a danger that they might not see what was being shown to them. Even in Venice where shimmering, disturbing, transcendent beauty is most tightly packed they might just kick cans, pick their noses, whine for Cokes and stare vacantly around saying, 'Old, innit?' and 'Funny having no roads'. It might take a jolt to open their eyes, but never mind. Once they were open they would never quite close. For for the rest of their lives these fifteen children would have a memory to call on: a memory of Something Else.

Kit had organized the jolt already. Since he had not thought it wise even to tell Anna the extent of his plans, the prospect of Molly Miles's finding out was explosive. By tomorrow night she would know. But he was himself again now, the dream forgotten, and it would take far more than Miss Miles to make him sweat again with terror. He turned on his side, yawned and slept again a deep, innocent sleep.

In the girls' compartment, Marianne Denver lay awake for a long time even after Miss Miles had glared accusingly round the door and silenced the whispering. Marianne was a big girl, busty for twelve years old, and there were stirrings within her which, she resentfully knew, were shared by few of her classmates. Natalie, for instance, might dress like a slapper in her mother's minis and stilettoes, or Leanne talk loudly of her 'boyfriend', but it was all a game to them. Even Sarah, who was rumoured to have almost Done It with her elder brother's football team-mate, was only after a bit of status and shock value.

Marianne knew that, and was secretly impatient with her giggling friends because for her it was different. To Marianne there was already a real and private urgency about the whole matter of flesh and embracing, about the hardness of male jaw lines and the set of masculine shoulders and the strange, leaping pulses you felt in private places.

It was something she had to bear alone, this early coarse flowering of primitive feeling; she half knew and wholly resented the fact that her ungovernable yearnings had overshadowed and withered the pale, dreamy flowers of childhood. Her own mother had been pregnant at thirteen the first time round and had summarily been taken to an abortion clinic. Marianne came six years and several partners later. Now, when Mrs Denver saw her fast-growing daughter being ambushed by the gene of early development, she became worried and irritable. Her own childhood had been cut short by the drive to experiment and she dimly knew that this had cost her much. She was afraid of history repeating itself. Not a woman to approach things directly, nor one of any notable patience or intelligence, she attempted a cautionary tale by telling her daughter, at least once a week and in a hectoring, aggrieved tone, the story of her own first pregnancy.

'I fell before I was fourteen,' Mrs Denver would say. 'Could've ruined me life. He was a right bastard, and all. Had to get rid of it. Went to the clinic, an' saw all these sharp shiny things hanging up, and they put me to sleep and got rid. Stupid little cow, I was.'

Marianne, unfortunately, never quite got the point of these tirades. She misconstrued the narrative as a veiled reproach to herself, the surviving baby. The central message seemed clear: she too could have been got rid of, and maybe should have been. Her life, so she understood from these remarks and from her mother's general bearing, had been a grudging gift and was now a much regretted one. Since Mrs Denver never mentioned sex as such, Marianne made no connection between her mother's bad-tempered account of her elder sibling's demise and her own private, troublesome desires. This feeling within her did not seem to have anything to do with babies, of the got-rid variety or otherwise. It was a clear, hot flame of unthinking desire. And – since boys of her own age were absurdly childish and older boys at school unsavourily coarse – that desire centred at the moment very firmly indeed on Mr Milcourt.

The train rattled through the exotic Continental darkness, bringing into her drowsy visions strange smells, bursts of strobing light, deep male laughter on the platforms, shrill whistles and obscurely exciting piston rhythms. Her long hair tousled around her on the hard pillow, as Marianne allowed her mind to curl softly and languidly around pictures of Mr Milcourt. She saw his broad shoulders and narrow waist, his shirt coming untucked at the back as he wrote vigorously on the classroom whiteboard, the lock of dark hair that fell over his eyes, to be swept impatiently back. She saw the glint of those eyes, and heard the bracing snap of his voice when he fired a question at you, followed by the gleeful laugh when you said something he liked.

Well, when *somebody* said something he liked. Marianne, for all her devotion, for all the heavy toil she put into her homework for him, rarely managed to get the amount of his attention that she wanted. Mr Milcourt was, she would gloomily reflect, more receptive to Andrew Murray's faltering, stammering questions, Leanne's bits of stupid poetry or Darren's brassy cheek.

All the same, she had been chosen for this trip. Well, not at first, but he had seemed really, really pleased when she said she could go instead of Maddy Arbon, whose mother had changed her mind and kept her back.

It was her chance, her destiny. On a foreign trip, surely Mr Milcourt would see her in a new light and realize she was more than just a kid. She had a vague notion of blue Mediterranean seas, with a backdrop of snow-capped mountains like on travel posters, herself sipping a tall drink with an umbrella as Mr Milcourt suddenly put his hand across the table to lay it on hers, so that her flesh caught fire at his touch.

Lying on top of the bedcover now, the real hand burned at the imagined contact. Slowly, Marianne raised it to her cheek, which burned as fiercely. Something would happen. She knew it for certain.

10

Molly Miles slept finally with the coming of dawn, and stayed blessedly unconscious for an hour and a half. When she awoke it was with a start: something was wrong in the compartment. There were no children, nor any sign of the Belgian salesman. Her heart hammered unpleasantly as she swung her solid legs out of the bunk and began to pull on her outer clothing. The children! Where could they be?

With a shock, she realized something else. The train had stopped. Where, she did not know, but somewhere far from all the safety that she knew, somewhere on the wrong side of Europe. Looking wildly around, shaking off sleep, she saw that the children's bags and untidily strewn possessions were still on their bunks. This afforded her some relief from panic, but with the relief came black rage. Kit Milcourt was responsible for this. She knew it. And sure enough, when she slid the narrow door open – too narrow, absurdly narrow for a woman of girth, a woman with a bust and in a hurry – the whole party was in sight just along the corridor.

Their noses were pressed to the glass and the man Milcourt was gesturing at something. She heard scraps of conversation:

'—Causeway. A causeway is a raised road, a rail track in this case, across water. This is the lagoon. Venice is on a series of islands, and the islands are cut up by canals. Two thousand years ago it was just a marsh. Like our marsh at home. Yes, that's right, like the marsh where you went to do pond dipping when you were little. Yes, probably with frogs. But now there are churches and palaces and statues, in wonderful colours, with gold and shining glass, and canals instead of roads.'

Darren asked something which Molly did not catch.

'No,' said Kit, 'no cars anywhere. Except at the Piazzale Roma, which doesn't count because it's on the edge. Otherwise, through the whole city, you have to walk or take a boat. That hasn't changed in hundreds of years, except that some of the boats have engines. Even the police and the dustmen and the firemen have to use boats instead of cars and lorries.'

Molly stood by the compartment door, feeling oddly unsure of herself. The children had not seen her; eager-faced, they were intent on Kit's account of a froggy, ancient, jewelled marshland. Looking the other way – for physical needs had suddenly become pressing – she saw the Belgian emerging from the lavatory. He gave her a small, neutral bow and moved away into the next carriage. He had his case with him, so she concluded thankfully that he would not be back.

Scuttling along the passage, she locked herself in the small lavatory compartment where male smells distressingly lingered. In the mirror she saw a square grim jaw on a face beginning to be coarsened by middle age, straight black hair, dark brows, square shoulders, a heavy chest. She rarely saw these things but on this unsteady morning, without knowing why, she found herself contrasting them with the vivid grace of Kit Milcourt and the children and was shaken by a sudden miserable anger.

When she had washed her face and hands as best she could, Molly walked, her shoes squeaking assertively, along the corridor towards the school party. The train was just beginning to move again, and through the breath-misted windows she could see that it had stopped on the long causeway into Venice and that the towers of the city were just visible. At least they were if you craned sideways and forwards, as all the children were still doing, with rather less grace than before. Kit turned to her, courteous without warmth.

'Ah, Miss Miles. We're here, as you see. A few minutes now.'

'Why have these children not packed up their bags?' She was almost hissing, tired and upset beyond reasonable measure. 'Our compartment is strewn with their things, they must pack up immediately.'

'Shouldn't worry.' His calm maddened her. 'This train stays

in Venice for ages. No rush to get off. It can't go any further, can it?'

'It could if it was an *am-amph-phibian*, sir,' said Marianne, removing her nose from the window, and was rewarded by a dazzling smile from Kit, accompanied by a friendly clap on the shoulder.

'An amphibious canal train. Yes, it could. Imagine it, rattling along the Grand Canal!'

'Marianne, Sally, Morrey, Mick, all of you – go and pack up your things, quickly, and *quietly*,' said Molly Miles briskly. 'Then bring all the bags into the corridor, and I want you, Joe, Sally and Natalie, each to do a thorough check on the compartment you slept in, to make sure nothing is left behind.'

The children scrambled into the compartments, leaving Kit and Molly alone in the corridor.

'I hope this Pensione is not far,' said Molly flatly. 'The children will need a rest, and so will I.'

'It's three minutes from the station, no more,' said Kit. 'But they all seem full of beans to me. We can drop the bags, have our breakfast and take our first walk round the city. Ferrovia to San Marco is only half an hour at most.'

'Will the hotel do breakfast?' Molly hated asking him questions, hated depending on him, but reminded herself fiercely that until yesterday morning she had had no notion of coming on this trip. She was being a trouper, doing the school a favour, and was owed some consideration and proper communication from her colleague.

And she did, now it had been mentioned, desperately want some breakfast. At home she had a Teasmade by the bed, and never rose without a strong and milky cup of tea.

'Yes,' said Kit. 'They're doing an extra day's breakfast. I asked them specially. There are too many of us to pile into a cafe all at once, they're all rather small ones in Cannareggio. We'd bring them to a grinding halt if we all piled in. Personally, I could eat a giraffe.'

'It'd be ever so tough, sir,' said Mick Harris, reappearing with a villainously orange and green backpack. 'An' tough, with all the muscles they got. Hey, cool, look!'

And, indeed, the train was edging into the station, and the

word *VENEZIA* could be clearly seen on the platform. More children reappeared with their bags.

'Sir,' said Kylie Chang Seng, after a moment of breathing mist onto the window and rubbing it hard, trying in her frustration to see more. Her neat dark bob of glossy hair swung as she raised her face to Kit's. 'In the night, sir, I woke up and I was on the top bunk so I could look out of the crack by the window. An' do you know what I saw?'

'What?'

'Mountains. I did. I saw mountains, wiv snow on 'em. I could see the snow because of the moon.'

'What mountains would they be?'

There was a moment's blankness.

'Anyone? What mountains?'

'Everest?' asked Josh, whose baseball cap, Molly noticed with loathing, was on back to front in defiance of Graham Merck's absolute ruling against this.

There was a general howl, and Nicky Pinter said with lofty contempt, 'Everest's in *Africa*, dickhead.'

Molly opened her mouth to correct them both, stretched out her hand to reverse Josh's horrible baseball hat, but thought better of both ideas and stumped towards her compartment to fetch her case.

Meanwhile Marianne, making an enormous effort of memory, said, 'The Alps.'

Kit nodded and, remembering that she was in his Latin for Louts group, waited. There would be more.

'An' the Alps,' she said carefully, 'is the mountains what Hannibal took the elephants over!' Flushed with triumph, Marianne stared at him, her eyes big beneath her dark, tangled mane of hair.

'Well done. Indeed.' He smiled, and at his voice and smile Marianne seemed to herself to be melting, almost fainting. 'The Alps, backbone of Europe. We have crossed them, in the night.'

'Pity we didn't have any elephants,' observed James Madden.

'True,' said Kit. 'Not an elephant in sight.'

It was unfortunate that at this moment, leaning forward to pull her case behind her on its wheels, Miss Miles backed out of her compartment in a broad, grey skirt. The children should not have laughed, and nor should Kit.

They turned left outside the station and followed Kit with his big suitcase. Behind them, embarrassingly noisy on the rough stones, buzzed and clattered the wheels of Molly's suitcase. Curious eyes darted right to the *vaporetto* taking on passengers by the Scalzi Bridge and left at the pavement stalls selling beads and masks. After a few moments they turned left again, away from it all into a quiet, narrow *calle* where several signs hung proclaiming minor hotels. Kit stopped at the third, dived in, and by the time the group had assembled round him was in rapid Italian conversation with the clerk. After a moment or two he turned back to them.

'The room for Miss Miles is ready now. The rest of us have to put our luggage by the mirror there, in the alcove, and the rooms will be ready by twelve. So we can go for a walk after breakfast and get our bearings.'

He handed Molly a key; it was the key to the double room originally intended for him and Anna. Kit had hastily arranged for himself to be relegated to an airless sliver of a servant's room, hardly more than a broom cupboard, on the ground floor.

As they went into the little dining room, a surge of excitement passed through the children. As Persephone found to her cost in Hades, the first meal in a foreign land brings you to a new, more committed level of intimacy with it. When they had eaten in Venice, a city of which they now expected unrationed excitement, they would truly have arrived. Under Molly's stern direction they lined up at the buffet and filled their plates with the makings of a solid Continental breakfast, uttering low awed cries.

'Hey, that's cheese!'

'Look, *slarmy*!'

'For breakfast? S'weird!'

'Sir, can we have cereal too?'

'Anything,' said Kit. 'Fill up. We've got a lot of walking ahead of us.'

The children fell to, in rapt and concentrated quiet.

Ten minutes later, gratefully contemplating her second cup of tea (deplorably weak though it was), Molly broke her third roll open and made a decision. Her head was swimming with fatigue, she felt dirty and travel-worn and there was a tremor, a distinct tremor, in the hand which she reached out for the butter. Nor was she happy to be seated opposite her reflection, square and white-faced and drably pudgy, in the chipped but splendid gilt mirror which ran along one wall of the room. She turned in her chair and said to Kit, who was on his way to the buffet, 'Mr Milcourt, could I have a word?'

Kit paused politely. Molly stood up, turning her back on the munching children at her table. She hated to admit weakness, so her voice was even more clipped than usual as she said, 'I think it would be best if I stayed here for the morning, to get some sleep. There is apparently a second bed in my room, so if one or two of the children feel extra tired they could stay. Would you be all right with the rest?'

Kit looked at her and she saw on his face an expression of dawning, grateful joy which she had never seen before. He looked younger, less patrician and more approachable ('less snooty' was how she put it to herself) and with a brief pang she saw that it might be pleasant to be on terms of friendship and not enmity with this man. But since the soft expression on his face had been conjured up only by the news that he was rid of her for the morning, her thawing towards him was of brief duration.

'That's fine,' said Kit. 'I thought I'd just take them on a short walk, down to San Marco to get a flavour of the city. Then back here by *vaporetto* to stow their things and have a rest. Then we could all go out later, and maybe go up the Campanile if it stays clear.'

'Could I have a copy of your proposed schedule of visits? Just to look at while I take my rest?' asked Molly. 'I suppose you've got all the opening times of the galleries and so forth?'

'Y-yes,' said Kit, looking a little sheepish (as she had meant him to). 'I haven't got it typed – it's a bit illegible.'

A bit imaginary, thought Molly. This man had no schedule, no proper organization. He was plainly capable of bringing fifteen children to Venice and *not even bothering* with the Accademia or the Doge's Palace. She had heard him in the staff room quoting some nonsense from John Julius Norwich about never going inside more than two buildings on your first visit to Venice, and how one of those should be Harry's Bar. Molly had read the guide books, and knew better than that.

'You can see the English programme folder,' offered Kit. 'I ran off a good few copies. It's a sort of anthology I made up. You know, the poems and famous prose on Venice, from Ruskin to Jan Morris. I thought we could read them together in the evenings, after diary writing.'

'Oh,' she said. 'Yes. Excellent.' Foiled again.

Not one of the fifteen children chose to stay and rest with Miss Miles, so within a few moments of finishing breakfast they had pulled their anoraks back on and spilled out into the cold thin February air at Kit's heels. Happy again, relaxed and adventurous, their Pied Piper grinned at them. He was wearing a longish, floppy black coat with wide sleeves which he had bought years ago in Istanbul, and Marianne, for one, thought him a most romantic figure.

'*Avanti!*' he said. And he loped off in the weak sunshine towards the banks of the Grand Canal, the children running and skipping around him, up the Scalzi Bridge and down the other side into San Polo.

They had not taken three turnings (mysterious, crumbling, canal-scented Venetian turnings) before abruptly Death reared up ahead of them.

He was all of six foot five, wrapped in a black shimmering cloak with a horridly frivolous silk frilled collar; and his face, under a black tricorn hat, was a skull. They met him in a dim *sottoportego* under the shadow of some crumbling apartment which overflew them, a crazy housebridge with crooked windows. Two of the girls screamed, and Marianne, walking next to Kit, shrank against him. Josh alone stood his ground.

'Issa bloke inna mask!' he said. 'S'a bloody *wicked* mask!'

'Wick-ed!' agreed two other boys, their voices fluting up to a higher note than they intended. Death bowed gravely, sweeping off his tricorn to reveal powdered white locks, and moved on past them. The girls squeezed against the wall in horror as he passed.

'That is *sick*,' said Kara, fervently. 'Goin' around scarin' people.'

'Prob'ly a flasher,' said Sarah Midali, sagely. Sandmarsh girls knew all about flashers; the reedy common land at the town's edge was rich in them.

But then round the corner came a Moor in a turban, his rigid clay face unmoving above the wet, real human mouth. With him walked a harlequin with a long, drooping gold nose, and a female figure whose vast red cloak was overlaid with a black lace cape. Her face was smooth and young, and only her eyes were covered by her swooping sequinned and feathered mask. High nodding pink and purple plumes rose from its centre to bob high above her brow, and long black hair streamed out behind. All bowed as Death had bowed, and brushed past the children without further ceremony. Andrew Murray let out a little crow of mingled fear and pleasure, and Mick Harris muttered, 'Phwoo, well weird!'

But Josh, more prosaic, taught by hard knocks to square his shoulders and face down any situation, demanded fiercely of his teacher, 'Whass going *on*? Do they always carry on like loonies here?'

'No,' said Kit. 'Normally, you would find the city quiet and thoughtful and foggy and fairly empty in winter, or crammed with tourists just like us in the summer. But this happens to be something in between. Carnival.'

'Wicked!' said Josh. 'So it's just for fun, like?'

'Exactly,' said Kit. 'From *carne vale*, farewell to the pleasures of flesh. On Shrove Tuesday, which is next week – you know, pancake day – the Christian tradition decrees the beginning of a strict fast to repent your sins. People used to do without meat and sugary things and drink and parties, right through until Easter. So they needed a really good party to say goodbye to it all. *Carne vale*, goodbye to flesh and fun. Carnival.'

'Did they used to do that everywhere?' asked Kara. 'Even in England?' The group had, by unspoken consent, sat down on the steps of a little bridge to gather their wits.

'Yes. Hence the pancakes,' said Kit. 'But in Venice it went on and on, from Christmas to Easter. People wore masks and disguises so you didn't know who was rich or poor, who was important, who was foreign and who belonged to the city. There used to be games and drinking on the streets all day and all night.' He pulled a roll of paper out of his pocket. 'There's a report on it written three hundred and fifty-two years ago. Do you want to know what happened then?'

A few nodded, and the rest were silent, unsure of themselves, their thin veneer of cynical street wisdom stripped from them by the uncertainties of a city with no streets and stiff primitive clay faces. Kit leaned on a broad windowsill, unrolled the paper, and began to read from John Evelyn's *Diary*. The children listened, unnerved, anxious for any clue to the place:

> *All the world repaire to Venice* [read Kit] *to see the folly & madnesse of the Carnevall; the Women, men & Persons of all Conditions disguising themselves in antique dresses, & extravagant Musique & a thousand gambols, & traversing the streetes from house to house, all places being then free to enter: there is abroad nothing but flinging of Eggs fill'd with sweet Waters & sometimes not over sweete; they also have a barbarous custome of hunting bulls about the Streetes & Piazzas, which is very dangerous, the passages being generally so narrow in that Citty.*

Kit stopped, and rolled the paper up again to push it in the pocket of his black coat.

The children were silent, then Natalie Morrison said, 'Will there be bulls? It's ever so narrow, like he said.'

'Probably not bulls,' said Kit.

'My brother went to a rave once,' began Morrey Hart, rather wildly, but then paused and said, 'They could be all sorts of muggers, in them masks.'

'Yes,' said Kit. 'There probably were in John Evelyn's time. It isn't the same now. I don't think you'll find anything worse than a few pickpockets. The carnival more or less stopped a hundred years ago. It got a bad reputation. Only recently it's come back. People just liked the idea.'

'Are they all Venice people? The dressed-up ones?'

'Well, some are, some aren't. Some are tourists and foreigners, some come up from Rome or down from Milan, some are actors, a lot of them are probably students. Nobody's going to know who's who. You can't tell who they are, can you? Not unless you see through the masks.'

Andrew Murray had stood up and climbed to the summit of the footbridge. He was looking down at the smooth brown surface of the little side canal, and his small, peaky face was frowning. After a moment he asked intensely, 'Will there be anybody dressed normal?'

'Yes,' said Kit. 'Lots of people, I should think. People in churches, and people out doing their ordinary shopping, and policemen, and newspaper sellers. But you'll probably see a lot of masks.'

Andrew had his elbows on the parapet now, his chin on his hands. He shuffled his trainers impatiently. '*We* oughter have disguises,' he said.

'Funny you should say that,' said Kit.

Three hours later, in wild exhilaration at the sights they had seen, sore feet and sleepiness forgotten, the children tore back into the quiet *pensione* and, with difficulty, piled into Kit's tiny room. He heaved his big brown suitcase onto the bed, pushing children aside to make space for it, and opened the lid.

There, neatly folded as Nellie Armstrong had put them away after a ragged summer production of *Dracula, The Musical*, were piles of long full cloaks of thin black cotton. The sides were gathered into rough sleeves, so that when the wearer raised an arm, the scalloped form of a bat's wing appeared beneath it. On top of these, thicker and shinier, were stiff black linen masks made like bags with eyeholes and pointed ears. The contents of the suitcase were sufficient to costume a chorus of sixteen vampire bats.

Kit pulled out a larger hat and put it on his own head. His eyes gleamed through the holes and he raised his arms, still in his floppy black coat, into a reasonable semblance of a giant bat. With trills of glee, the children grabbed for the cloaks, boys and girls equally excited, weariness forgotten in the exhilaration of setting out into this weird and beautiful city in disguise.

'We could make *bat noises*!'

'Yeah, did you see those people by the big tower, that was all penguins?'

'Did you see the big bird, with the fevvers?'

'Did you see the huge big hat with the red things and the wire?'

'An' the cat lady?'

'There was hundreds of cat ladies, stupid.'

'The one with the big silver whiskers!'

Kit smiled inside his bat hat. The jolt had happened. On the far side of it, teaching could begin. They were no longer lumpen children of a lumpen land, resistant to anything new or strange or difficult, liable to whine at missing *Eastenders* (as Natalie and Leanne had done the previous night at the Gare de Lyon). They were all his now, ready for anything. Liberated by the strange, stagey city in carnival they would soak up anything offered to them.

They had already learned that a seventeenth-century diarist could be right. Now he could read them anything at all about Venice – Ruskin, Byron, Henry James, Wordsworth, Thomas Mann – and young as they were they would listen, and at least want to understand. He could take them away from the carnival crowds to show them melancholy corners: the brooding quiet of San Michele, the horses of St Mark in their high eminence, the hypnotic swirling and waving patterns of a hundred mosaic pavements, the glassworks of Murano. They would see now with clear eyes and heightened emotions, grope for language to express what they saw, and understand in doing so the power that language holds. They would gain memories, have their dreams fed and thoughts freed by glittering excess and ancient beauty. Morrey Hart had stood half an hour ago in the centre of St Mark's Square, spread his arms wide and said, 'It's like being on a rollercoaster, only not moving.'

As Kit contemplated his troop of small bats a wave of love swept over him, almost choking him.

Molly had slept well on the blissful stillness and softness of a real bed, and woke at mid-morning to the sound of some clock chiming. Venturing out in search of tea, she found the *patrone*'s daughter, a dumpy smiling girl in her twenties, writing something at the little desk in the lobby.

Chiara had done a degree in English at Padova, and was

entranced to have the chance to practise. When she had fetched the tea with her own hands, she hovered for a moment by the table where Molly sat and ventured the opinion that the party was very wise to come by train at this time.

'Yes,' said Molly. 'There are advantages over coaches. I suppose.'

'No more coaches today. No coaches after nine each morning, now,' said Chiara. 'And I have heard on the radio that the causeway' (she pronounced it cows'-way, which confused Molly for a few seconds) 'is to be closed to cars also. Many people.'

Molly gaped. 'At this time of year? But surely in winter it's far quieter – I have heard that summer in Venice is a problem, but not the winter months!'

Chiara looked at the Englishwoman in amazement, and began to spill out information in increasingly broken English, with much shrugging and exaggeration.

So it was that Molly learnt what Kit Milcourt had done, without mentioning it to his headmaster, his colleague, or the trustees of the Dewar fund. This monstrous, irresponsible man had brought a party of young children, on their maiden trip abroad, into the most confused and crowded European street event of the year.

He had done it deliberately, that she knew. Chiara had made it quite clear that one had to book and pay a large deposit to a hotel like theirs a full year ahead where *carnevale* was concerned. Her description of the surging, crowding rowdiness of Venice at this season froze Molly with horror.

Granted, they were travelling home on the Monday night sleeper and would be gone before the culmination on Shrove Tuesday. But before that there were two nights and two days in which any catastrophe could befall them.

'Last year,' Chiara was saying with relish, 'we have had many visitors falling into the canals, which is not good, you know? Not clean. They are drunk, I think. There is much dancing in San Marco, even in the daytime.'

Molly's mood was not improved, half an hour of helpless fuming later, when she came out of the hotel telephone booth after failing to contact the headmaster to find herself surrounded by bouncing, exultant pantomime bats.

Mary and the children left Anna's house after breakfast on Saturday morning to drive down to the coast. Lee had been up since half past six, revving up and doing handbrake turns along the landing. Anna had woken at much the same time and been sick.

'You ought to come with us,' urged Mary, mopping streaks of cereal from her small son's jersey. 'See Mike and Barbara. You can keep away from the exhaust fumes.'

Anna, however, pleaded tiredness. The thought of Barbara's greasy frozen beefburgers and oven chips made her stomach revolt. So, if truth be told, did the thought of Mike's loud enthusiasm, his horrible cars and the scowling figures of the twins Dirk and Deelya. It was a source of faint guilt to Anna that she had grown so far away from her own brother; but then, he was nearly nine years older. Mike had left home for a brief unsuccessful career in the army when she was only eight years old. Even before that, she privately remembered, he was always noisy and prone to step on one's dolls.

Mary, five years closer to him in age and a far stronger personality in childhood, rather enjoyed Mike's racket. By extension, she even enjoyed Barbara's blatant, sluttish sexiness and her children's mean and moody adolescence. Perhaps having two sons of her own made it easier to enjoy the machismo of Mike's household. Perhaps, thought Anna queasily, if her own child were to be a boy she would gradually come to value her brother's abrasive brand of masculinity and see it as part of her own son's heritage. Lee certainly appeared to worship his rackety uncle.

But she need not face them all today. 'No,' she said to her

sister's coaxing. 'Even the drive would finish me off. I'd be throwing up in every gutter. I'll stay here and correct some of my GCSE Italian.'

'Swank,' said Mary fondly. One of her qualities was to remember other people's points of pride, and she recalled from the summer how exultantly proud Anna was of her Italian set, five girls and eight boys. It was rare for Sandmarsh children to attempt a second language, and virtually unknown among the boys, but a year earlier Kit had helped her set up a pen-pal fan group with two Italian football clubs, and the response had astonished everybody. The modern languages classroom was festooned with scarves, posters, and slogans in felt pen. As she left, Mary said teasingly, 'Go on then, spend the morning gloating over your bambini.'

Anna watched her sister go, the children skipping beside her to the car, then turned back yawning and moved the ruins of breakfast onto the counter where she did not have to look at them. She pulled the folders out of her briefcase and sat down to work in the warm kitchen.

But it was no good. Her head drooped, her eyelids grew heavy, and spidery teenage handwriting wobbled and weaved as she looked at it. Outside, the early sunshine faded into a greyness more like evening. Kit's mother's old clock ticked loudly in the silence, and chimed the quarters. 'Never be ashamed to have a nap when you need one,' said the dog-eared pregnancy book which Mary had passed on with due ceremony to her sister. At ten o'clock those words came back to Anna with irresistible force, and she hauled herself up from the table and, for the first time in her life, went back to bed for a morning nap.

Sunk in the hollow of the soft mattress, the thick white duvet like a snowdrift over her, she twisted and shivered for a few moments before sliding with pleasant helplessness into a deeper sleep than she had enjoyed for days. As she rolled onto her side a lock of hair fell across her face, soft and tickly; her hand reached up to brush it aside and all of a sudden in her dream she was swimming, stretching through warm buoyant water with the sun on her back. It was a deep sea, with shapes that moved darkly far below her. Huge bubbles, wobbling ever brighter towards the sun, broke against her bare limbs and became fizzing streams which spiralled up to lose themselves on the surface.

In the dream Anna knew who it was who swam so distant and so dark below her. She knew that they were Kit's air bubbles, breaking from his mouthpiece as he breathed his slow way along the bottom. She hung there, happy, suspended in his breath but content to float high and naked in the simple sunshine. Her world was up above, buoyant and easy; she had no wish to follow him into the deep and the cold and the dark, or be strapped up in tanks and rubber and hoses. He would come back up to her sunny, coloured realm soon enough. She sighed, and kicked, and sprawled with dreams of swimming until she lay spreadeagled across the wide bed. The edge of the sheet lay cold against her leg and some jump of her nerves turned the dream bad. Abruptly, the swimming Anna in the dream saw that the bubbles had stopped coming.

The dark figure still moved far below her on the sea bed, a vague frog shape; but no air rose from it. In panic Anna doubled up to dive towards him but could not get so far. Rising again to the surface, gasping, panicking, she looked around and saw no dive boat, no Ahmed or Aziz waiting vigilant on a stern deck to haul the divers out. No other divers. Only the desert and the bland sea surface, and somewhere Kit: unbreathing, sending no bubbles, lost to her far below amid the dark tangle of rock and weed. Drowned.

Anna's body gave a great jerk in the bed and she half woke, teeth chattering, staring in terror at the bedroom ceiling. She looked at the clock to bring herself to the present: it was half past twelve. But she was clawed back into the dream against her will. Twelve thirty! The time itself butted into her dream, making it worse. Had he been trapped down there for two whole hours? He would be dead, long dead. But the firemen were coming at least, the police and the ambulance and the Egyptian coastguard (which turned out to be Poppet Melville's Positively Plump class, jogging along with coils of rope). Anna told them to hurry, to cut Kit loose from suffocation. She could hear their bells as they approached.

She could hear the telephone bell. Fighting her way out of sleep, Anna rolled to the far side of the bed and groped beneath it for the receiver which Kit kept on his side. She picked it up, almost falling out of bed in her haste.

'Yes. Hello. Three eight seven nine.'

'It's me.' Kit's voice was tinny with distance, and sounded also as if he were keeping it low so as not to be overheard. 'How are you? Is Mary there?'

'Gone to Mike's. Back tonight. I couldn't quite face it.'

'Are you OK? You sound funny.'

'Yes, yes. Been asleep. Bit sick this morning. But fine. How's Venice?'

'Excellent. All I wanted. The thing is, Anna – Molly Miles is a bit upset.'

Behind the glazed mahogany door of the hotel phone box, Kit picked at a piece of flaking cream paint. This was not the way he had hoped to break it to his wife about the *carnevale*. He could have told her months before; she would have been wary, perhaps a bit annoyed with him for creating such an extra pressure on an already complicated school trip, but he knew that she would eventually have agreed that it was not a bad idea. Somehow, though, Kit had become gripped by the notion of making it a surprise. He had wanted to see Anna as amazed as the children when the first wave of masked figures came round some alley corner or floated beneath a canal bridge in a gondola. Now he cursed his whimsy and steeled himself for a bald confession.

'Why is she upset?' Anna was asking. 'Was the journey bad?'

'No,' said Kit. 'Clockwork. Apart from a bit of bother with a Belgian travelling salesman. Don't ask. No, sweetheart, she's upset because the city's a bit wild. A lot of people about. It's carnival.'

Anna gasped. 'Do you know, Mary was chatting on about pancake day falling in half-term, and I never made the connection! God, how we do get out of touch with these things. What a weird coincidence!'

Far away, tinny and distorted, Kit sighed heavily. 'She's worked out it isn't a coincidence. I couldn't have booked the hotel unless I'd booked it last year. She knows I did it on purpose. Seemed a good idea at the time.'

Anna was silent. She did not want to reprove Kit; besides, part of her was still exalted, singing with relief that the dream was not true and that he still lived and breathed and disrupted things.

Kit, too, knew better than to rush in with self-justification. After a moment his wife said into the crackling silence, 'Will it be all that bad? There are two of you to keep an eye on them. You needn't go out when it's dark or anything. It's not a criminal sort of thing, is it? Carnival?'

'No, but there are just thousands of people, all in masks and cloaks, and lots of eccentric busking and distractions and the odd banger being thrown around underfoot in San Marco. And teenagers in rather daring costumes tightrope-walking on the parapets of bridges. Not very Molly. Well, imagine. She hasn't even been out and seen all that yet, and already she's trying to ring Harding to bale us out. She says we shouldn't be here, and the kids will get lost in the crowd.'

'Well, they'd better not. Put them in groups. A crocodile, even. Pity they don't wear uniform, in a way.'

'Well, they do, in a way,' said Kit. 'In a way.' He felt far more comfortable now that Anna knew and was his accomplice. 'I pinched the bat costumes from the drama cupboard.'

'Whoo!' Anna exhaled, for the first time in weeks feeling not at all sick or fraily pregnant, but full of vigour and delight in the vividness and brinkmanship of life. 'God, I wish I was there. It must be amazing. You and Venice and a pack of underage bats.'

'*I* wish you were here,' said Kit. 'But look, will you do something? Will you ring Harding and find a way to explain it? Make it sound as if it was always quite understood between us all that it'd be carnival? Molly tried to get through to him but she couldn't. She will in the end, though. If by that time he's all laid back and aware of everything and sanctions it, she'll shut up and make the best of a bad job. As it is, she's barking furious. I only got to the phone because she went to the bog.'

Anna sighed. 'Is the hotel number by the downstairs phone? Right. Stick around for half an hour and I'll get on to Ron Harding. I happen to know where he is. He's at the Legion Hall arranging this Badminton club idea with Graham Merck. I heard them discussing it yesterday. If he rang Molly to say it's all OK, would that be a good idea?'

'It would be,' said Kit fervently, 'a fucking miracle.'

All her life, Anna had known that she was deliciously, quite edibly charming and possessed of power over men. Over daddies, in particular. Settled, tranquil knowledge of this kind is one of the most powerful weapons which a truly doting father can place in the hands of his small daughter, and Derek Melville had worshipped Anna as a baby. Mary was plain and angular and prone to wriggle from embraces and crawl away to make a noise with her big brother. Anna, five years later, fulfilled his dream of a baby daughter by being blonde and cuddlesome and full of giggles.

For the first twelve years of her life, therefore, any struggles or worries that Anna met – in her school life or with her commanding mother – were offset by the sure knowledge that to her daddy she was a peerless princess who could do no wrong. Being a fair-minded child, she rarely asked for special privileges, but it was nice to know she had the power to wheedle them if necessary. Only when she began to look more womanly did Derek, in whom there ran a deep vein of primness, feel it no longer appropriate to cuddle and extravagantly praise her. He withdrew to admire from afar with wistful pride his new-fledged swan, and indulged himself only by buying her ever fluffier angora pastel sweaters every Christmas.

So Anna – who dimly understood the delicate feelings that underlay her father's new distance – was left with his legacy. She had a particular kind of confidence where older men were concerned: she saw the doting in their eyes and the burning chivalrous desire they felt to help her through her life in any way they could, and she knew she could exploit it. Her fair-mindedness, however, endured into adulthood and she rarely did exploit it. In the case of Ron Harding, whose core of lonely sentimentality made him dangerously prone to dote, she had always been scrupulously careful to take no advantage at all. She had backed Kit's application for the Dewar trip fund, but done so as much with argument as with eyelashes.

Desperate situations, however, require desperate remedies. Anna stared into the bedroom mirror for a few moments, gathering her wits. After some hesitation she peeled off her navy sweatshirt and replaced it with her father's most recent Christmas present, a pale blue mohair jersey with a scooped neckline. She brushed her hair back, shook her head to let it fall forward, and found in the drawer a pale blue plastic Alice band which had not yet been discovered and snapped in half by a disapproving Kit. Five minutes later, looking anything but a thirty-year-old wife and prospective matron, she was walking purposefully down the road to the Legion Hall.

The *pock!* of shuttlecock on racket greeted her as she pushed the heavy swing door open. There, sure enough, standing morosely on the sideline was Ronald Harding with his hands thrust deep into his pockets. He was, without enthusiasm, watching his deputy head in white shorts playing against a young man of athletic build who was presumably the coach. Anna had heard Merck, the day before, chivvying his superior into coming along to meet this Mr Dangerfield about badminton club. But it was a piece of unsought luck that she would find the deputy so deep in combat that he could not interfere in their conversation. *Pock!* went Merck and *pock!* went Dangerfield, and Anna was able to sidle up unnoticed to her headmaster just as he sank in boredom onto a hard Legion bench.

'Hi!' she said, sitting down beside him. 'I thought I'd find you here. I just wanted to say that Caroline Chang is feeling a lot better. She can go home tomorrow in a walking plaster.' For, such was her duplicity that Anna had taken the precaution of ringing the ward to gather this piece of information.

'Good, excellent,' said Harding, looking down at her with yearning paternal affection. He wanted to pat her shoulder just where her smooth glowing young neck met the pale fluffiness of the sweater, but restrained himself.

Anna saw the look in his eyes and disliked herself, but for Kit's sake blinked prettily a couple of times and said, 'I've heard from Kit. It's going splendidly. They're so lucky to be able to show the children *carnevale*. I bet not many schools have done that.'

'Oh, er, yes.' He was momentarily lost and, distracted by a particularly loud *pock!* turned away from her to look at the players.

Anna rattled on, 'It was a terrific idea. He says it's really bringing the texts alive to them. Seeing all the costumes, actually in that setting. I'm sorry to be missing it. But the children's diaries should be splendid.'

Harding turned back to her. 'Yes, splendid,' he said, still vaguely. 'And, er, Molly Miles? Is she enjoying herself?'

Anna looked up at him, a picture of innocence. 'Well, she seems a bit disconcerted. Obviously, she didn't quite realize it wasn't just a standard sort of museum and gallery trip. We all forgot to tell her about the carnival theme, and the work we've planned round it – what with her standing in at the last minute. Obviously, Caroline was in no state to run through the details with her. So Molly . . .' Anna pouted, a pout her mother would have been proud of.

The headmaster sighed heavily. 'Creating, is she?' He would not have ventured on a disloyal remark about one of his staff had Anna not been a model of kindness, team spirit and discretion.

She smiled and said, 'Yes, a bit. I think maybe she just needs to know that everything's all right with you. There just *wasn't* time for a proper briefing, was there? You had Caroline to think of.'

Thus was planted in Ronald Harding's mind, painlessly and even flatteringly, the idea that it was up to him, as the responsible authority and the man who knew the full picture from the beginning, to make good his omission and reassure Molly Miles that everything was going according to an approved plan. It would not have been so easy had Graham Merck been party to the conversation. But Graham Merck was 14–3 down – *pock!* – and fighting back hard, on the grimy Legion parquet.

The headmaster made his excuses between points, hastily agreed to let the deputy have his way over the badminton instructor, and walked up the road with Anna to make the call from her telephone. Then, his duty done, he stayed to drink a cup of cappuccino from her machine. It was as frothy, as light and as sweet as Anna herself. For a short while Ronald Harding was a happy man.

As dusk fell that night on San Marco, Molly struggled grim-faced and maskless through a nodding, bobbing, blank-eyed nightmare throng of travesties: skulls, cats, courtesans and jesters. Again and again, peering from a variety of cloaks and hoods, she was tormented by the same horrid symbol of the city's long depravity: the white harlequin face with the nose that grew obscenely, insolently, into a stabbing beak. Around her the small bats tumbled and squealed and squabbled, circling too fast to be counted, looking everywhere but at their teachers, masked too thoroughly to be recognized and scolded. Kit, a tall and imperturbable senior bat, seemed to be smiling under his mask and Molly hated him with all her heart. The black old passions of the city entered her, and if she had had a knife she would have slid it, then and there, beneath his ribs.

It was only half past seven when they reached the hotel, but already on the Grand Canal the gondolas bore flaring torches illuminating still more masked dreams and horrors, and a heavy rock beat shook the city from the Campo San Polo. Unbidden, several of the children demanded their diaries and began, feverishly, to write.

Josh, with Leanne at his side, began in his big untidy scrawl, 'You defnately safer in a mask. Withote it peple can see yore scared of there masks. In mask world to show yore face is to die.'

'Oscar Wilde,' said Kit, 'wrote, "Give a man a mask and he will tell you the truth."'

An argument broke out over this. Leanne held strongly that it was true and that her mask made her braver. Andrew said masks were nothing but lies made solid. Molly went to bed early, and Kit stayed up to read, beautifully, to the children.

12

Mary and her children came back on Saturday evening tired, grimy and full of high spirits. Lee had been allowed to help strip down an engine, taught the lore and language of the pits, and given an old spanner and a torn check flag by his uncle. With these treasures he dived immediately beneath the kitchen table to make growling pit noises and bang the floor tiles. Maggie was whiningly exhausted, having discovered that motor racing did not after all speak to her soul. She sat on Mary's knee, thumb in her mouth and big eyes blank, refusing to go to bed.

Since Lee would plainly take some time to return from the exalted realms of mechanical fantasy, the two women accepted the situation and sat together finishing the kitchen wine box and talking. Ravenous now that her sickness had passed off for the day, Anna picked at the children's rejected sandwiches.

'I suppose I shouldn't be drinking,' she said once or twice, but Mary brushed her scruples aside.

'One glass a day. Good for you. *The Times* doctor says so.'

'Well, one glass. Gosh, it's good not to be feeling sick.'

'You will again tomorrow. Face it.'

'I do. I know. But it's still good for the moment.'

Maggie began to whimper, burrowing into her mother's neck with inarticulate babyish noises of discontent.

'How were Mike and Barbara, anyway?' asked Anna.

'Fine. Deelya's playing up a bit. Boyfriend with a ring in his lip.'

'Well, Dirk's got rings in his ear, or had when I last saw him.'

'That's different. Ears are OK apparently. Not lips.'

'Yes, but Dirk had a ring in the top bit of his ear as well as the one on the lobe. It was the size of a curtain ring.'

'I know. But Barbara is still one hundred per cent adamant: ears are OK, lips are beyond the pale. Ugh, imagine kissing it.'

'I wanna, wanna oh, I wanna neooow. Mummeeee,' said Maggie from the depths of Mary's chest.

'Sorry,' said Mary, stretching her head back so she could take a swig of her wine over the child's head. 'She doesn't approve of my talking to anyone else when she's whingeing, do you, sweetie?'

'I wanna make *fudge*,' said the child more distinctly. '*Now*.'

'Bed now. Fudge tomorrow,' said Mary. 'Ow! You little sod!' Lee had hit her foot quite forcefully with the small spanner, and was now emerging from his improvised pit under the table waving the chequered flag. 'Monster!' Mary hauled her son up onto her other knee, and sat weighed down by the two children, an arm round each. Anna watched her with admiration.

'You must have incredibly strong knees by now,' she said.

'Oh, one is not a *person*,' said Mary. 'One is a sort of rocky outcrop. A prehistoric barrow, jutting out of the landscape. A mother is there to be scrambled over. I know my place.' She gestured towards Anna with one hand, keeping the arm stiff to support Lee's back. 'You'll know yours, soon. No more "yes, miss", no respectful silence when you come into the room, no holidays, no clocking-off time. For the first nine months you are just a milk bar and sewage disposal operative, thereafter a lackey and large indestructible toy.'

'It can't be more difficult than clearing up the chaos Kit causes,' said Anna. 'He rang today, as a result of which I had to put on a dab of placatory pink lipstick *and* an Alice band to go and see the headmaster and smooth things over.'

'Why?' asked Mary. 'The Alice band sounds pretty serious. Did you have to simper?'

'A bit. It now turns out that Kit deliberately booked the trip bang in the middle of the Venice carnival. The place is heaving with revellers and quite rowdy. He has also disguised all the children as masked bats. Molly Miles is not happy. I had to get the head to ring her and say it was all right.'

Mary slid her children off her knees and pulled herself stiffly to her feet, ignoring their complaints.

'I love that man,' she said reverently. 'If he wasn't already spoken for, and I wasn't a rocky outcrop, I warn you that I would make a very serious play for Kit. Come on, sausages. Bed!' She began to drag her children by the hand towards the kitchen door.

Anna reached gloomily for the last Marmite sandwich and said, 'It's all very well for you to say that, but I'll still be damn glad when this trip's safely over.'

'Fudge tomorrow?' said Maggie from the doorway.

'Fudge tomorrow,' said Anna. 'Good night, sweeties. Do you mind if I don't come up? My back aches.'

Natalie and Kara were annoyed with Marianne. When Kit had finished reading to them – Charles Dickens' description of a gondola ride, all mysterious alleys and strange echoing cries – the children had dispersed to their rooms willingly enough. Natalie had been put in charge of Room 7, where she and Marianne occupied the standard twin beds, as close together as a double, and Kara being the smallest and lightest took the rickety folding cot under the window. But Marianne would not settle down. Instead, she stood precariously on Kara's bed with the curtains open, looking out of the window. There was a sliver of white moon above the alley and an iron lantern threw mellow light over the peeling ochre and rose of the houses opposite.

'You're on my *feet*,' said Kara peevishly. 'Mr Milcourt said we had to go to *sleep*.'

'I can't sleep,' said Marianne.

'You ain't tried.'

'I know I can't, *little girl*,' said Marianne crushingly. 'When you grow up a bit you'll know why.'

'Wooooh!' said Natalie, in satirical respect. 'Get her! What's 'is then? You got a feller? You got hot knickers?'

'You wun't understand,' said Marianne. She showed no sign of moving from the end of the rickety folding bed, so Kara flounced up out of it and buried herself under the bedclothes in Marianne's own bed. She and Natalie waited a moment for the expected explosion of wrath, but none came. Marianne continued looking at the moon and the lamp for a while, silently, then laid herself down without complaint, almost absent-mindedly, on the bed which was too small, too narrow, and too lonely for her comfort.

In the morning the city was quiet. Kit, aware of the fragility of their official truce, suggested meekly that Molly – who had an impressive knowledge of art history – should lead a trip round the Accademia gallery and that the children should remain unmasked in the interests of sobriety. He would come with them, await them by the entrance, and then take over for an hour after lunch to do some 'local architectural walking', as he rather wildly called it, before the whole party set out again to have the gondola ride and supper in a *trattoria* which Kit had booked, and watch fireworks from the Rialto Bridge.

Offered this firm, comprehensible timetable, Molly felt more secure and became more pleasant. As the party walked sedately, unmasked and unharassed, through the clear winter light towards the Accademia, she gradually relaxed. She even joined in a conversation which had been going on all through breakfast among the boys, about how Byron took four hours and twenty minutes to swim the length of the Grand Canal in 1818.

Kit, inevitably, was the origin of this thrilling snippet of information, but Molly took it graciously, because by chance she knew enough about swimming to keep her end up. She had swum for her county as a girl, and discussed currents and stamina and fatigue curves with some authority.

'Didn't he die of the sewage?' asked Sally, seriously.

'They din't have sewage in the old days,' said Morrey Hart, contemptuously.

'Course they did.'

'Not chemical toxic sewage.'

'You are such a *dickhead*.'

'Children! Language! Please!'

'Well, he is. Mr Milcourt says they had such bad sewage people got butronic plagues.'

'I think you mean bubonic.'

'This Byron din't get ill, did he?'

'He worked out a lot, prob'ly.'

Kit kept himself in the background, walking between Kylie and Marianne in comparative silence. He felt oddly tired, and there was a nagging ache in his chest. When, accompanied by the spirit of Byron, they came out of the final alleyway and saw the Accademia Bridge, he was glad enough to sit on a bench outside the gallery and wait for them, alone with his thoughts.

Molly's tour, however, was not a success. The indoor gloom of the gallery depressed the children's spirits. Outdoors in the clear cold air the city and the lagoon had sparkled like a living Canaletto with moving boats and bright figures. It irked them to be indoors with Miss Miles, in a museum hush with only the dim flat splendours of high art to look at. Veronese and Bellini, Giorgione and Carpaccio were wasted on them; they said their feet hurt, that they were hungry. A few found flashes of interest, even if only in the vastness of the canvases, but there were too many galleries, not enough light and no freedom to roam. Molly gathered them round canvas after canvas, guide book in hand, and told them things they did not want to know about painters who were dead. And, in the opinion of most of the children, deserved to be. Before long rebellion set in.

'Miss, Andrew pushed me.'

'Can we go an' see the lion on a stick again?'

'Miss, will we be in our bat suits later?'

'I'm hung-ary!'

'Fatty!'

'Fatarse yourself!'

Molly battled on for a while, achieved two-thirds of her planned itinerary and emerged into the sunshine again, the children punching and snarling behind her. Kit was sitting on the same bench where she had left him but with two large paper carrier bags by his side.

'Lunch,' he said. 'The cafe over there did sandwiches for us. I thought we could start our architectural walk from here when they've all eaten.'

'Aw, sir!' remonstrated Darren and Joe Baldwin together. 'Then we won't have our costumes!'

'Give them a rest. We aren't going to San Marco, or Rialto, or any of the big *campi*,' said Kit. 'We're just going to walk for an hour and look at the way the buildings and the canals fit together. Then we go back for an hour's rest, then out for the evening. That's correct, isn't it, Miss Miles?'

Molly was not to be wooed with false deference. Coldly polite, squaring her shoulders in the sensible brown jacket she always wore for travelling, she merely said, 'Are you sure you can manage? If so, I will spend some time in the gallery and then meet you at the hotel.'

'Fine,' said Kit. 'I did get you a sandwich, if you, er . . .'

'No thank you,' said Molly, and turned back towards the great door. She particularly wanted to see Paolo Veneziano's polyptych 'Coronation of the Virgin', and had not been able to face any more of the boys' silly giggling at the V-word.

The rest of the party ate their lunch, drank lemonade from a stand outside, panicked briefly over lavatories, found one, and finally set off on their exploration. As the street crowds were thickening every minute, Kit split them into five numbered groups of three.

'Only one rule,' he said. 'Everybody, at all times, must be able to see both their partners. And the chief partner – Andrew, Darren, Morrey, Sally, Natalie – each of you must be able to see someone from the group numbered one ahead of yours. And Andrew, as number one, you have to be able to see me. That way we won't get split up going round all the corners. I shall stop every few minutes. If we do lose someone—'

'Have you got Miss Miles's whistle?' asked Sally Addams. There was a general shout of laughter. Molly's games whistle had been in frequent use during the early stages of the morning walk. Kit grinned.

'No whistle,' he said. 'This.' He held up a little bell of thick purple Murano glass: a tourist gewgaw. 'Listen.' When he shook it, the little bell emitted a surprisingly penetrating sound. 'I hope I won't need it. And let me say that if anybody falls into any canal whatsoever they will *not* get the gondola ride tonight. *Avanti!*'

Their spirits restored by food and the prospect of adventure, the children followed him, clustered close enough to make separation unlikely. Kit threaded his way blithely through the alleys and over little bridges, cut across great *campi*, waited patiently while the children clustered round the windows of mask shops, dived occasionally into churches for a few moments then out again into the fast-fading sunlight.

'How do you know the way, sir?'

'I don't. But look – on the wall.'

'It says *per Rialto* – arrow – *per Ferrovia* – arrow.'

'Yep. Follow *Ferrovia*, and we end up near our hotel, don't we? Who remembers what Ferrovia means?'

Before they reached it, though, the party found themselves in a big square unfamiliar to Kit. In the centre was an unexpected building, a round neoclassical stone ring with doorways into it. It blended so well with the *campo* that it took a moment for them all to realize that it was no building at all but a plywood painted structure, like a stage set. Curious, they moved towards it and looked through the archways.

'It's a market, sir!' said Kylie. The others pushed round her, and squeaked with excitement.

'It's a mask market!'

Sure enough, stand after stand was filled with carnival masks, and racks of ruffled cloaks stood alongside, black and gold and purple and silver.

'Wicked!'

'Can we look?'

'Wish I had some money!'

The mask shops which had fascinated them on the walk had not tempted the children in: their boutique size and air of taste and craftsmanship intimidated them. This, however, was a market, but better than the stands they had seen at St Mark's or the Rialto because it was less crowded and sold only disguises, not plastic gondolas and postcards. From stand to stand they surged, carefully picking up and trying on the light cardboard and thin plastic faces, the turbans and wigs.

'Oh, we got no money!' lamented Leanne.

'We gave Miss Miles our pocket money,' mourned Morrey Hart.

'It was in English anyway,' said Nicky. Then they all turned to look at Kit.

'Well,' he said, 'I did, as it happens, take charge of the pocket money. I also happened to change it into Italian money. What's Italian money? Anyone know?'

'Pesetas.'

'Francs.'

'Lire?'

'Correct. So you can have it. There are two thousand five hundred lire in a pound, more or less. So ten pounds is . . . ?'

The children went into a huddle. 'Twenty – twenty-five thousand – nah, can't be, thass huge!'

'I'm quite glad poor Miss Chang isn't here,' said Kit. 'She'd be mortified. Take a pull. Come on. You're not getting the money till you do the maths.'

When he was satisfied, he gave each of them a bundle of notes and let them loose among the stalls. Leanne, he noticed, was sticking close to big Josh and gently helping him to count the noughts at the end of the absurd prices. The other girls stayed in one group, the boys in another; except for Andrew who stood alone, entranced before a display of golden suns and silver moon faces.

When those who wanted had bought masks, they suddenly saw a display of red and yellow cloth hats for L 8,100 and raided those. Within ten minutes they were back at his side: three curly-rayed suns, a number of harlequins, several feathered birds – Kara, with her red hair, was a particularly striking owl – and Marianne, who had spent the whole of her L 25,000 on becoming a slinky effigy of a cat, in a dim gold half-mask with a veil of black silk loops which fell like a curtain over the bottom half of her face. As she walked along beside him, Kit saw to his amusement that the black tassels kept blowing into her mouth.

Back at the little hotel, they dispersed to their rooms and rested gratefully enough, some with books or magazines, a few with tapes, others dreaming or talking. Kit, who rarely slept during the day, lay down on the bed and knew no more until, surprised, he woke from a deep sleep at ten to five. Emerging blearily from his hot little room, he found Molly Miles having a cup of tea in the tiny lounge area near the reception desk.

'I've sent the children to get ready,' she said. 'We want to leave at five. You said.'

Kit nodded and looked around, hopeful himself of a cup of tea. Chiara, however, had vanished and already the children were reappearing one by one. Molly stared, aghast, at the unfamiliar faces.

'What is all this?' she asked, an octave higher than usual. 'What? Where are your bat masks?'

'Oh, do we *have* to wear bat masks, miss?' said a plaintive voice from behind a gilded, slit-eyed sun. 'Only these are real Venice ones.'

'Venetian,' said Andrew Murray's voice. 'These are, like, proper.'

Molly moved aside and turned to Kit. In a low, almost hissing voice she said, '*How* do you propose to keep track of fifteen children in masks if they aren't all the same? At least in the black costumes –' she could not bring herself to speak of bats again, this was all just so nightmarishly *silly* – 'in the black costumes we had some chance of keeping the group together.'

'The cloaks are still the same,' said Kit defensively. 'Surely – well, whatever you think.'

But Molly was defeated. She could not bring herself to order the group back into their bat masks.

As they left, Sarah Midali, a quiet, sweet girl, Molly had always thought, turned sequinned harlequin eyes to her and said, 'Miss? If we're all in our new masks, there's plenty of bat hats left. Would you like me to go back and get you one?'

There was real solicitude in the child's voice, and Molly felt a pricking of tears behind her eyes. More gently, she said, 'No thank you, Sarah. I'll be fine. There should be somebody you can all easily recognize. Just in case.'

13

As the group came round the great church of San Giacomo di Rialto, Kit called a halt and pulled a black bundle out of his coat pocket. It was an imitation silk cord, intended probably for a curtain pull in some grand room, and all of thirty feet long. He knotted it in the middle with a loop, slid his hand through the loop and said to the children, 'In the crowd, I want you to hold on to this rope. It's what French schoolchildren do. It will keep us together in a clump and stop anybody wandering off. If Miss Miles brings up the rear, nobody will go missing.'

'Unless Miss Miles does.'

'Or the rope breaks.'

'Better tie it onto Josh's loops,' giggled Leanne. Josh's trousers were fashionably military, with a camouflage pattern and abundant loops for commando knives, water bottles and heavy belts. They had been the subject of much half-envious jeering from the rest of the boys, who were still too short to shop at army surplus stores.

Molly approved the system, particularly since Kit artfully added for her benefit, 'It was Anna's idea.'

In good accord, they moved along the crowded waterfront, crossed the teeming Rialto Bridge and plunged into the lighted busy streets beyond. Kit had booked a six o'clock supper for them all at a *trattoria* close enough to San Marco for the rising evening tide of masks and musicians to be intoxicatingly visible through the wide glass windows. They piled their masks and cloaks in a corner and settled, happy and excited, to eat.

There were two tables for eight with one extra chair squeezed in, giving just enough room for small Kara. Molly presided over one table, mainly of boys although Leanne would not be separated from Josh. Over on the other table Kit had Andrew Murray, Joe Baldwin, and the other six girls. Glancing round halfway through her spaghetti carbonara, Molly saw with horror that Kit had ordered red wine, and was giving each child a taste of it. Andrew was looking up at him over his glass, and Kit was leaning over, inclining his head as if to listen to the boy while on his other side, gazing at him, sat the moon-faced Marianne. That child, Molly noted grimly, was wearing both rouge and mascara. Must have put them on under her mask before leaving, the artful little minx. Kit was saying, '. . . the best wine comes from the toughest, hardest soil. It's the stress, the suffering of the vines, which makes the grapes sweet and good.'

Molly made another mental note. Her report to the head would be full, frank, and incontrovertibly damning. Milcourt might be getting his own way this week but she would make very sure that this was the last Dewar trip – or school trip of any kind – that he was ever entrusted with.

'Can I have my diary, sir?' Andrew asked.

'Sorry. It's at the hotel,' said Kit. 'Do you need to write something? Is it about the grapes?'

The little boy nodded, solemn-eyed.

Kit proffered his own fountain pen and the restaurant's napkin. 'Will that do?'

Andrew nodded, bent and wrote, sauce from his spaghetti staining the edges of the napkin and the sleeve of his sweater. Kit looked on approvingly for a moment, then turned to talk to the girls. Molly returned to the last of her carbonara and to a clamour which was rising at her table regarding ice creams. The ordering of these was somewhat delayed by the abrupt entry with accordion and collecting bucket of a gold-faced harlequin in ballet tights and a turbaned and feathered blackamoor. Molly felt a headache coming on.

Outside again, the cold air refreshed them. Kit led them by his silken cord down through the alleys to the little canal of San Zulian, where he told them to wait while he swung down onto a pontoon. Half a dozen gondolas gleamed darker black against the night and as they bobbed on the water, their high prows like silver combs caught the light from a single street lamp. It was quieter here, and the fifteen masked children stood shivering slightly, their silhouettes odd and humped where the black cloaks rested on the padded shoulders of their anoraks. After a brief rapid conversation, Kit called them down.

'Three boats of four, one with five. Kara, you'd better go in the five, you'll fit better. Careful.'

Cautiously, handed by impassive gondoliers in the darkness, the children stepped into the boats. Leanne and Josh, still inseparable, found themselves chaperoned, to their disgust, on the opposite red cushions by Molly and Nicky Pinter. Marianne, by discreet use of elbows and treading on feet, made sure of a place by Kit. More of them were shuddering now from the cold and the insecurity of being down on the canal, smelling it, wobbling on its ripples. It seemed a more vital, threatening element now than when they looked at it from firm ground or from the high deck of a *vaporetto*.

'Weird,' said Joe Baldwin quietly, speaking for them all.

Kit spoke again briefly to the four gondoliers, who nodded and grinned. Then they pushed off, one by one, leaning to their single oars with lounging casual grace.

All through their various lives, each of the fifteen children would remember that night and that ride. Some talked of it to their own children: of the way the long boats slid silently under arched bridges and through dark ravines of tall houses, of the snatches of music that echoed plaintively round distant corners, of the splashing of the oar and the ghostly cry of 'Ey-o!' loosed by their gondolier at each sharp turn.

They would remember the excitement and the fear as one dim, dank passage followed another, and the relief of the moment when suddenly they came out onto the Grand Canal and all was light and glory after the murderous darkness of the back canals. Even those who did not talk of it remembered; they wrote their diaries that night, kept them through the careless teenage years, found them again in the detritus of some house move, read them again and put them carefully aside. As Kit had intended, the night and the city stayed with the children for good. In that half-hour each laid down a layer of necessary splendour, a cushion to stay hidden but perennially comforting beneath the hard banality of life.

The boats, as Kit had asked them to, separated as soon as they could. Mick, Morrey, Joe and James found themselves alone, being swiftly taken through God knows what dark waterway by their silent Charon. They were at first scared and then exhilarated. Kara, Kylie, Sarah and Natalie were glad to have Darren in their boat, because he was chunky and solid and somehow comforting; but even so there was one point, in a particularly dark and dank ravine, when all five of them simultaneously decided it would be good to take off their masks for a moment and see one another's pink, familiar human faces glimmering in the darkness.

Molly looked around a little wildly when her gondolier broke away from the others, but fortunately concluded that her own boat was the only one to do so and made no fuss. Indeed, she enjoyed the ride, but would have enjoyed it more if the presence of the children had not been so incongruous. This was not her idea of a school trip, not at all. 'Too much rich food and excitement,' her mother used to say, and 'It'll end in tears.' As for the cost, she had glimpsed the half-hourly gondola rate on a board by the pontoon, and resolved to make the headmaster fully aware of the frivolous way the Dewar subsistence fund was being spent.

But Kit and Marianne, Andrew and Sally Addams were, in every sense, transported. Kit was now extremely tired despite his afternoon's sleep; even to him who had planned it, this Venetian adventure was becoming uncomfortably surreal. It was an overwrought, over-ornate departure from normality. He wished Anna was with him. Yet he could not but be moved by the ancient, watery perfection of the night city, and obscurely excited by the distant invisible sounds of carnival. Wisps of music came to them from doorways; they glimpsed some kind of dance going on behind great windows in a Grand Canal palazzo above watersteps lit by flaring torches. Turning back into the side canals, they moved in swift silence for a moment and then in the distance heard a shriek of unconnected laughter, a sharp cry, a small stony splash. At his side, Marianne huddled closer and he glanced down at the child with amusement.

'What was that?' she asked. 'That didn't sound ordinary.'

'This ain't ordinary,' said Andrew. 'It ain't *modern*, is it, sir?'

'No,' said Kit. 'Timeless. Think how many centuries these buildings have stood here over the canals, listening to – what's the line? "Distant sounds of revelry and rape."'

They were almost back; as they glided up to the pontoon they saw the shadowy shapes of two other gondolas behind them, and Molly's group already disembarked and standing huddled on the pavement.

'Wicked,' said Morrey's voice out of the darkness astern.

It would have been better, Kit thought a thousand times after-wards, if they had all gone straight back to the hotel and to bed. Quit while you're winning, bow out on a high note, leave 'em laughing. But the children had been promised fireworks and even Molly was sufficiently gripped by the spirit of the evening to feel a greed for more sensation, more show. So in the time-honoured tradition of carrying on a bit too long with carnival, the seventeen of them with their silken cord walked on towards the shore of the lagoon, and found the fireworks just beginning.

When the last long shiver of light had passed and the lagoon lay black and empty once more, they turned back to walk through the Piazza San Marco, past the 'lion on a stick' and the high triumphant horses over the Basilica's door. As Kit came level with the Campanile, shouldering his way through the crowd slowly so that the children on the line could keep up, he felt a sudden urgent tug on the curtain cord round his left wrist.

'Si-ir!' hissed Andrew Murray. '*Look!*'

All the children stopped and followed the boy's pointing arm. On the low wall round the Campanile were two statues, fourteenth or fifteenth century by the look of them; they were monks, tonsured and robed, in pale marble. One had a hand raised in blessing, the other looked piously aloft with his palms together. Their white marble feet in monkish sandals were carved in calloused detail, their fine-boned hook-nosed ancient faces were turned inward towards one another as if they were preparing to chant an antiphon from their choir stalls.

'The statues!' said Andrew. The lights shone easily on his pale face.

'So?' said Josh. 'We seen statchoos. Hundreds of 'em.'

'One *moved*,' said Andrew. He had pushed his mask back to see better. 'It *did*!'

As the children watched, amused at Andrew's intensity, the praying monk's hands seemed to grow further apart. Against the carven stillness of his robe, the right hand moved upward as if in supplication. The children gasped.

'The other one!' said Kara. 'The other one! Look!' While their eyes were on the second monk, whose arm was moving in a great sign of the cross over them, the first one must have moved fast. When they whirled back, the statue was kneeling, arms outstretched, palms upward, as if he had been doing it for five hundred years through indignities of weather and passing birds. Not a tremor broke its stillness.

Kit, who had seen this variety of busking once or twice before in European cities, smiled at this unsought bonus. In front of him, head barely up to his breastbone, little Andrew was trembling violently, transported out of himself by the extraordinary excitement of the sight. The other children, after the first shock, had returned to normal levels of pleased arousal and were chattering among themselves.

'Imagine keepin' still like that!'

'Do you think their feet get cold?'

'Do you think if we tickled his feet with Kara's feathers off her mask . . . ?'

'That is so cool. Look how white his face is. If he smiled, that'd crack off.'

'The one over there just winked. He did!'

Andrew Murray, however, had been the first to see them. He had not been alerted by the others to look, but had felt the full shock of expecting statues and finding living, if chalky white, flesh before his eyes. He continued to shiver, his teeth chattering, and Kit placed gentle, calming hands on each of the child's shoulders.

'They are good, aren't they?' he said conversationally, to lower the emotional temperature. 'There's a man in Paris, a mime artist, who teaches it. It's always very odd when you see the living statues walk away, even sometimes to get a hot dog.' The boy slowly stilled under his hands. His shoulders, through the cloak and padded anorak, felt as frail as the bones of a bird beneath its feathers. Kit let him go, put his hands in his pockets and looked round to rally the others.

There was no sign of Molly Miles. Kit counted up the children – with some difficulty given the crowd around them and the variety of their masks and hats – and found only fourteen.

'Who's missing?' he asked sharply. 'Who isn't here?'

'Kylie, sir,' said a voice from between some red and pink feathers and a black cloak.

'I'm here,' said Kylie's voice through a gold sun. 'P'raps it's Natalie.'

'No, I'm here.'

Kit rapidly called the register from memory. It became apparent that the missing child was Marianne Denver. Around them, the crowd was growing denser as people drifted back from the fireworks and began to point and laugh at the living statues. Kit pulled out his Murano bell and tinkled it, loudly, above his head. Then a thought struck him.

'Miss Miles isn't here. Is she with Marianne?'

'P'raps they went to the toilet.'

However wide their differences, Kit knew that Molly Miles would never have left the group, least of all with a girl child in tow, without notifying him. But perhaps she had said something while he was standing with Andrew, deep in the moment of the statues. Perhaps he had not heard.

'Does anybody,' he said, slowly, 'know where they are?'

Whereon Miss Miles returned, alone. She had been barely three metres away, crouched by a wall trying to tie together a broken shoelace on her sensible English brogue. While she did so she found herself jostled and tousled by bustles and breeches, velvet and cotton and nylon cloaks that crackled with static electricity. The way the revellers brushed past her so unheedingly made her want to lash out at them. She was tired now, her brief flame of carnival spirit extinct, and she wanted her bed.

Marianne stood by the lagoon, enjoying the way her hair streamed down her back and lifted in the night breeze, enjoying the sensation of being cloaked and masked and alone in Venice waiting for her fate. If she was unbalanced by hormones and high art, puppy love and carnival, she did not feel it. Marianne Denver, aged twelve, felt at that moment utterly and calmly and timelessly in control: a mistress of intrigue. She had lost herself on purpose in order to be found. She knew who would come to find her. She hoped, more than she had ever hoped anything, that he would be alone.

Kit jumped on the low wall between the statues and amused the careless crowd by tinkling his glass bell and calling Marianne's name as loudly as he could. Molly was torn between the terrible urgency of finding the child and the terrible embarrassment of the group's making a spectacle of itself in front of foreigners. Kit was still wearing a bat headdress. After a few moments she said crossly, 'If we stand around in this crowd we'll only lose the other fourteen. See how tired they are.'

Kit looked at her, saying nothing.

Molly continued, 'Suppose I take them back on the *vaporetto* and you carry on looking for Marianne. If she doesn't turn up in ten minutes or so, you can ring the police.'

He sighed. 'Yes, you're right. No point losing the whole lot.' He tossed her the bundle of curtain cord. 'Better have this.'

'Sir,' said Leanne unexpectedly. She was holding Josh's hand, Kit noticed. 'Would you like us to stay and help you look?'

'It would be another pair of eyes,' said Kit. 'Or two pairs. On the right level, as well. Yes, OK.'

Molly quashed the proposal – which Kit thought had been made in genuine kindness – with ruthess contempt. 'Certainly not. What nonsense. We can't risk any more of you wandering off and falling in the lagoon.'

There was a snivelling sound from behind more than one feather mask and, beneath them, lips began to tremble.

'D'you think she's drowned, miss?'

Molly saw her mistake, and as usual this enraged her further. Her corncrake voice became harsher, her delivery savagely clipped as she hectored the fourteen children into lines, seven holding each of the silken cords, and towed them off towards the *vaporetto* pontoon.

Kit followed to ensure that none of the whimpering children fell out of the convoy, watched from a short distance as they moved into the floating shelter, then turned away once he was confident that no harm would now befall them.

As he turned, he saw a few feet away a small figure, black-cloaked, with hair that streamed over its shoulders. Moving towards it, he was swept aside by a woman with a whitened face, hair dyed blue and a metre-long gondola on her head. Through his irritated panic he saw that her spreading robe was embroidered most beautifully in gold and black threads with likenesses of the great buildings of the city. The Campanile swished past him on her train. Somewhere close to them in the crowd an accordion had started to play. As he looked wildly around for the figure he took to be Marianne, her voice spoke from his other elbow.

'I'm here.'

Whirling round, he saw the pussycat mask with its black fringes through which red lips could be glimpsed, smiling. He clapped a hand on her shoulder, hard, as if afraid she would run away.

'Where the *hell* have you been? Why did you let go of the rope?'

'I had a cramp, sir.' All Sandmarsh girls knew, by the time they were twelve, that the authority of a male teacher would crumble to powder at the most oblique invocation of monthly female mysteries. Karen Dodbey had got out of a detention from Mr Atkins only the week before by saying she had a cramp. Kit was unconvinced, but recognized the checkmate and merely grunted.

'Speak to Miss Miles about it. She'll look after you,' he said, not without spite. 'I'll ask her to come and see you this evening.'

Marianne's eyes gleamed through the holes in her mask, pupils dilated in the dim light. Kit's hand on her shoulder was firm and thrilling, and he did not remove it as he turned her round and began to march her towards the *vaporetto* stop. She was glad he was annoyed, at least for the moment; the edge of roughness in his handling of her was pleasing. And, crazy with love as she was, she had enough sense left to know that if he were less annoyed or less worried that she would bolt, the precious hand would leave her shoulder.

As they got to the stop the boat was moving away, with

Miss Miles and the others aboard. Kit hesitated, then let go of Marianne's shoulder and said, 'We'll walk. Probably as quick as waiting here.'

So they walked together through the city, out of the maelstrom of the Piazza into quieter alleys and along embankments. Marianne murmured dreamily as the sounds faded, '"Distant sounds of revelry and rape".'

Kit glanced sharply down at her, alerted by her tone. Idiot! He had always been slow to notice when girls took a fancy to him. At this moment an outbreak of calf love was the last complication he needed. He wished they had taken the *vaporetto*. The fact that they were both masked suddenly felt dangerous rather than festive or protective. He pulled off his headdress and became not a giant bat but a white-faced, aquiline, wearily distinguished-looking Englishman in an eccentric black overcoat. He hustled Marianne ever faster through the narrow passages until she stopped suddenly and said, 'I got a stitch.'

They paused for a while and she propped herself against a sill, one hip jutting, her cloak thrown back to show her leg beneath a short skirt. She kept her mask on and pouted redly through its dangling black fringes.

Kit stared moodily down into a drained, muddy canal which gave a hint, even in the cold air, of how vile it might smell when the city grew warmer. His mood about the city had changed, and he saw its decay now more clearly than its beauty. Suddenly he remembered a particular chest of his mother's, in the attic of his childhood at Priory Shore School.

He had opened it one rainy, dull winter holiday afternoon to find it full of velvet and silk clothes folded and abandoned decades earlier. The small boy Kit, always fond of his dressing-up box, thought to replenish it from these treasures; but when he lifted the first velvet layer a smell of must and rot assailed him, and he saw that the cloth was eaten into ragged holes by moth and that – worse – the insect's fat papery grubs were clinging to everything in the box. From the trunk rose a terrible, rank, sharp smell of unclean antiquity. He had slammed its tin lid shut and avoided the attic for weeks.

That smell came back to him now, together with a pain in his chest which was becoming familiar. Only by fixing his thoughts on Anna did he banish a wave of violent depression.

Marianne was standing up now. They walked on silently for a few minutes and then she gasped, making a retching noise and clawing at her mouth. Kit looked down and saw that the black fringe of her mask had blown into her mouth. From the sounds he guessed that one of the longer loops had touched the back of her throat, making her gag and panic. Swiftly he pulled the mask from her face, and the gagging stopped.

'Silly bit of design,' he said lightly, to spare her embarrassment. 'It's bound to happen.' But Marianne, bare-faced, threw herself onto his chest. Her arms rose and clasped his neck as if she were drowning and her eyes, upturned to his, said everything. It was not a child's face any more.

Gently, Kit removed her arms from his neck. He did not want the child to feel humiliated; best to pretend he did not understand.

'Phew,' he said heartily. 'Yes, I bet that choking made you feel faint for a moment. Not far now. Perhaps the hotel would do us some hot chocolate.'

Within minutes they were opposite the station. They crossed the Scalzi Bridge and walked rapidly along to the hotel without further conversation. When they arrived, he found Molly by the reception desk and saw relief and the inevitable dawning anger on her face.

'She's fine,' he said. 'Just lost the rope for a moment. She was close to where we were, ironically. We only just missed your *vaporetto*. Thank you for taking charge of the rest.'

Molly began scolding Marianne, who looked at her with big sombre eyes, turned her back and went to her room. Molly made to follow, but Kit put out an arm to prevent her.

'She's a bit upset by being lost. You know how they get at that age. It's a mixture of feeling frightened and feeling silly for being frightened.' Molly glared at him, but said nothing and retired to her own room.

Kit let himself into the stuffy walnut-panelled telephone kiosk and rang Anna because he needed to tell her the outline of what had happened. Far away, sleepy in her empty kitchen now that Mary and the children were gone, Anna said, 'Is

Marianne all right? Do you think you convinced her you didn't notice?'

'Hope so,' said Kit. 'Bloody girl. You sound very solicitous. Did you hurl yourself at male teachers when you were a kid?'

'Not explicitly. We all had a few fantasies about the biology teacher. I have to say, I thought all that business of yearning for older men had died out now. I thought, what with the boy bands, they all fancied other infants just as they should. Not old wrinklies like you.'

Kit laughed, happy to be out of the stifling mouldy velvet of the night and back in Anna's clean and breezy hilltop world.

'I love you,' he said.

'I love you too.'

He slept after that, deeply and peacefully, only waking once to cough for a while.

Natalie and Kara were annoyed with Marianne again. Instead of getting into bed to discuss the evening in drowsy cosiness, she stood balanced on the camping cot, looking at the lamp in the alley.

'Miss Miles was horrible on the way back tonight. It's your fault, winding her up,' said Kara.

'Where'd you get to, anyway?' said Natalie.

Marianne did not answer. At last she pulled the curtain shut and got down into her rickety bed.

'You're just kids,' she said. 'Babies. You don't know nothing.'

14

After breakfast, Kit gathered the children in the reception area and made them spend an hour with their diaries. The gondola ride featured largely in most of them, but Natalie composed a poem about fireworks over water and Darren wrote the imaginary diary of a living statue busker: 'Got up. Poured plaster all over me and rubbed wihite stuff in my hair. Draped some sheets and gave the tourists a mega shock. Feet got very cold on the stone. Wish old style statues sometimes got carved with warm socks on but I suppose it would be difficult to do the woolyness.'

Kit told him and Morrey Hart the story of Pygmalion, and Morrey observed that it was a bit like the story of Pinocchio. Natalie said it would make a good play, and recruited a group of friends to devise one, with much shrieking and self-consciously glamorous statue posing.

Andrew Murray had pulled out the crumpled paper napkin from the restaurant and painstakingly copied out the poem he had written during supper. Then he paused, attention distracted by the Pygmalion game going on beyond the reception dcsk, and said, 'Is it all right in a poem, if you change the last line?'

'It's your poem,' said Kit. Eventually the boy brought it across to him.

THE GENEROUS GRAPE

The vine had a hard hard winter
It struggled for water and air
The grap's had to fight to be born

> *And fight to be sweet*
> *The vine suffered miserable times and died*
> *But it left the grapes behind*
> *So that they would make people warm in their tumies*
> *And laugh when they drank the wine.*
> *The grape's hard life and sadness took people's sadness away*
> *And made dead stone statues move again.*

Andrew's anxious eyes were on him. 'Is it all right?'

'Yes,' said Kit. 'Oh, yes.'

He was brought down to earth by Josh and Leanne's joint effort of a limerick, erratic as to scansion, concerning an old gondolier called Bud who got his boat stuck on the mud.

The hotel wanted the rooms clear by twelve, so Molly seized upon the children one by one as they finished their diaries, and chivvied them to pack up their scattered possessions. Kit, still tired, was moved by a sudden compunction at the sight of her bustling the children around and solving problems about combs and inhalers while he read poems and talked of Pygmalion. Martha and Mary, he thought. The New Testament story, which he had never thought much about as a boy, had been brought home to him when Anna, in a brief spell of supply RE teaching, had burst into the house one evening full of indignation.

'It's the most insidious, unfair idea,' she said. 'Mary does naff all, sits around googly-eyed at the feet of the Master, thinking beautiful thoughts. Martha runs herself ragged doing all the work and making the food for dozens of disciples to eat. Then it's Martha who gets told off. Pah! Men!'

Kit guiltily suspected that men, by long tradition, were more inclined to side with Mary. It had never occurred to him to do otherwise. On this occasion he felt himself actually to *be* Mary, and his dumpy, bustling colleague to be the Martha who would efficiently get these children on the train with all their packing done.

He also knew that if he had been with Anna or Caroline Chang, he would have done more of the mundane chivvying and organization of the school trip and left them more of the intellectual excitement. But he and Molly, like two charged particles, would always fly to opposite extremes of any situation they found themselves sharing. In a small gesture of reconciliation, he approached her with Andrew's diary when the boy had been sent off to pack.

'Look at this,' he said in a low voice. 'It's very good. Perhaps it would be one for your exhibition.' Molly set some store by her summer exhibition of English department work. She took the little book from Kit – even her gestures were abrupt and unforgiving – and scanned the page. Her lips remained pursed.

Kit looked at her but glanced away immediately. Her frumpish aggressive vulnerability troubled him. Her head inclined over the book, Molly nonetheless felt his revulsion as if it were a solid object.

'I'm not sure,' she said coldly, 'that parents will be very impressed by a child this age writing in praise of alcohol.'

Kit took the book away with a sense of finality.

Leaving the luggage packed and the bill paid, they set off again for a sandwich lunch and a final excursion. The two teachers had conferred briefly at breakfast, agreeing that a boat trip on the lagoon, round the main island and to the monastery of San Michele, would provide the restful afternoon they all needed. Everybody's feet hurt. The weather had turned: in the street a veil of drizzling rain ran down the peeling walls of the houses, and out on the lagoon aboard the No. 52 *vaporetto*, great waves of fog blew over them. They walked around the cemetery, subdued by its atmosphere, the children gazing in quiet wonder at angels of white Istrian marble. In the church, ranks of candles burned with the sad, rich smell of warm wax and Kit handed out the remains of their money so that each of them could light a candle for the late George Hamilton Dewar.

'Sir,' asked Darren in a whisper, his black brows knitted in concentration as he lit the long taper and put it on the spike, 'why did this Dewar bloke want to give the money for school trips?'

'I suppose he wanted to broaden your minds,' said Kit. 'Some children get the chance to travel all over the world, and some don't, and he didn't think that was fair.'

'I like seeing the world,' said Darren, admiring his candle. 'My dad says it's the worst thing about prison, seeing the same walls every day and the same people. My mum says he used to think prison wouldn't be so bad, but he's got fed up with it being all the same every day.'

'Stay out of prison, then,' said Kit. 'Perhaps Mr Dewar just wanted you to see the point of staying out of trouble.'

'What, go straight just so's you can come to Venice?' said Darren.

'I don't know,' said Kit. 'It's as good a reason as any.' He was suddenly tired of answering questions and felt unaccountably hot despite the marble cool of the church. He pushed a lock of hair back from his perspiring brow. Marianne Denver, lighting her taper close by, looked at his face in the worshipping candle-light and breathed a long, trembling breath.

Anna slept badly on Monday night. Her sickness had persevered through the day and left her tired, hungry and disorientated by bedtime. She wanted Kit and was cold without him, but the electric radiator she switched on in the bedroom made her wake up sweating soon after midnight. Stumbling from the bed she bent to switch it off, and felt so dizzy that she had to rest her arms on the windowsill with her brow on the cold glass. They had never curtained the smaller of the two bedroom windows; neither of them cared enough to bother. Money was for spending on journeys and adventures, scuba kit and seeing friends. Not on curtain material.

But something, Anna thought, really must be done to make this house cosier when the baby came. Suddenly she had a vision of roseate, ruffled curtains drawn against the winter blast, tender flowered wallpaper and a plump chair in which she sat feeding a sleepy milky child.

She turned from the cold window and the thought dissolved again. More than anything she wanted Kit home. He would be on the sleeper by now, she thought gratefully, halfway across Europe, and there were five more days of half-term. Perhaps when he had rested from the journey they would go up to London, see a film, have supper, spend the night with old friends. Look at curtain fabrics, even. She glanced back at the window and saw beyond the cheerless, moonless emptiness of the marsh the dull sodium glow of the docks. It would be good to get away from this dull estuary town for a few days.

As she crept back into the bedclothes she remembered the sweaty dream she had awoken from. Something to do with Ron Harding. Something horrible. Shuddering, she closed her eyes and fell into a blessedly blank sleep.

'I got a secret,' said Marianne to Natalie in the night. Both had woken wanting the lavatory, and in a whispered pact between their lower bunks had crept along the jolting corridor together to wait for one another outside the door. Now they were holding on to the rail by the window, held there by curiosity, shivering a little and looking out at the dark anonymous streaming country-side. They had been close friends until quite lately, inseparable at primary school and neighbours on the estate. At Sandmarsh the pressure of other girls and other interests had driven them a short way apart, but in the confidential dim-lit corridor of the train those pressures seemed distant and unreal. They were nine years old again, heads bent together in the traditional nit-spreading pose of small girls anywhere.

'I got a secret.'

'Tell,' said Natalie.

'I got a boyfriend. A proper *man*.'

'You never! Who?'

Marianne, sleepy and triumphant from a very good dream, smiled into the darkness. 'Mr Milcourt. I get to call him Kit.'

'What?' Natalie was incredulous. 'Whass been going on?'

'When we walked home on our own that time. From the fireworks. He kissed me. And we did more than that, only I shouldn't tell. It was dark. By a canal. Nobody could see. And he said it had to be a secret, but when I'm sixteen we can get married.'

'He is married,' said Natalie. 'Mrs Milcourt won't be too happy.'

'She's not right for him,' said Marianne confidently. 'He said it was a marriage of convenience. She gives him a hard time. It's me he loves.'

'Get away!' said Natalie.

'Only, you won't tell?'

'All right.'

'Cross your heart?'

'Yeah,' said Natalie. She did not believe a word of it anyway.

Ron Harding had lived alone for too long. He ate badly, took no exercise, and grieved every day for his distant Eileen. At first he had almost hated her for wanting him to retire early and be a gardening drone at fifty-four. Gradually, though, as Sandmarsh became a millstone so her image had shone brighter. He longed for the comfort of a woman and a home. On Saturday, drinking frothy coffee with fair, soft, smiling Anna, he made up his mind. He would retire in the summer and never go near a school again.

All through Sunday the headmaster walked on his own across the marshes, refining his plan with growing hope. Eileen, he knew almost for certain, had no other entanglements. If he went to Burford and threw himself on her mercy she would eventually have him back. If her ménage with her sister had become too fixed a habit to break, he would not even mind it continuing. He liked Sandra. They could all rub along together. He would do the garden and read Sherlock Holmes and accept that he had done his bit and earned his rest.

A great peace flowed into his mind, and every muscle seemed to relax. That night – the same night that on the other side of Europe his English department managed to mislay Marianne Denver in the masked Venetian crowds – he went to bed early the better to enjoy the dream.

There, alone and without knowing it, between sleep and waking Ronald Alexander Harding died of a massive and unheralded heart attack at the age of fifty-nine. It was not until Wednesday that, humming cheerfully and crashing the vacuum cleaner against the paintwork as usual, his cleaning lady found him there.

15

'Oh, it's horrible,' said Eileen McCafferty for the fifth or sixth time. It was Wednesday afternoon and she was in the Milcourts' house, huddled in the warmth of the kitchen with Kit and Anna. The cleaner, distressed and helpless, had called the police out to Harding's boxy little house on Romsey Road. The police, on hearing that he was a teacher, had rung the local Education Authority; the Authority had failed to contact Graham Merck and instead picked Doreen Nixon. Doreen, in her wheelchair and with her little car in dock, could do nothing but ring Eileen McCafferty; so it was poor Eileen who with heavy heart had identified the body, found the number and telephoned her namesake in Burford, the estranged wife of the late headmaster.

'It was horrible,' she said again. 'She just kept asking how long he was lying there alone before they found him. I told her that it didn't make a difference, that the doctor said it must have been instant. It was probably in his sleep. But poor Mrs Harding just wailed. She said she should have been there. Her sister's away – the one she lives with – and she was hearing it all alone by telephone. I should have driven there and told her in person, shouldn't I? I didn't think. Even if I had, what with the kids all home from school, and Bill working . . .'

'You did what you could,' said Anna mechanically. She was much affected by the death. A little later, when Eileen had calmed down, she unburdened herself of her own guilt, saying, 'The last thing I did for the poor bastard was to hoodwink him.'

Kit looked at her, complicit in the crime and powerless to give her any reassurance. Eileen looked confused, and Anna, driven to confession, told her the full story of Saturday's encounter. 'In the end,' she concluded tearfully, 'he came back here and rang Molly and said it was a misunderstanding. He even said it was his fault for not going through the details with her, and that everything was all right. And I made him a cappuccino and he stayed for about an hour, chatting about when he was first married.'

Eileen, leaning her elbows on the scrubbed table, glanced around the kitchen where Ron Harding had spent his last social hour. She saw the gleaming cappuccino machine and the dried flowers and the stone crocks for bread and butter and the cups and plates with splashy yellow sunbursts on the little dresser. She said, 'He probably enjoyed that, you know. He was lonely, I always thought. We had him round a couple of times, and even when the children were being atrocious he seemed to sort of enjoy it.'

'But that's it. He was lonely, and I flirted with him to get my own way.'

'But you didn't have to ask him for coffee afterwards.'

'I wanted to,' said Anna. 'It was nice.'

'There you are then,' said Eileen. 'He had a nice, affectionate, sociable human hour with you. He would have seen that you were enjoying his company. You didn't con him about that.'

'N-no,' said Anna. 'No. I wanted to give him a kiss on the cheek when he went. He reminded me of the way my Dad looks sometimes. Only I didn't, obviously.'

'He would have seen that you wanted to,' said Eileen obstinately. 'So you gave him something. If that was the last he saw of anybody to talk to, it was a good meeting. Better than if he'd just walked home from Graham's ping-pong session on his own and not seen anyone, and died.'

'Badminton,' said Anna automatically, twisting her empty mug between her hands. 'Yes, I suppose so. I've got to think of it like that. And he was terribly sweet about the baby coming. Asked what we wanted to call it. Oh, poor old Ron!'

Kit watched the two women as they cosily mourned and intensely tried to make friendly human sense of the old man's death. He loved them for it. Despite their youth and prettiness they reminded him of the middle-aged matron at Priory Shore when he was small. She was a dumpy little woman with a keen eye and a sharp tongue, hard on misdemeanours, ruthless about the changing of pants and socks, but with a comforting core of pure human kindness. He never forgot her withering comment on a visiting preacher, a suffragan bishop.

'Pooh,' she had said, labouring up the chapel back stairs with a pile of surplices for the laundry. 'Full of wind, that one. Nasty piece of work. You only have to look at him. Bishop or no bishop, you don't get a face like that at sixty by thinking good thoughts and loving your friends.'

Kit, who had been made to take tea with the bishop in Headmaster's House, had himself felt a profound instinctive revulsion against the bishop's thin-lipped, cruel, intellectual face. The matron's comment was of ineffable comfort to his eight-year-old heart; it seemed that even when people were important you were allowed to make your own mind up about whether they were nice. He never forgot the moment. In later years, when he found companions of his own sex all too easily seduced by the trappings of power and suavity, he placed a secret hope on women and would measure up every girl he met against the memory of Matey Dawson. Socialite women, glamorous women, competent women and brilliant ones failed to draw his approbation unless he could see in them some trace of the solid humanity displayed by the snappish old lady on the back stairs. He saw that humanity now, in Anna's and Eileen's mourning for Ronald Harding's lonely death. He wished that he, like them, could feel that he had contributed some warmth to the life of the man who now lay cold and alone. He suspected that he had not. He shivered. He had felt cold all day even indoors.

After a while Anna turned to him. 'Kit,' she said. 'What happens now, at school?'

'Graham Merck, I suppose, until they appoint someone. Knowing the LEA they'll drag their feet to save half a year's salary.'

'Will it be him who tells the children at assembly on Monday?' said Eileen. A pall of gloom fell over the company at this possibility.

'Ah well,' said Kit. 'We'll pick up the pieces in class.'

*　　*　　*

In the event, it was not Graham Merck who took the first assembly. He sent a message to say he would not be in until lunchtime because of an urgent meeting. Molly was unaccountably absent as well. Doreen Nixon, Kit, Eileen, Anna and Ian Atkins hastily devised a short half-secular service in which they told the children the news, led a prayer for the head's family and all those who mourned him, and then each spoke for a minute about their memory of Ronald Harding. At the music department's suggestion they played his favourite music, Vaughan Williams' 'The Lark Ascending'. Then two of the seniors, a boy and a girl, read a short bland funeral poem and the school dispersed in silence to their classrooms.

'That was OK,' said Anna to Ian Atkins.

The science teacher nodded. 'Yes, it was fine, I think. It helps that they all thought he was terribly old.'

'Well,' said Anna, 'all their parents are so incredibly young, aren't they? They're going to think I'm a freak getting pregnant at my age.' She was feeling better now, and had not been sick for two days. Despite the sombreness of the moment she found herself smiling idiotically, hands on her miraculous belly.

Kit took his form register, absent-mindedly as usual, only raising his head when a silence met the name 'Marianne Denver'.

'Is Marianne not in school today?'

Natalie and Kara, supposed to be Marianne's best friends, looked blank.

'Oh, all right. Mick Harris. Angela Harsten. Morris Hart . . .' The children answered their names dutifully. They looked jaded, far from glad to be back in school after the excitements of half-term. Back among their peers, those who had been on the trip to Venice were starting to take on protective colouring. Among themselves they half pretended that they too had merely spent the time hanging around the Odeon, watching telly, or rollerblading round the precinct annoying shoppers. Kit looked at them affectionately. He understood. They had to live in the world that lay around them. But he was confident that deep within the lucky fifteen the experience of a journey into strangeness would go on working its magic. He must devise more trips, for more children.

'OK,' he said, closing the register. 'Wake up. Outside, I think. The past-and-present tenses game.'

A mile away, in the Victorian town house which served as headquarters for Sandmarsh Social Services, Mrs Denver sat clasping her surly daughter's hand. In a crescent formation before them sat Eric Danby, an experienced child protection officer, Sarah Beale, an inexperienced but suitably female one, WPC Pam Morrison, Molly Miles and Graham Merck.

Danby looked uneasy. He did not approve of the child's being confronted with quite so many figures of authority. He did not like the way that this stand-in headmaster had jumped on the allegation and convened an instant meeting. Old Harding would have taken things far more slowly. It was not as if there was immediate danger, for God's sake. But Graham Merck had contacted police and Social Services within minutes of Mrs Denver's telephone call, and together with the furious mother had whipped up such a fuss that here they all were, on a Monday morning, making an issue of it before the child had even been properly, professionally questioned about this dubious diary her mother had found.

He sighed. At least the little girl seemed unfazed by it, merely regarding them with big calm eyes. Her dark hair cascaded over her shoulders, her full lips pouted slightly, and in her short black skirt and sweater she looked any age from eleven to eighteen, depending almost entirely on the expression on her face. The social worker glanced at his notes. Twelve. Well, that was a bad business. If it was true. But there was something spooky about the child all the same. Her calm was so intense as to make him suspect repressed hysteria, or at the least a taste for drama. Most children in these circumstances looked either blank or embarrassed. This one had a little smile . . .

Danby checked himself sternly. He must not think this way. This way lay anarchy: the kind of cultural obfuscation and moral collapse which led to condoning of paedophilia and the hateful molester's whine that the child 'asked for it'. Even if a child did seem to 'ask for it', even at fifteen going on thirty, it was the bounden duty of any adult to ignore immature advances. A child is a child, however provocative. If this male teacher really had taken gross advantage of a school trip, as the girl's ramblingly salacious diary claimed, the man must be uncovered and punished and never have charge of children again. Perhaps Merck was right to whip up such an instant storm. Perhaps he, Danby, was allowing too much doubt to cloud his mind because of the child's odd, almost adult bearing.

But, dammit! This meeting was all wrong. If the mother's tearful allegations were right, this was a case of statutory rape. The victim must be assumed to be traumatized. She should absolutely not be sitting in front of such a group of adults of both sexes. It was neither right nor decent.

He raised his hand and said, 'Before we go any further, I think it is best that Marianne has a chance to talk more with her mother and with Sarah. Mr Merck, I think there is plenty of time to go into the business of witnesses,' he gestured towards the grim-faced Molly Miles, 'and police involvement. Could I suggest that Marianne and Mrs Denver stay here with Sarah and have a cup of coffee, and the rest of us leave for the moment?'

Merck opened his mouth to protest, but Danby swept him from the interview room, followed by the police officer and Molly Miles.

Outside, Merck said peevishly, 'I have the teacher to think of. I felt it best to involve the proper authorities directly, as he will have to be immediately suspended. I'm not happy about his being with a class at this very moment.'

Danby resisted an impulse to point out that a class of thirty-five was a rather less sexually risky arena than a Venetian back alley at night. Goodness, how he disliked this pompous little man. Poor old Harding. No wonder he died early.

'That's up to you,' he said mildly. 'But remember that suspension always causes a lot of gossip. Inside and outside the school. The allegations may prove to be quite unfounded.' For a crazy moment, Danby thought that a shadow of disappointment crossed Merck's face at the idea. Glancing at the other teacher, the Miles woman, he saw the same expression amplified.

Merck said, 'I did of course take that into my consideration. But I have heard Miss Miles's full account of the trip, which Mr

Milcourt arranged, and I am afraid that we have to consider very strongly the possibility that the entire exercise was designed for one end only.'

The policewoman, who had been silent, said, 'I would like to go through all that with you, Mr Merck. And Miss Miles. Could we have a room here, Mr Danby?'

Back in the interview room, young Sarah Beale began, haltingly, to question Marianne. It was difficult because every few moments her mother broke in. Often, Mrs Denver furiously quoted from the diary: 'Hand between my legs . . . pushed me down . . . our tongues together.' Actually, the diary said 'tongs'. Marianne might have put more eloquence and imagination into her private diary than her school one, but her spelling was no better.

In contrast to her mother, the child was calm and almost brusque. 'I'm not a kid,' she said. 'Mr Milcourt knows I'm not a kid. We're gonna get married when I'm sixteen. Or we might go to that place in America where you can get married at fourteen.'

'Can we go back to what happened that evening, dear?' said Sarah Beale. 'Just tell me in your own words what happened.'

'I got lost,' said Marianne. 'He came 'n found me an' we walked back.'

'Was anybody else with you?'

'No,' said Marianne proudly. 'He got rid of them all onto the boat, so he got a chance to say he loved me.'

Mrs Denver sniffed. 'More than say he loved you. Dirty old man. And you,' she turned on her daughter in sudden wrath, 'you led him on, didn't you? You're no better than I was. If you're in the club . . .'

Marianne's eyes were hooded, unreadable. As her mother ranted in blind, misguided, angry love, Marianne sat wrapped in sullen silence and looked out of the window. The social worker felt control slipping from her, and wished herself anywhere else. Then, brightening, she walked over to a drawer in the corner and pulled out the device known in the trade as an anatomically correct doll. Marianne looked at it in bewilderment. She didn't do dolls any more. Plus, this doll had naff curly hair and was fat.

'You don't need to talk about it,' said Sarah Beale, in the tone she would have used to a four-year-old. 'Just show me where he touched you.'

'She don't need to show,' snorted Mrs Denver. 'It's written down here. And she's not short of words for it, either. Or can't you read?' She peered down. Even to her the spelling 'nippal' looked wrong.

'Merck wants to see you,' said Ian Atkins, putting his head round the staff-room door at break.

'Turned up, has he?' said Kit. 'That's nice. What does he want?'

'I dunno,' said Ian. 'Been leaving windows open again, have you?'

'I want you to think very carefully before you answer this,' said Graham Merck, who wanted no such thing. 'On the Dewar trip, did anything occur which seemed to you untoward?'

'No,' said Kit. 'It went very smoothly, considering the last-minute staff change. Miss Miles is very efficient, and the children have produced some cracking good work.'

'Would it surprise you,' continued Merck, 'to hear that there have been allegations of improper contact between you and one of the children in your care?'

For a moment Kit stood frozen. *Terrified*, thought Merck, and a pulse of triumph moved in his heart. Mr Oxbridge wasn't as perfect as he made out, then. He waited.

Shakily, Kit said, 'Yes, I *would* be surprised to hear that. What do you mean? Which child?'

'The girl in question is being interviewed by Social Services,' said Merck smoothly. 'But I ask you again, is there anything you want to tell me?'

Kit, fully in command of himself now, spoke with some vehemence. 'No, there isn't,' he said. 'If some little girl has developed a crush on me, you know quite well that these things happen. I certainly have not molested anybody, in Venice or elsewhere.'

He knew as he spoke which girl it would be. Poor bloody little Marianne. He had forgotten until that moment her brief collapse on his chest in San Polo. The short, light conversation with Anna on the telephone had exorcised his embarrassment on the subject, leaving only a faint caution and a memo to himself to avoid being alone with that particular child for a week or two.

'Her diary suggests otherwise,' said Merck. 'In the circumstances, I am afraid the immediate course of action is laid down for me. I have to suspend you pending investigations. You had better go home now. I'm sorry.'

'You're not,' said Kit scornfully. 'You're thrilled. Who's going to take year 7 and 8 English?'

'We'll ring the agency,' said Merck absently, as if the teaching of children was the matter furthest from his mind. 'You'll be paid, obviously, during the period of suspension.'

'Oh, fuck off,' said Kit. He had not sat down for their brief conversation; turning on his heel, he left.

He did not really take in the seriousness of what had happened until he arrived home to find two policemen on the doorstep with a warrant, demanding with neutral, impassive politeness their right to search through drawers, cupboards, shelves and computer disk drives. They were still there at four-thirty, putting things into boxes, when Anna came home.

Marianne came back to school two days after Kit left it. The Social Services had got little from her beyond the surly reiteration of her marriage plans and of the diary's accuracy.

'It's not lies,' she said when the policewoman who had joined Sarah Beale gently suggested that she might have made it up. 'It's not lies, but it *was* private.' At this, she swivelled to glare at her mother.

'Nobody should ask you to keep secrets,' said Sarah Beale soothingly. 'It's not wrong to tell about these things. It's right.'

'It was me that *wanted* it to be secret,' said Marianne. 'Because I know what *she's* like. She wanted to get rid of me before I was even *born*. Now she's just jealous of me getting married, because her blokes always take off.' Indeed, Mr Denver had removed himself from the ambit of Mrs Denver when Marianne was three years old.

So with nothing much resolved and the police still ploughing through Kit's notebooks and computer disks, Marianne came back to Sandmarsh High.

Nobody knew officially what had happened, but everybody knew by rumour. In the staff room and among the cleaners, in other neighbourhood schools and at the leisure centre, conversation returned to the subject again and again.

'That's terrible. I can't believe it. Nice man, I thought.'

'Bit standoffish. Upper-class, like.'

'Well, I wouldn't think it of him. No, really. Not Kit Milcourt.'

'The girl wrote a pretty explicit diary. Tom Beale told me that his wife was quite shocked, down at Social Services – she works there now full time, did you know?'

'Yes, but really. He's married to that lovely girl.'

'Yes, but Anna's always looked so young, hasn't she? Almost like a schoolgirl. And now, of course, she's pregnant. Madeleine Atkins told me.'

'Yes . . . I suppose. If the tendency's *there* in a man, the time it's going to come out is when you've got a pregnant wife. You can't kid yourself your wife's that young when she's pregnant.'

'They haven't said which kid it is. But I heard it's Annie Denver's daughter. Sullen-looking, busty kid. Right little Lolita, actually.'

'Have you ever felt . . . ?'

'No, no, perish the thought. But you can't close your eyes to it. There are people who find these nymphet types pretty irresistible. Jailbait.'

'I always think of jailbait as older. Fifteen or so.'

'They grow up so young these days.'

Anna, dazed with horror and misery, knew what they said. Sometimes at school she half heard it, entering a staff room which suddenly fell quiet. Doreen Nixon and Eileen McCafferty took her aside one day and told her frankly and flatly that they believed none of it, and that neither did Ian Atkins only he was too shy to tell her so. This did not help, because it merely confirmed to Anna that the rest of the staff either did believe it or withheld judgement. Her overwhelming impulse was to corner Marianne Denver and get her to tell the truth, but she had been warned by the police that she must do no such thing. She went through the days' work automatically, spiritlessly, her mind absent in a place of torment.

When they were alone one afternoon in the staff room during games she said to Doreen Nixon, 'Would it help you to know that Kit rang me, the evening he walked this benighted child home? He told me that he thought she had developed a crush on him. So there was warning of this fantasy of hers. It isn't just out of the blue.'

'You don't need to tell me that,' said Doreen. 'I know he's not guilty. He'll be vindicated. Without a stain on his character.'

'But how?' said Anna. 'How? The girl's absolutely refusing a medical examination even.'

'And she might not be a virgin even if they did one,' said Doreen steadily. 'Anna, you mustn't get upset. There's your own baby to think of. Something will happen. Kit will be cleared.'

'Maybe,' said Anna wretchedly. 'But maybe it'll just drizzle on. Unresolved. It's been a week now. Some people get clouds like this over their head for years. They have to move, and then someone finds out in the new place and everyone assumes they were at it for years beforehand, and they get hate mail and fire bombs and—'

She began to cry, and sank to her knees in front of the wheelchair, head in hands. Doreen leaned forward and gathered Anna to her, cradling her on her breast, murmuring comfort. As she looked over Anna's bowed head, though, her face was bleak.

Kit stayed at home, uncommunicative and grim-faced. He seemed to Anna to be forever pushing the main issue aside in favour of absurd complaints about detail. The police had messed up his desk drawers. They had taken the computer disks he was working on, the ones labelled 'Lesson.plans' and 'Anthol.kids, Venice'. They had ransacked his bookshelves and removed treasures, including a first edition of Thomas Mann's *Death in Venice*. The road outside was noisy. The time switch on the central heating boiler was functioning erratically, so the house became hot or cold at inappropriate times. It was raining. He had a pain in his throat, and difficulty swallowing. It seemed to Anna when she got home each day that Kit was complaining about everything except the central unmentionable fact: that he was suspended from school on suspicion of sexually abusing a child.

She tried to raise the subject with him in a natural, brightly supportive way. Usually he would only grunt and say, 'It's crap. She's fantasising. Merck and Molly Miles just desperately want to believe it. They want me out so they can bore the children to tears in peace.'

'Yes,' said Anna, who privately thought there might be some truth in what he said. 'Molly is being very odd. Won't speak to me. Purses her lips and spends time with Merck. Did you know she's now Acting Deputy Head? Ian Atkins is rather fed up about it. But there must be something we can do.'

'What? We can't talk to Marianne, and it all hangs on Marianne.'

'The police haven't brought any charges, which must be a good sign.'

'The police,' said Kit, 'spent two hours asking me why I took the children to Venice "given its reputation". I said, what reputation? As a repository of art treasures?'

'You haven't been too aggressive, have you?' Anna was alarmed. 'Oh, sweetheart, you do know what happens when you make people feel silly? They get angry. Like Molly over the Dracula play.'

Ignoring her, he rattled on. He had not said much for days so Anna fell silent to encourage him to speak.

'Then they changed tack, the plods, and started asking me about Thomas Mann, and wasn't it a book about paedophilia? And I told them to grow up, and if they wanted a good book on why children ought to see Venice, to try James Morris. And they said aha! Did I mean *Jan* Morris? The one who was born a man? Well, you can guess the rest. They think I'm a thoroughgoing pervert. They asked me if I had read *Lolita* and what I thought of it, and didn't literary types consider it a book of great merit? And I said yes, some critics did, but I found Nabokov a bit florid and self-indulgent for my taste. And they looked really pleased and said ah, so I had read it then? And so on.'

He looked so bleak, so angry and yet so weak that Anna, riven with pity and love, wanted to take him in her arms and tell him how she loved him and trusted him and always would do, to the death. But he turned away abruptly, and began to complain again about the heating.

That night, though, he lay with his arms round Anna and his head on her breast, and sometimes seemed to her to be weeping when he thought she was asleep.

Anna accosted Molly in the corridor next morning.

'Can I have a word?' she asked, and guided her into an empty science room. Molly stood looking at her, arms folded, chunky and impassive as a prison wardress.

'Molly,' began Anna, 'we've been friends. Can we talk about

this Kit business? You don't really think he did anything to Marianne, do you?'

'We are not supposed to discuss the case even between ourselves,' said Molly primly. 'You know that. Especially we are not supposed to mention the child's name.'

'Everybody's bloody discussing it,' said Anna. 'So don't give me that. Molly, are you convinced he did it? Is that why you were involved at the start, with Graham? Is it you that's keeping this going?'

'The Dewar was,' said Molly flatly, addressing the wall beyond Anna, 'a very unconventionally organized school trip. Frankly, I was surprised that you went along with it. It has rather changed my view of your judgement. There was a completely strange adult man billeted with us on the train. The hotel was not listed in any schools' directories as approved. I was not happy with the hygiene standards of the plumbing, for one thing. And the children were actively encouraged to disguise themselves and interact with provocatively dressed adult strangers.'

'What's so provocative about feather masks?' said Anna grimly.

Molly smirked. 'Your husband was heard quoting some poem to the girls – to the girls, note – about "revelry and rape". He encouraged the children to drink alcohol. He engineered a situation in which he had to walk a twelve-year-old girl back to the hotel alone in the dark through deserted streets.'

'Engineered it!' Anna was furious now, but exhilarated too. She was beginning to see how the circumstantial case against Kit was being built up, and once they knew that, then it could surely be fought detail by detail. They could demolish it before charges were even brought. '*How* did he engineer it? As I understand it, the bloody child went missing.'

'He volunteered to look for her. Alone,' said Molly.

'Didn't any children offer to come and help him?' said Anna. It was a shot in the dark, but Molly's eyes glinted with irritation.

'He refused their help,' she said. 'He deliberately went alone to find her. She wasn't far away. It points to collusion. He could have made a prior arrangement with her. She is a particularly silly child. I'm sorry for your sake, Anna, but it's better you find these things out now and face them. Before your own child is put at risk.'

Anna had never struck anybody since childhood fights with Mary. Now she took a clumsy swing at Molly, who stepped aside with her small, grim smile intact. Anna's open palm struck the sharp edge of an equipment cabinet and she winced in pain, cradling the hand against her chest and glaring at Molly Miles.

'You wait,' Anna said. 'You just wait.'

Later, she asked Kit about the children's offer. Carelessly, still riffling in distracted irritation through his desk drawers, he said, 'Oh, I think Leanne and Josh did offer to come and help look. I thought it was quite a good idea, because their eyes would be on a level with hers. It's important in masks, seeing the eyes. There were an awful lot of those fringey cat masks around. But Molly said no, they'd fall in the lagoon. I remember that, because half the others started crying that Marianne might have drowned. Tactless old bat.'

'But that's it!' said Anna in triumph. 'It's the evidence! It's proof that you didn't plot to be alone with Marianne! Josh and Leanne could give evidence that it was Molly who insisted you went alone.'

Kit raised his head to look at her, and she saw that he was pale, and oddly swollen around the face. Wearily he said, 'What does it matter, anyway? Smoke without fire, all that. I won't be teaching again, will I?'

More days passed, with still no word of a police charge, no arrest, no caution, no end to Anna's torment. She picked up the telephone several times to ring Mary, but put it down again before she finished dialling. The shame was too great. Innocent as he was – of course he was! He was Kit! – she felt disgrace creeping into her heart, coating it like slime. Even to be associated with such a charge was shaming. Every newspaper she picked up seemed to be full of paedophiles, rapists, unspeakable acts of depravity visited on children. Every pop psychologist and columnist seemed to know all about the 'profile' of molesters, rapists, perverts, killers. A whole natural history of pederasts appeared to have grown up, and everybody was an expert but her.

She tried not to read these things but her eyes was drawn inexorably to them. The tabloid headlines about various current crimes – SEX BEAST, MONSTER, MAN OF EVIL – disturbed her less than the more discursive articles in broadsheet newspapers. God, how much they seemed to know! How smugly confident they were of their ground! *'These men seem ordinary enough . . . often intelligent . . . fixated preferential paedophile . . . obsession with pre-pubescent girl . . . process of "grooming" . . . the offender may seem genuinely to love children, often taking a job involving their care . . . ability to delude himself that the child enjoys the seduction . . . exhibit extraordinary cunning and ability to plan seduction . . . often apparently happily married . . . difficulty of bringing cases to trial results in many men abusing for years with impunity . . . by the time they are first caught or suspected, it is likely that they have been seriously abusing children for many years . . .'*

Anna saw with horror that Kit could well be right. People would say there was no smoke without fire. Even if there was no formal charge, how could he stay at Sandmarsh and have such things thought about him? How could he apply for a job teaching elsewhere, with a record of several weeks' suspension on such disgraceful grounds? The blasted child had scuppered him, she thought hysterically, scuppered him for good and all.

And what about *her* child? Would pressure be put on her not to raise the baby with Kit in the house? Would Social Services have the power to separate them, or take the baby away on mere suspicion? She had heard of such things but paid no heed. Now they loomed monstrous and black and blotted out the future.

Kit, listless and pallid, offered no help or hope. It was as if he did not care what happened. She had no idea what he did all day, but from his heavy eyes guessed that he spent much of it sleeping. At the weekends she urged him to come walking on the marshes, or drive down to the sea. He came on the first weekend, but by the second pleaded tiredness.

'He's ill,' she said at school. 'Some sort of flu.' Again she sensed the murmuring of rumour all around.

'Collapsed, apparently.'

'Well, it must be a strain.'

'Even worse strain if it's true. A decent man like that, think of the remorse. Sometimes the fact of being found out brings it home to people.'

'You hear about suicides. Oh, poor Anna.'

'There's still no charge, though, is there?'

The police returned Kit's books and disks without comment. Eric Danby summoned Sarah Beale and asked her whether any progress had been made over the matter of medical examination. It seemed not. The police were unwilling to bring charges without at least some indication that the child was not a virgin, and appeared to be growing increasingly sceptical about the whole case.

'I want it cleared up,' said Danby.

'We don't have to—' began Sarah, but he cut her off abruptly.

'I know. We can just keep the file open. But that won't do this teacher any good. What do you make of the girl?'

'I would say,' said Sarah Beale, with some vehemence, 'that the worst thing about her situation is the way her relationship with her own mother seems to have broken down. As to whether she's been abused, I do not have the faintest idea. But we must believe the child.'

'It was a diary,' said Danby. 'Never heard of fictional diaries? Adrian Mole, Bridget Jones, Charles Pooter?'

'She says it's true,' said Sarah Beale.

'She says that to her hysterical mother,' said Danby. 'Have you pointed out to her what the effect would be on the teacher if a case were brought? And that she'd have to give evidence to send him to prison?'

'She's a child,' said Sarah. 'Children don't lie about these things.'

'Teenage girls fantasise. They always have.'

'She's not a teenager. She's twelve.'

Frustrated, Danby stabbed his pen into his blotter and said, 'OK. Give it another week.'

As part of the Social Services inquiry, the parents of all the other girls in Kit's classes were contacted and asked whether any untoward reports or unusual behaviour had ever disturbed them. In turn they asked their daughters, some tactfully, others more dramatically. It was a dull time of year in a dull town and any drama was welcome. Before long, every child in the school knew exactly why Mr Milcourt was not teaching English at the moment.

Year 7 were not best pleased with the situation. First of all Miss Miles had sent down worksheets, very boring worksheets where you had to underline adjectives in red and nouns in blue. Then came a young supply teacher who could not keep order. They walked around in class, turned their backs on him, giggled at him, wrote obscenities on the whiteboard, asked deliberately silly questions and finally ignored him until he wandered bleating through the classroom, his nerve gone.

His replacement after a week was the elderly, choleric Mr Parker who usually stood in for maths teachers. He could keep order all right, but English was a subject he secretly despised, and neither he nor the children enjoyed the experience. He was usually late for classes, and at the beginning of his third week, while they sat glumly waiting for him, Josh said to Leanne, 'It's real crap without Mr Milcourt, yeah?'

'Yeah,' said Leanne. 'I wish he'd come back.'

'So do I,' said Andrew Murray, who had been less quiet and far less studious since Kit left, showing an unsuspected streak of rebellion which the girls were beginning to admire. 'I like him. He's the only good thing in this crap school. Why can't he come back?'

'Police investigations,' said Kylie. 'Like on *The Bill*. Investigations on whether he shagged that Marianne in Venice.' Kylie liked to be blunt and explicit, especially to boys and most especially to big-eyed, rather nervous boys like Andrew. 'She told the coppers he had sex with her.'

'In her dreams!' said Natalie. 'She told me that on the train, but she's a bloody liar. That's what I reckon.'

'Yeah,' said Kara. 'She fancied him, all right. In Venice she was all stupid. She spent all her time standing on that cruddy folding bed thing, looking at the moon. I bet she made it all up then, while we was trying to get to sleep.'

Marianne, as it happened, was out of school for yet another interview with Social Services. She would reappear from these visits looking distant and martyred and communicating little, and in her absence feeling was beginning to run high among those children who had best grasped the situation.

'Tell you what,' said Madeleine Cooper, a tall drooping blonde child who had not been on the expedition. 'You lot that went to Italy. You oughter have a word with her. Tell her to knock it off. Then he could come back.'

'Yer,' said Josh slowly. 'That's true, that is.' It had not previously occurred to the children that the power to stop this impasse and return their favourite teacher lay with one of their own number. Because police and council and headteachers were involved, the thing had been assumed to have an adult momentum of its own. The idea that it might not have – that it could be ended by a word from Marianne – was new and intoxicating.

'So who gets to tell her?'

'I will,' said Natalie. 'She used to be my mate. There's no point just being horrible to her, like bullying her. And Kara, you come too. She'll have to listen to her mates.'

On the morning after the Year 7 indignation meeting, Anna woke up, looked at her sleeping husband and made a discovery. He was ill. Physically ill, she thought, not just depressed by his awful circumstances. She was amazed that she had not seen it before. The Kit she had known for a decade was energetic, decisive, cheerful, voluble, enthusiastic and affectionate. It would surely, she thought, take more than one absurd accusation to transform him into this dull, depressed and indifferent creature?

Leaning on her elbow, watching him carefully, she felt a new clear certainty about this. The Kit she knew would have raged at the charges, passionately denied them, made black jokes about them or at the very least begun to sketch out alternative futures in the event of his being unable to clear himself. Anna reproached herself. Why had she not thought about physical illness? Had pregnancy made her so self-absorbed that she could not see past the end of her nose?

He was pale, with an unhealthy sweaty pallor. He had lost weight. His skin was dry and flaky, and on his neck – at least on the side she saw as he lay with his head sideways – there were puffy swellings. *Glandular fever!* she thought. Then, in sudden terror, the baby! Will I get it? Then came shame: did pregnancy, she wondered, make every woman so self-centred? Then the panic came again, for the baby. Rolling away from the sleeping Kit she crept downstairs and rang the surgery. It was not yet eight thirty, so there was no receptionist and at the third ring Dr Ransom answered the phone himself, out of breath from puffing up the stairs.

'God, I'm sorry, it's just that I'm so worried about the baby,' began Anna.

The doctor listened, spoke a few calm and reassuring words, and suggested that they both come down to surgery together.

'Oh, I'm not sure he would. He's not been out much since . . .'

Behind the surgery counter, tapping his pencil on the desk, Dr Ransom cursed himself for forgetting. He knew, of course. The whole town knew. Poor little Anna Milcourt, so tremulous about her pregnancy, and now with all this to put up with. He knew Kit only slightly, but allowed himself to be fairly well-convinced of his innocence. For one thing, he had heard on the professional grapevine that the girl was being very odd about the medical examination. For another, like most men the doctor found it hard to imagine anybody married to Anna even glancing elsewhere, let alone at a sullen child who could end his career in a flash. The doctor knew this last instinct to be illogical but felt it all the same.

'Yes, of course,' he said now. 'Suppose I come by on my rounds. One thirty or thereabouts?'

'I feel terrible asking for a house call,' began Anna.

Jovially, he cut her off. 'I told you. When you're pregnant, you suit yourself. Anyway, I haven't seen hide nor hair of your husband since he broke that tibia a few years back. It can be an effort getting these sporty chaps along to the surgery.'

Grateful, Anna put down the telephone and pushed back her tangled hair. She was still in her nightshirt, standing on the freezing tiles of the hall, and sleet was falling outside. She picked up the phone again and rang the office at Sandmarsh High. As she had hoped, the school secretary was not in, so she was able to leave an impersonal and unchallenged message on the machine to the effect that she would not be in 'because of illness'. Anna had never found it easy to lie, even to machines.

When Kit woke, he met the news of the doctor's visit with a lethargic indifference which made Anna doubly glad she had taken action.

'He won't find anything. I'm just tired,' he said. 'But he's welcome to try.'

'But Kit, it's not normal tiredness. You were only just yourself when you left for Venice, and by the time you got back you were flatter than I've ever seen you. Ever since then it's got worse and worse, however much you sleep. That isn't like you.'

'I might just be getting old,' said Kit.

'No,' said Anna firmly. 'You're thirty-eight, for God's sake. You've got to get whatever it is sorted out. There's the baby to think of.'

A cloud of pain passed over his face. 'Yes,' he said. 'The baby.'

Natalie and Kara conferred, and decided that morning break would not give them long enough to put their case to Marianne. Lunchtime would be better. By ten to one most of the Sandmarsh children had either grumbled their way through school dinner or eaten their packed lunches. Classes did not begin again till one forty-five. A number of clubs existed, officially at least, but with the exception of Ian Atkins' Space Science Club, they were moribund. The seniors had a rundown common room but most of the younger children played in the yard or the noisy echoing hall, sneaked out to the town to supplement their lunch with chips and a smoke, or sat around in whatever classrooms had been carelessly left unlocked, usually by Ian Atkins.

The Year 7 group which had discussed the problem co-operated neatly to ensure that by one o'clock Marianne was in Science 2X, and that everybody but Natalie and Kara had mysteriously melted away. Josh and Leanne stood guard at the door, frowningly deterring any more invaders. Science 2X was a popular retreat, being far from the staff room, rarely locked, and equipped with a much-admired tank of tropical fish.

Marianne was staring at the fish when Natalie opened fire.

'I s'pose you know why Mr Milcourt can't come and do English any more, an' we've got these crap supply teachers?' she began. 'It's all because of you.'

'You,' said Kara, 'and that stupid made-up diary.'

'Wasn't made up,' said Marianne sulkily. Then, with a return of her dramatic style, 'We're lovers. He's going to marry me.'

'Oh, bollocks!' exploded Kara, who despite her size had an enviable building-site vocabulary. 'That is just such crap. Get real! He's just a teacher! He's married! He thinks you're a little girl who don't spell very well. That's all.'

'*You're* a little girl. You don't know anything,' said Marianne. 'I tell you, he kissed me.'

Kara and Natalie regarded her carefully. They were struck by the sudden reduction of the charge to 'he kissed me', and not sure for the moment how to proceed. Silence turned out to be the best policy. Marianne continued talking, and her tone perceptibly changed. She sounded more like her old self and less like the programmed automaton she had lately become.

'He did kiss me. We took our masks off.'

'Then why,' said Natalie coldly, 'did you say he did all the other stuff?'

'I never *said*,' said Marianne fretfully. 'I *wrote*, an' my bleeding mother found it in my bag. Nosy cow.'

'So the other stuff was *definitely* made up?' Like a skilled advocate, Natalie decided to demolish one layer of the story at a time. The moment to challenge the kiss could come later. 'You made up all the sex bits?'

Now it was Marianne's turn to be silent. Her state of mind in these past weeks had been a strange one. In love, deluded, romantically desperate but sheltered by a beautiful and carnal dream, she had been shocked to come home to the flat reality of life. Home to her mother's perpetually smouldering resentment, to the tawdry ugliness of the little house on the estate, to the February drizzle and the spotty boys who whooped after her in the street, to the generally hopeless boringness of the estuary town. When the diary first disappeared on the last weekend of half-term, she thought nothing of it. Her mother's slapping, screaming explosion of wrath on the Sunday had thrown her into a kind of shock. The only thing she could hold on to was the dream.

She was ashamed to have her mother know the detail of it, lifted as it was from video films, giggling conversations with the widely-read Kylie (whose big brother had a startling paperback library) and teen magazines. She was even more ashamed to know that thanks to her nosy bloody mother the diary had been read by all those police and council people, and perhaps even – her blood ran cold at the thought – by Mr Merck. The only way to protect the beauty of what she had invented was to keep on repeating her own private dream truth: that Kit loved her and always would, and that they would one day be married and go away from all this ugliness.

As long as she repeated this and did not recant the diary, she was listened to with respect and sympathy. If she were to say anything else now she would just be a naughty, dirty, lying little girl. A girl in deep trouble.

But Natalie and Kara, unsentimental and brutal, slipped easily through the chinks in her armour.

'Even if he did kiss you—'

'Which I don't believe, 'cos he's not *stupid*—'

'Even if he did, that's not the same as all the other stuff. If you keep on saying that, he could go to *prison*, Marianne. He could.'

'Then he'd *never* come back and do English. Or Dewar trips.'

'An' Mrs Milcourt would go too.'

'An' you know what kind of teachers we'd get. *Miss Miles*.'

'Let's get everything back to normal, yeah?' They were wheedling now, friendly again as they saw the changes in Marianne's face. At primary school they had been an insepa-rable trio.

Marianne pouted and her eyes filled with tears. But despite the dismaying vista of reproof and disgrace ahead of her, there was a kind of comfort in being twelve years old again, awake not dreaming, a child not a romantic heroine. The queer feelings about men had led her too far, too fast, away from being just one of the girls round the fish tank in Science 2X. A growing part of her wanted to come back to that.

'What can I do?' she asked slowly, consideringly. 'My mum will kill me.'

Kit pulled his shirt back on and gave Dr Ransom a small, tight smile. 'All OK then?' he said. 'Told you I was just tired.'

Anna had gone through to the kitchen so that she did not seem to be fussing over him like a child. The door was ajar, though, and she strained to hear. Ransom's voice spoke next, muffled as if he was leaning over to put the stethoscope and syringes back in his bag.

'I'll send the blood in,' he said, 'but I'd place a substantial bet that you're anaemic. And I don't like the look of that groin.'

Kit said something Anna did not catch, but to her delight it must have been a joke because the doctor laughed. Kit laughed too. Then Ransom's voice said, 'We don't know anything until we get the blood tests back, but it all takes so long that I'm going to book you in at the hospital now, for another useful little test. Have a proper look at those glands. They won't need you more than a couple of hours. Unless they want to run a scan.'

'For glandular fever?' said Kit. 'You don't scan for that, do you?'

'Oh, they scan for everything these days,' said Ransom evasively. 'Wonderful technology. In the meantime, could I prevail on you to take iron tablets, one a day? Over the counter at the chemist's. The anaemia won't be helping.'

'Get more iron in your diet, eat a bicycle today,' said Kit. 'OK then.'

Anna, coming through from the kitchen with two mugs of coffee, quietly noted that the doctor's breezy maleness seemed to have perked Kit up. Maybe a surfeit of her exclusive company was partly to blame for his depression. He had not, after all, been out of the house much since his suspension; not to play squash, or swim, or even to run. She must get Ian Atkins and his wife round to supper. She could distract Madeleine Atkins in the kitchen for half an hour so that the two men could talk and joke by the fire. Returning to the kitchen, she wrote 'Iron Pills' on the shopping list.

'So what do I do?' repeated Marianne, restlessly. She had gone back to staring blankly at the angel fish, and with only five minutes to go before the bell the other two girls were anxious that she should not slip away from them.

'Tell them the truth. That nothing happened. You made it all up,' said the ruthless Natalie.

'S'not gonna be easy,' said Kara, *sotto voce*. 'Trouble is, they might not believe it.'

'She's gotter try,' said Natalie stubbornly.

Marianne turned round, and sat down astride a chair, her skirt rucked up with childish casualness.

'I thought of something,' she said. The others grinned. There was an understanding between them that they were all on the same side now, and the strength that this alliance gave was savoured by all three.

'C'n we help?' asked Natalie. 'Will you be all right?'

'Yeah. C'n I come and sleep at yours for a night or two?' asked Marianne. 'Only I've thought who to tell. I can't talk to that soppy Miss Beale any more.'

'Stay at mine as long as you like,' said Natalie. 'I got bunk beds.'

Eric Danby picked up the telephone irritably just as he was packing up his briefcase to go home.

'Yes?' He thought the department secretary would be on the line, filtering calls, but she must have gone down the corridor. It was a child's voice, breathless, from the tinny acoustic of a telephone kiosk.

Squashed into the glass box outside the gates of Sandmarsh High School were three girls, and the voice that spoke to the social worker was Marianne's.

'Can I come and see you?' she said, after giving her name and demanding his. 'Now?'

'You want to see Miss Beale?' said Danby.

'No. You. You're the boss bloke that was there the first day, yeah?'

'Yes, I'm supervising your case. But you should talk to Miss Beale.'

'I don't wanna. I wanna talk to you. On your own. I got something important to say. About Mr Milcourt.'

Danby frowned. 'Oh, all right. Come round now. We'll be here.' He would have to be home late, that was all. When he had put the telephone down he strode into the corridor and called 'Sarah!' to a retreating figure laden with carrier bags. She was not over-pleased to be delayed either, but when Marianne arrived a little pale and breathless half an hour later, Danby and the despised Miss Beale were both waiting for her by the reception desk.

'I wanna talk to you on your own,' she said, exclusively addressing Eric Danby. 'It's really important.'

'Does your mother know you're here?' asked Sarah, coaxingly.

Marianne dropped her head, then raised it again to meet the social worker's eyes with flat insolence. 'No,' she said. 'I got rights. Even against my mother I got a right to be heard. I don't have to tell her. An' I don't have to talk to anyone I don't feel comfortable with.'

The lessons of Childline and the Children Act, reflected Danby, were really getting through very satisfactorily to the new generation. All the same, no way was he going to sit unchaperoned in this dangerous child's company. He glanced at Sarah.

She said uncertainly, 'If you do have something to tell Mr Danby, and you don't want me to hear it, I think that is one of your rights, Marianne.' Turning to her colleague, she said meaningfully, 'Room seven's free, I think.'

Since all the rooms were free and everybody had gone home, it took a moment before Danby, tired and fuddled at the end of a long day, realized what she was telling him. Room 7 adjoined Room 6. In Room 6 there was a monitor and video recorder, in Room 7 the camera linked to it. They had rarely used the equipment, installed for recording interviews and disclosure play sessions with very small children where abuse was suspected. But it was there. He beamed at his younger colleague. This was, he thought benevolently, perhaps the first time he had known her to show tact and intelligence simultaneously. There was hope for her yet.

Kit went back to sleep after the doctor left, and Anna went into town. There she bought two bottles of iron tablets, some fresh spinach, a piece of liver, some Spanish onions and a quantity of broccoli. When Kit woke up late in the afternoon and found her in the kitchen conscientiously preparing this aggressively iron-rich meal he actually laughed.

'Couldn't I have just had a suck of your bicycle?'

Anna smiled at him, pushing her fringe back with the back of her hand so as not to make her hair reek of liver. She hated the shiny, slithery stuff and had rarely cooked it for Kit, much as he enjoyed it.

'Man of steel,' she said. 'Humour me. I want you well.'

* * *

Marianne found it hard to tell Eric Danby the truth, but she managed it. It did not, after all, take long. Again, as she had with her two friends (now kicking their heels in the street outside), she stressed that she had never said anything about the sex. Just written it down and then not denied it and said the bit about getting married.

'Why are you telling me this, after all this time?' said Eric, quite kindly. 'I don't understand.'

'Because you can save me having to go home to my mum,' said Marianne. 'You're Social Services, right? You're the boss. And I don't want to be at home with my mum. Miss Beale keeps going on about how important my mum must be "at this difficult time".' Her mimickry was cruelly accurate, catching the breathless sincerity of Sarah Beale.

Danby smiled. 'Why don't you want to go home to your mum?'

'She'll kill me. For writing the diary, and that. And now saying it's not true.'

'Perhaps she thinks it *is* true. Perhaps she thinks you're protecting Mr Milcourt. Perhaps you are.'

'No,' said Marianne, and there was an adult sadness in her voice which made Danby look at her curiously. 'No. He never would've looked at me, would he? I made it up. I fancied him. I think I was a bit barmy.'

'Why should we believe you now, and not believe what you said before?'

'Because my mum ain't here, is she? She does my head in, my mum. Honest, I haven't had sex. Not ever. If you have to get a doctor to say that, I s'pose I'll do the tests, all right? And all the stuff about Mr Milcourt was made up. Now I want everything back the same's it used to be. Except not living with my mum. Even before all this stuff, I hated living at home.'

Danby sighed. One problem was now replaced with another, and if things fell this way it was his problem rather than a police case taken mercifully far from his hands.

'We had an idea though,' continued Marianne. 'Me an' my friends. About what to say. We can say I just started my periods an' went barmy, hormones an' that. And now

I got some medicine for that, and now I've come round, all right? Ameenzia. No, am-knees-ya. Like in the *X Files*, when the aliens stole her brain only it turned out to be government chemicals.'

'Er, *have* you just started your periods?' asked Danby, startled by this ingenuity.

'Nah. Had them start when I was at Colton Primary. When I was ten,' said Marianne. 'I was the first in the class. Kara still hasn't got hers.'

Her brittle courage touched Danby very much. 'All the same,' he said gently, 'it isn't necessary to make excuses or pretend you're ill. You're a child. You're only twelve years old. Everyone makes mistakes when they're upset and when they're in love. Don't blame yourself.'

There was a silence. The girl looked at him, with tears behind her eyes, and gruffly said, 'I think it would be best if we said the stuff about the periods. Mr Milcourt might not be so cross. Then he could come back and I could still be in the class. Being mad's a good excuse, all right? You get let off if you get barmy. I did try it on with the poor bloke. All he really did was pretend not to notice and offer me some hot chocolate. He's ever so sweet.'

'Do you not want to go home tonight?' asked Danby, practical again. He did not want to see any more of her tears.

'It's all fixed,' said Marianne, blinking them away. 'I'm staying with Natalie. She's got bunk beds.'

Danby rang the police with his news. Tinny questions met him, to which he gave terse answers. 'No, quite satisfied . . . on video. Pretty certain our psychologists would identify a common enough fantasy syndrome and an explicable recovery. Offered to submit to medical examination, previously refused. We can do that if you insist. I'd rather not. It's all right. I really think he's in the clear. I've known these cases before, but it's unusual for the child to let us off the hook this early.'

The police had found nothing remotely untoward in any of the papers, cassettes and disks removed from the Milcourts' house. Such a complete clearing-up of the matter was welcome. All the same, Kit's sharp-tongued comments on the day of the interview were still smarting, so D.I. Markham rather spitefully resolved not to contact him or his headmaster with the good news until morning.

18

Anna thought of it ever afterwards as the Last Night. The last night of the Marianne business, the last night of illusion, the last night of her youth. Kit ate his liver and spinach and broccoli, took his iron pill meekly with a glass of red wine and talked little. The brief cheerfulness which had marked the doctor's visit seemed to evaporate, and he wilted visibly towards nine o'clock. They watched the news headlines together and then, wearily, he said, 'Bed for me.'

By the time she followed him up after the weather forecast, he was asleep, his swollen face heavy and pale on the pillow. Anna slipped in beside him and turned out the light. For an hour she lay with her own thoughts, not sleepy, wondering whether to read awhile with Kit's small battery book light. She had bought it for him, she reflected amazedly, only three months ago at Christmas because he was usually the one who read late into the night, and woke fresher than she did after hours less sleep. Now, he hardly seemed to read at all.

She reached up for the place where the torch with its long flexible neck was kept hooked over the bedhead, and in doing so pulled at the duvet which covered her husband. With a start, sweat glistening on his brow, he woke.

'Anna? Oh, thank God. Thank God. I dreamed—'

She put her arms round him. 'What?' He was shaking all over, gasping as he fought off the nightmare. Again she said, 'What? Sweetheart, it's all right. What did you dream?'

To her surprise he sat bolt upright, propped himself on pillows and switched on his bedside lamp.

'I can't take any more of this,' he said, but without vehemence.

'It won't go on much longer,' said Anna. 'I know you're going to be cleared. It's an absurdity. Nobody with any brains at all could possibly think that you could molest a child.'

'Oh, but I could,' said Kit, still flat and expressionless. 'But that's why it's absurd. It wouldn't have been a girl, though, would it?'

Anna switched on her own bedside lamp, as a motorist will hopelessly flick his lights to full beam in the illogical hope of piercing the advancing wall of fog. She stared at him: pale, dishevelled, unhappy, and with an edge of anger she had never seen.

'What?'

'I mean that it would be a boy, wouldn't it? Good public-school chap like me. We molest boys, don't we? Not girls.'

Anna fell back against her pillow with a wave of relief, not daring even to register it as relief. Not daring to acknowledge what she had momentarily thought.

'Oh, that's rubbish,' she said. 'People aren't that cliché-minded about public schoolboys any more. Don't be paranoid. I know people gossip, but they'd never say that about you.'

Kit shifted, still staring ahead at the uncurtained window, the marsh and the faint lights of the distant dockyard.

'More fool them,' he said. 'I'm telling you, if I wanted to kiss a twelve-year-old in a Venetian alleyway, it wouldn't be a girl. You might as well know. Everyone might as well know. Safer that way.'

Anna drew her knees up and fought to control her breathing. 'Kit, don't joke. Don't make awful jokes. It's been horrible ever since half-term, but it *will* be over.'

'Never,' said Kit. 'Not till I die. I have to live with it. I always have had to.'

For a time neither said anything. Then Anna, with an effort she felt would almost cost her her sanity, asked in a low, steady voice, 'Are you telling me that you *are* attracted to children? To little boys? I mean, like that?'

'You mean sexually,' said Kit. 'Yes. It is a sexual disorder. The only one left these days, really. All the others are sexual *orientations*, to be proud of. You can have marches and rallies and magazines about them. Paedophilia, on the other hand, is not even to be hinted at without hissing and cursing.'

Anna was silent, plucking at the sheet, looking down at her fingers with studied concentration. She could not speak.

Kit continued, flat, unemotional, weary. 'If the human creature you instinctively desire is a boy of eleven, you do not deserve to live. Anybody can tell you that. I agree,' he added. 'I don't deserve to live. But here I am. A paedophile, what they call a fixated preferential paedophile, and not even a sensible one. Sensible ones jump off high buildings or drive into trees as soon as they understand what they are.'

Anna's heart was beating so violently that she still could not speak. This was a bad dream and she would wake from it. His flat tone frightened her almost more than what he was saying. After a few moments she climbed out of bed and went to the dark window where she stood in her long white cotton nightdress, light hair streaming down her back, while Kit watched her sorrowfully from his pillow. Eventually she turned and walked back to sit on the end of the bed, shivering slightly.

'Why are you telling me these horrible things? What have I done? Why do you want to upset me?'

'I don't. You've done nothing. I can't live like this any more, that's all. I can't bear all this indignant defending of my purity. You're too good and sweet and decent to be deceived. I want to speak the truth, and when that's done, whatever happens will happen. Anna, I am attracted to boys. Young ones. Physically. I dream about them.'

'How long has it been?'

'Probably all my life. I think I first knew at school. But it never mattered. I could pack it away. Sweat it off. This last year has been the worst.'

'Why?'

'Because it just came back, that's all. Stronger, worse than ever. More directed. More personal.'

Anna did not yet have the strength to ask which child. Blindly, she battled on towards understanding.

'Why did you marry me?'

'Because I loved you. I will always love you.'

'Do I – disgust you? Physically?'

Kit sighed, and pulled aside the duvet for her to return to her place beside him. Cautiously, avoiding touch, she did so.

'No. You know you don't. You're pure warm goodness and I adore you. It's more complicated than that.'

She stared at him, her eyes wide, a rabbit in a car's headlights. 'When we make love, do you think about – do you pretend—'

'No! No, no, no!' He was vehement now, almost angry, and she found this easier to bear than his previous defeated listlessness. 'For God's sake, no. Of course not. I never think, or pretend, or indulge, or fantasise. Ever. I fight it off. All day sometimes, every day and half the night.'

'Is it because you're ill that you're in trouble with it now?' Anna grasped at straws. 'Perhaps it's part of the illness.'

'No. It was there before. When I'm ill it's worse in one way because it's harder to fight, and harder to hide from you. But in another way it's better. I don't have the strength or the desire in me to do anybody any harm.'

'You know it would be harm, then? You know it's . . . impossible?'

'I do.'

'Then why do you want it?'

'It doesn't work like that, does it? People don't only want good things. If they did there would be no need for laws. But sweet Anna,' he looked at her now more like his old self, 'sweet girl, you might not understand that. I really think that it's possible that you only want good things. Just naturally.'

Anna sat upright, pulling her hair back with both hands. 'No,' she said. 'I do see the difference.' She reached over and switched the lamp off on her side. Directing her gaze into the darkest part of the room she said, 'Kit, will you tell me the most important thing. Have you ever? Have you ever . . . oh God. Have you ever done anything about the feeling? Involving a child?'

'Never. If I had I think I would have killed myself.'

A long silence fell between them. Kit thought of Andrew, transported with delight and shivering with glee at the living statue buskers in the Piazza San Marco. About the way the child's shoulders had trembled under his hands.

Then Anna asked, steadily, 'Never? Not even in a small way?'

Kit sighed. 'Whenever I have felt confusion about the way I am with a child, I have moved further away. Never a grope, never a leer, never an unchaste brush past in a lift. All in the mind. And I fight my mind, Anna. Like I said, all day, every day, half the night. Never done harm. So far. Does that answer the question?'

'So far?'

'I told you. I'm at the end of my rope. I'm so tired. I don't know what could happen. I've got to the bit where sensible perverts jump off the high building. That's why I'm telling you.'

'So that I can *help*?' said Anna incredulously. 'You think I can *help*?'

'I don't know,' said Kit.

19

Sleep overcame them both, a blessed image of death. *Eternal rest give unto them, O Lord*, said Kit to himself before he slipped into unconsciousness. He felt that he had indeed committed suicide and was now reaping its sweet oblivious reward. Before the relief of sleep, though, there came a wave of sorrow that in his attack on himself he had wounded Anna. *Eternal rest* . . . He felt that the guilt would haunt him even through his weariness, but in the end he slept deeply, sweetly and dreamlessly as he had not done for years. It was mid-morning before he woke and remembered the life that must be faced.

Anna was gone. She had woken early, suddenly free from the morning sickness, pulled on a tracksuit and gone out to run along the marshland path. It had been a habit of hers before pregnancy, sometimes a shared habit, but neither of them had been out for weeks. It was still dark as she reached the open ground, and she panted slightly from the forgotten exertion. The more she ran and panted, the less she had to think about the night's strange conversation.

Fatigue at last stopped her, and she sat, wheezing slightly, on a bench at the end of their road. The sky had lightened and a pink dawn was breaking beyond the brick turrets of their house. She wished very much to believe that she had run out of the nightmare as well as the night. For a moment she told herself that it was all an aberration, a delirium to be banished by the cool dawn. But as she looked back down the years she found enough clues to confirm at least that Kit had been afraid and cautious. He had always avoided being alone with his small nephews and nieces, pleading incompetence. He had refused suggestions from his teacher training college that he specialize in primary teaching, since there was a dearth of male recruits in that area. He had originally planned to teach at A level standard, but had not been able to find a job in a state sixth form; then he had protested when Ron Harding confined him to Years 7 and 8 rather than let him teach the GCSE years. Presumably fifteen-year-olds were less attractive, she thought. But . . . gay men were always making passes at fifteen-year-olds, weren't they? But of course – ugh – this was not the same as just gay, was it? Anna shuddered. None of it made sense. It was disgusting. Horrible.

She did not want to think about the Venice trip: so many children, so many boys, some small and pretty like Andrew Murray. Kit had taken them to a setting which was famous for heightening emotion, to a city of lovers. Regarding Marianne, Molly certainly believed that it had been a plot. The police were suspicious – 'given its reputation', they had said. Why had he done it? Why so secretly? He had planned the masked carnival element long in advance without her knowing about it. He had said he wanted it to be a surprise.

Paedophiles show remarkable patience and persistent cunning in achieving their ends, said a voice in the back of her head, quoting from one of the dozen newspaper articles she had loathingly read during the past weeks.

But he had wanted her to go to Venice, hadn't he? If it had been a plot, he would not have wanted her, of all people, because she would have seen anything amiss. If her worst suspicions were right, he ought to have been pleased when she said she couldn't come.

A new thought occurred. Had he wanted her there to guard him? Should she have stayed by him at all costs?

Rising from the bench again and walking along the pavement in the first of the morning sunshine, Anna fell into her fatally bad habit of wondering whether it was all, somehow, her fault.

Kit was not stirring. When she had taken a shower and made herself some strong coffee, Anna resolved to go in to school as usual. She yearned for the familiarity of her classes. She was comforted by the very sight of her briefcase, with corrected Year 7 French homework stuffed untidily into its open jaws.

She needed the reassurance of known faces, of the children, of Doreen and Ian and Caroline Chang, who was now back in school stumping around in a walking plaster and crutches. She could not confide this horror to any of them, of course. But to see them would make her feel more normal. Normal! That was important. She had a powerful instinct that if she were ever properly to grasp the meaning of what had happened, even to speak rationally with Kit about it, she must first get her feet planted back on firm ground.

After five minutes of painful hesitation, she wrote him a note.

'Gone to school. Back 5.00. Please be here. Love, A.

She was early. The first children she saw, walking in through the wire gates of Sandmarsh High, were Natalie Morrison and Marianne Denver, deep in conversation. Natalie turned and saw her, and whirled back to say something rapidly to her friend. Marianne seemed to be agreeing, with some show of reluctance. Anna hung back, remembering the police warning not to talk privately to Marianne or to other children who might be witnesses. But the girls waited, and when they saw that she had stopped on the pavement, they walked purposefully back towards her.

'Miz' Milcourt,' said Natalie. 'C'd we have a word? Could Marianne, I mean?'

'It's difficult,' said Anna stiffly. 'There's a rule—'

'Yeah,' said Marianne. 'They explained that. Only it's finished now.'

'What do you mean?'

Marianne, face to face with the pale, unsmiling Anna, suddenly lost all the courage which had carried her through so far. She turned to Natalie. 'You tell her.'

Natalie said, 'Marianne's told the Social Services it was all rubbish. Mr Milcourt an' that. She had a hormone thing and got a bit weird in the head, but it's better now. She's sorry, an' that.'

'Yeah,' said Marianne, not looking at the teacher. 'S'right.'

Anna looked wildly around her. She sensed a monstrous joke, a wave of unheard derisive laughter somewhere in the cosmos. All finished now? Just like that?

She began to laugh and feared she might not be able to stop. Panic rose as she saw the two girls watching her with small scared faces. Mercifully, she found the strength to pull herself together just as Molly Miles appeared, squat and grim, walking down Drake Street with her thick black case.

'OK,' she said to the girls. 'Thanks.' And absurdly, because she had no words for this situation, 'Don't forget you'll need your *En Vacances* books for third period.' Normality. Routine. Anna craved these things at that moment more than anything else in the universe.

Molly Miles passed her without speaking.

Detective Inspector Markham rang Graham Merck at nine o'clock. No charges would be brought, he said, regarding the suspended teacher. The alleged victim had withdrawn all her allegations. The teacher could return to duty.

Merck, astonished and torn between relief and an obscure sense of let-down, said, 'But the child's in school today! I just saw her!'

'Good,' said the policeman. 'Meant to be, isn't she?'

'Yes,' said Merck. 'I just thought – obviously it's been some kind of trauma . . .'

'Ask Social Services,' said D.I. Markham. 'They seem to think the kid's fine. She's staying with a friend. Some trouble at home.'

'Right,' said Merck, and rang Eric Danby.

When Merck had heard the full story of Marianne's retraction, he sat for a while tapping his teeth with a pencil and then buzzed a summons to the school secretary. She appeared, without much enthusiasm. She had been applying for other jobs daily ever since Ronald Harding's death. 'Ask Miss Miles to come and see me at ten thirty break please,' he said. 'And Mrs Milcourt, at ten forty-five.'

He knew he ought to ring Kit directly, but didn't.

When Molly came to the office and heard the news she said flatly, 'I'm afraid I don't believe it. That is a very tricky child.'

'You think she's lying now? And wasn't lying before?'

'I think she's been *got at*,' said Molly, and described the scene at half past eight when she had caught Anna Milcourt, in defiance of the police instructions, deep in private conversation with the victim child and one of the key witnesses. 'They're fond of Anna, who is a very good teacher, even if she's been a bit unbalanced lately. I didn't like to tell you this . . .'

Whereon she told with well-timed relish the story of how Anna had tried to hit her in the science room, concluding, 'I'm sure she's been working on that poor child.'

Graham Merck was chewing the pencil now, so viciously that splinters from its end broke off and threatened to embed themselves in his tongue.

'It won't change the police's mind. Even if you could prove she talked to Marianne Denver before this morning.'

'No,' said Molly. 'But the decision about suspension remains with you.'

'I can't suspend a teacher if they aren't charging him!' said the acting head irritably. 'He hasn't done anything!'

Molly glared at him, and even her old ally felt the force of her will and flinched. 'What about the conduct of the Dewar expedition?' she said. 'And the resulting damage to the reputation and good standing of Sandmarsh High? These add up to perfectly adequate grounds for asking him to leave. Frankly, I'm surprised you can't see that.'

'I don't want an industrial tribunal,' said Merck fretfully. 'I shall have to go to the governors and the LEA for a ruling. I'm only acting, you know, at the moment.'

Molly's snort suggested that she knew very well he was only acting. He was as keen as she was to see the last of Kit Milcourt.

When Anna came up she found them both there, acting head and acting deputy, ranged together behind the desk. Molly stood at Merck's side. Graham Merck told her the news and suggested that she was the best person to convey it to Kit. What he meant was that she could convey it to Kit without any firm arrangement being made about his return to the school.

Anna looked distraite, far less thrilled and relieved than he had expected. Women, thought Merck savagely, were bloody odd. He was glad he did not have one in his life. All she said was, 'Yes – I knew, actually. Since this morning.'

Merck felt Molly Miles stiffen with triumph beside him. The young woman clearly *had* been discussing the case with the children. That alone should ease his task of removing Kit. Except, he thought with a stab of panic, that of course in that case Anna would have to go too. Or she would walk out. Then he would have lost his best modern languages teacher in the middle of the academic year, and what would become of the prized Italian GCSE group? And of his bid to prove to the governors that he was, indeed, a safe pair of hands to take over the headship of Sandmarsh High? Heads who shed good teachers were frowned upon, especially heads of struggling schools which most teachers would rather not risk adding to their CVs.

The remains of the pencil snapped between his fingers. Anna left, as glum and uncommunicative as when she arrived. Molly began talking again but he motioned her away. Bloody women.

Routine and determined normality carried Anna through the rest of the day. The worst time began during the enforced idleness of the lunch break. Unreeling again the night's conversation, she remembered how Kit had remarked, flatly and unemotionally, that sensible men in his predicament jumped off high buildings or drove into trees.

Panic swept over her. She had once read that the highest proportion of successful suicides was among active, practical, physically competent men: farmers and soldiers and sailors and climbers and vets and surgeons. They knew the limits of the human body and the properties of materials, and invariably arranged their suicides with the same brisk competence with which they had led their lives. No underdone overdoses for them, no botched jumps from too-low railway bridges, no incompetent routing of leaky exhaust pipes into cars which then stalled, leaving them to come round with no worse damage than a headache. Such men, said the article, put themselves down with the same swift competence they would use in breaking an injured rabbit's neck.

Anna had seen Kit handling rope often enough to be haunted all afternoon by the spectre of his hands competently and murderously twisting a coil into a noose. Her classes noticed that she talked much more than usual and more shrilly. She pinned her hope on her note: *'Please be here.'* She did not think he would refuse her that.

He was there. He was sitting in the five o'clock gloom by the dim glow of the electric fire. Anna resisted the temptation to snap the light on and merely stood in the doorway, saying with determined brightness, 'How're you feeling?'

Kit looked up at her in silence.

She persevered. 'When did you get up?'

'Eleven,' he said.

'Supper soon? I bet you had no lunch.'

'You don't have to feed me.'

'I do. Don't be silly. Besides, I've got some good news.'

He grunted.

Anna went on, 'You've been cleared. Marianne Denver has withdrawn all her story. She's told Social Services and the police that it was some sort of hormonal thing. PMT. All made up.'

'Poor little devil,' said Kit unexpectedly. 'It wasn't PMT at all. It was love and desire. She looked and sighed and longed and brooded, and when she couldn't take it any longer she risked everything. She made a daring plan and threw the dice. Think how much it must have hurt.'

Anna watched his face in the orange glow from the fire but said nothing.

'And now,' he continued, 'she has to face the humiliation of admitting what she was, and what she wanted, and what it drove her to.'

'You're very sympathetic, considering,' said Anna.

'Considering? Considering that we're twin souls,' said Kit, 'I ought to know how she feels.'

'How?' Anna did not understand.

'To want the wrong thing and be afraid you'll almost die if you don't get it. To know it's wrong and impossible. To confess publicly that you were disgusting enough to want it, and still to know that you'll never have it. The only difference between us is that I'm twenty-five years older, want even worse things and have more self-control.'

Anna knelt at his feet. A cold, dry resolution was in her.

She was a teacher and respect for knowledge of all kinds was ingrained to her very core. She had to know, whatever the knowledge was going to cost.

'Can we talk about all this?' she asked. 'Properly?'

'Nothing to say,' said Kit.

'Just a few questions? Please?'

He looked down at her face, shadowed so that he caught only the gleam of her damp eyes. Anna saw that he had poured himself a tumblerful of whisky, and divined that it was not the first. She reached for it and took a gulp of the burning liquor. Then she looked at him again, expectant.

'All right,' he said. 'Shoot.'

'There are things I have to know. First, is it men too? Grown-up men?'

'No. Never. Not a flicker.'

Anna shuddered, but went on. 'When did you know?'

'Eighteen, maybe nineteen. Small choristers. At college.'

'What did you feel?'

'Pass.'

'All right. What did you do?'

'Nothing. Left the choir. Took a few girls out. Tried to forget about it.'

'Did it ever go away completely after that?'

'No.' His face was as still and remote as marble.

Anna summoned the resolution to go on with the questioning. 'Did you ever tell anybody? Try to get help?'

'Once,' said Kit. 'In my last year. The college chaplain. He had some psychiatric qualification, and another guy I knew had seen him after he tried to kill himself over a girl.'

'Well, did that help?'

Kit looked at her, his eyes unreadable, dead. 'He said God gave us our desires, and that children have an unacknowledged sexuality which often torments grown men, but that we must have faith in God's wisdom in giving us our instincts. He asked me to write down everything I felt and wanted, and give it to him so we could read it together. He was quite excited about it.'

'Oh, Kit!' For the first time since they began, Anna was moved to sharp pity by the remembered shame and horror in his face. 'Did you write it for the bastard?'

'I was desperate enough to start. Two pages in, I tore it up. To write about a feeling is to feed it. I sent him a two-line note saying I never wanted to discuss the subject again. I still don't, actually.'

Anna ignored this. There was another question. 'Why did you take up teaching, if you knew?'

'Because you told me to. On the turtle day, remember? Because I felt strong by then. With you. I love you. I thought it would go away. Besides, I worked out that I could always opt to teach ages above my danger level. It's a very precise level.'

'But why risk doing any kind of work with children? You would have been safe in the bank.'

'Because . . .'

He paused, and she scanned his face in the firelight. It grew softer, some of the haggard, strained look ebbing from it. He sipped the whisky.

'Because I love them,' he said simply, at last. 'All ages, and the girls, too. I love the innocence, and the possibilities. I love the way their minds are supple and clean and fresh. I wanted to make their eyes shine. I wanted to give them mental armour against all the demons of the world. The kind of armour that got me through it all for years.'

He glanced down and saw her face screwed up, working desperately not to cry. He understood. He knew the torment of carnal imaginings he had accidentally unleashed when he said 'supple and clean and fresh'. He had lived with the horror for years, with the crawling of his flesh in shame at its own desire. It gave him a stab of agonized grief to see this woman, fresh and clean herself, confronting his corruption so bravely.

Again he said, with gentle force, 'I loved the children. Cleanly enough, I swear it.'

She mumbled something. He made out the words, 'How can it be clean, if . . .'

He sighed. 'Anna, I've had years to think about this. The thing you have to hold on to is that Freud was wrong. The whole world is not driven by sex. Sex can be pushed to the edges. Think of Plato's Cave, the real glory and the dim reflections. Hang on to that. Sex is just a tarnished, distorted mirror of love.'

'For us it wasn't.' She looked at him. 'Was it?'

Kit was silent. Then, 'Let's just say that sex is dispensable and love isn't.'

Anna recovered herself. 'One more question,' she said. 'Were you – interfered with, as a child?'

Kit stared into the fire. 'You want to build up a theory about cycles of abuse, out of the Sunday broadsheets and the psychology books? Was I buggered at Priory Shore, hence left forever fixated on the bodies of boys?'

'Yes,' said Anna. 'And don't use that word, I can't bear it. Not now, not knowing that you dream—'

'Sorry,' said Kit, and meant it. 'But the answer is no, I wasn't.' He gave a small, dry, private smile. 'And no, I don't believe in recovered memory therapy. I remember quite enough bad things to trust my total recall.'

'You've never got on with your father, have you?' said Anna. It was a wild and unpremeditated shot, but the change in the atmosphere was so palpable that she held her breath for a moment in fear.

'No,' said Kit after a silence. 'But no, he didn't touch me up either. He never touched me.'

He was silent, and Anna did not speak for a few moments. Then, 'There's more,' she said softly. 'Kit, tell me!'

But he told her nothing else that night. They shared a bed as usual, because Anna was still afraid of what he might do if she left his side. But there were no embraces or reassurances. It seemed to her that they were pressed apart by the dead weight of something he had not said.

20

By morning the news of Marianne's retraction was all round the school, and Kit's friends rejoiced unashamedly as they confronted his few enemies and the majority camp of worried doubters.

'It was all a fantasy!' said Ian Atkins. 'Girls. Dangerous little swine.'

'I didn't believe it,' said young Nellie Armstrong from the IT department. 'Only Molly Miles was *there*, you see, and she seemed so *sure*, and you do hear such stories. And children have to be believed, don't they? So it was hard to know what to think.'

'Well, shame on you,' said Caroline Chang, hopping in on her crutches. 'You know perfectly well that Molly can't stand Kit. If he was up on a charge of sexually assaulting a council bin wagon she'd swear blind she always knew he was that way inclined.'

'When's he coming back?' asked Eileen McCafferty. 'Anna hasn't said. I saw her this morning and she still looks weepy.'

'Shock,' said Ian Atkins knowledgeably. 'And perhaps he doesn't want to come back. Not with Ron Harding gone, and all the embarrassment there'll be with the children.'

'I don't think he embarrasses easily,' said Doreen Nixon. 'If I know Kit, he'll be back in the midst of his sets stirring things up on Monday as if nothing had happened. Little Marianne actually went to Anna Milcourt and apologized, you know. She's got some quality, that child.'

'*Minx*,' said Ian Atkins. 'I don't know how you can say that. Butter wouldn't melt. She is a danger to decent men. It's all very well for you, Doreen, nobody accuses innocent middle-aged women of lunging at boys. Men are the victims. Anybody with testicles is mad to teach co-ed secondary. I tell you, girls are trouble.'

'Funny, isn't it, how they never fancy science teachers?' said Eileen McCafferty mischievously. 'I detect the green-eyed monster there. You'd quite enjoy a bit of adoration, Ian.'

He snorted.

Doreen Nixon said reflectively, 'All the same, I'd like to hear from Anna and Kit themselves whether he's coming back. I can't bear to imagine the school without them.'

'Merck can,' said Caroline Chang. 'So can Molly.'

'And they have taken over the world,' said Ian.

The little group of teachers, friends in adversity, looked gloomily towards the noticeboard where a dozen new proscriptive notices, sharply printed in the school computer's most uncompromising fonts, had sprung up in the past three weeks. All were signed *Act. Headteacher* and *Dep. Act. Headteacher*. They were about windows, stationery, punctuality, care of textbooks, abuse of computer equipment, locking of classrooms, stationery again, texbooks again, complaints from cleaning staff regarding abuse of felt markers, and (yet again) stationery. The latest one was a sharply worded rebuke to Certain Staff Members who had written letters to persons outside the school without using the correct size of school headed notepaper. Above it hung five hundred words of indignation about an in-service training module in 'communication skills' which had been offered as a weekend Skill Enhancement opportunity but had received no applicants whatsoever from Sandmarsh.

'Couldn't we organize for Molly to get the push, instead of them?' said Ian reflectively. 'Do you know, poor little Anna tried to deck her the other day for saying that Kit as a molester would be a danger to his own child.'

'Missed, did she?' said Caroline Chang. 'Pity.'

'Bloody big target,' said Atkins. 'Poor kid must have been seriously distraught, to miss all of Molly.'

Towards Anna they were all warm and affectionate. Those who knew her best were worried by her listless response to their congratulations. She would not say when Kit might be back, only that he had not heard 'anything official'. She supposed that there were 'routine channels'. This was so unlike Anna that Eileen, Caroline and Doreen went into a huddle of worry together at lunchtime, the result of which was that Eileen cornered her in the afternoon and brightly suggested that she drop round at the Milcourts' that evening with the bottle of malt whisky and victory card bought after a hasty whip-round among the staff.

Anna stalled. 'Oh, that's sweet of you. Kit will be thrilled. He loves malts. But to be honest, he's not well. He's got a hospital appointment at the beginning of the week, and I think the more he's left in peace, the better.'

So, immediately, the rumour began to spread that Kit's appointment was with a psychiatrist.

'Bloody child!' said Ian Atkins again. 'Thrown him right off balance. They wreck lives, these knowing children who make allegations. I blame the television. Chap in Dorset chucked himself off a cliff—'

'Oh dear, I hope he'll be all right. Specially with Anna in her condition.'

'Christ, I forgot! Bloody awful luck.'

Molly and Graham, in their official redoubt far from the staff room, talked with equal earnestness. Molly, in the role of Lady Macbeth, stiffened Graham Merck's resolve.

'If Anna Milcourt walks out, then she walks out. I really think that the continuing disruption and irresponsibility of Kit Milcourt does more harm than her presence does good.'

'Yes,' said Merck. 'I suppose so.'

A tap on the door from the disaffected school secretary brought an unexpected visitation. Josh Bannerman, Natalie Morrison, Darren Oxtey and Kylie Chang Seng stood in the doorway, all unnaturally brushed and tidy.

'Well? Who sent you? What have you been up to?' began Merck irritably. 'Josh, I thought I told you I didn't want you on report *one more time* this term.'

'We're not on report,' said Darren Oxtey with dignity. He had been chosen at Natalie's insistence because he was known to be impervious to the thunderings of authority: a hard man like his father. Now he fixed the Acting face of authority with hard, sharp little black eyes.

Josh, who had been chosen because his great height and bulk gave the others courage, said, 'That's right. We're a detupation.'

'Deputation,' said clever Kylie, with a slight frown. 'We've got a letter from all the Year 7s.'

'Except Rosalie, 'cos she's ill,' added Natalie. 'But it's all of us. Marianne signed.'

She held out the orange folder to Graham Merck. Inside was an A3 sheet with, carefully printed across the top, the words, 'WE WANT OUR ENGLISH TEACHER BACK (MR MILCOURT)'. Underneath were sixty-eight signatures. Graham knew there were sixty-eight because they were carefully numbered. What he did not know was how the children knew that there was any question over Kit's return.

He asked, 'Why are you sending me this?'

'Because,' said Darren, after glancing around and seeing that everyone else had fallen silent, 'we've got a lot of projects to finish, about Venice an' carnivals an' that. We were going to do a big thing with all the others that didn't come. We need our diaries, an' he's got those.'

Merck, who thought that the diaries were probably still in the hands of the police, looked at the child uncertainly. He was small, but there was a chunky, insolent determination about him that the acting head could not quite stare down.

'You'll get them back, of course,' he said. 'As for Mr Milcourt, you'll be told in due course what arrangements are being made.'

'Will he be back before the end of term?' asked Natalie.

'Will it be next week? Only if we had the diaries first . . .' said Kylie.

Josh cocked his head, his usual freckled grin folded into seriousness.

They all waited for their headteacher's reply. After a moment Molly Miles chipped in.

'Back to class now,' she said briskly. 'The bell's gone. You heard what the headmaster said.'

The four children's faces plainly showed that they did not think he had said anything. Nor did they count him as a proper headmaster. Then Darren Oxtey held out his hand.

'Can we have our petition back?' he said.

'Well, it's – it's for me, isn't it?' said Merck peevishly.

'You seen it,' said Darren. 'We might need to take it around a bit, like.' And, stepping forward, with great daring he picked the folder up from the desk and skipped backwards to the door, hugging it to him. The others followed.

'Well!' said Molly explosively as they left. 'Of all the cheek!'

'What do you think the boy meant?' asked Merck. 'You don't suppose the Authority?'

He looked at his erstwhile ally. Molly seemed to him to grow uglier every minute. Her features, he thought, were not actually ugly at all. It was the expression which made her so unpleasant to look at. Not for the first time, Merck wondered whether she had her own eye on getting the headship once he had lost favour with the authorities by shedding their two best-liked teachers.

Anna got home and again found Kit morose and alone, this time at the kitchen table. She told him she had made a decision.

'Look,' she said. 'I'm very tired. I'm confused. I want to go away. To Mum's, or Mary's if she'll have me. Just for the weekend and perhaps Monday. A few days. But I need to know you'll be all right.'

'You mean, will I jump off a building while you're away?' said Kit. 'Probably not, is the answer. I'd be too tired to get up the stairs in the first place.'

'Are you taking the iron pills?' said Anna. 'Nothing will be sorted out unless you're well again.'

'I will,' said Kit. 'I will take them. I promise.'

'I'm going to ask Eileen McCafferty and Ian Atkins to look in,' said Anna. 'And I'm going to leave stuff in the freezer. Are you sure you'll be all right?'

'Look,' said Kit, 'are you worried I'll fall downstairs, or that I'll top myself, or that I'll hang around outside school gates with a dirty mac and a bag of sweeties?'

'You are *foul*,' said Anna, vehement and tearful. 'I am *trying*. And,' she hated herself for adding it, but felt compelled to, 'I am *pregnant*.'

Kit regarded her sombrely. 'I am sorry,' he said. 'I wish I could be nice to you. But at the moment I can't. All I can say is yes, please do go away on your own, see your family. You need them. I have written to Graham Merck saying that I can't work again until the hospital tests are over. They're a good excuse. I have also said that you are under stress and ought to be offered a week's compassionate leave.'

Anna hesitated. The day before, she would have been horrified at the idea of losing the lifeline of work and the company of colleagues. Now she was overwhelmed with longing to get away from Sandmarsh, out of the county, away from all of it. On the walk home, looking out at the marshes, she had been intoxicated by the possibility of moving herself physically far from it all. But here in her kitchen with her husband she felt a wiry web of memory and affection and habit and hope holding her down.

'I ought to stay,' she said. 'I ought to come to the hospital with you.'

Kit stood up. He looked at Anna's pallor, her trembling lip, the dank blonde hair that once sprang exuberantly from her head. He raised from deep within himself every last remaining ounce of compassion. He was desperately tired, aching with tiredness, his skin dry and itchy; it took heroic effort to summon up an imitation of his old manner and counterfeit his flippant and loving and confident way with her.

'Sweetheart,' he said, 'go. I will be fine. I'm only ill. Glandular fever or something. I will go to the hospital, I promise. The rest can wait. But I do solemnly promise you that I will be here when you come back, and that I will do nothing stupid and nothing wicked. For a week or ten days nothing will change for the worse. Trust me. I am still Kit the Invincible.'

A sob tore from Anna, and she flew across the kitchen to bury herself in his arms. He held her, feeling her warmth, rubbing her trembling back. But over her shoulder he looked at the wall with dull, exhausted eyes and in his heart he felt only numbness.

Anna was duly offered compassionate leave, and left Sandmarsh on Saturday morning, taking the car. Kit said he would get a cab to the hospital appointment, and had no plans to go anywhere else.

'I'll ring every night,' said Anna, as she clung briefly to him on the pavement.

'Don't,' he said sharply. 'Better not to ring at all. Get clear of me. I just think it's the best thing.'

'All right,' said Anna. 'If you're sure.' She was very much dismayed at the idea of not even telephoning. 'I could write?'

'Don't,' said Kit. 'Go away, you and the baby in there. Rest. Go to naff West End musicals with your mother. Get your eyebrows strimmed, or whatever you do. Be a Barbie doll. But just get away from all this.'

'And you?'

'Like I said, nothing will have got worse. Just give yourself a week.'

So Anna drove away along the flat estuary road, under the broad river and round the M25 motorway to Richmond. And Kit, after making himself a cheese sandwich, went back to bed and fought against his dreams.

21 $\int$

It was almost April. Unnoticed in the Milcourts' troubles, winter had passed away. Anna was into the second trimester of her pregnancy; the sickness had passed and a neat bump showed under her long cotton sweaters. On Sunday morning, walking round her parents' garden in the early sunshine, she felt for the first time a real and physical excitement at the quickening life within her. Pamela favoured a half-wild garden and when Anna stopped at the bench just out of sight of the patio doors she could sit among tall grass and exuberant daffodils, their tall green blades glittering with beads of dew. There were primroses under the trees at the end of the lawn, and birdsong clear and sharp from the branches.

It was necessary to sit out of sight of the dining-room windows because otherwise her mother would have seen that she was up, and charged out to ply her with breakfast. Pamela Melville was frankly appalled at her daughter's thinness. At three months pregnant, she regarded it as nothing short of perverse. 'A bump on a stick, dear, that's all you are, and you'll have *no reserves* if anything goes wrong. Eat!'

Lunch and supper had both been rich and solid, and Anna really did not want breakfast. The sickness might have abated but its memory was still with her and anything more than thin toast before mid-morning was unthinkable. This garden, on the other hand, was nourishing her every minute that she spent in it.

How come she and Kit had so ignored their little garden? They mowed the grass and let it be. What bulbs had originally grown there had gradually lost their potency, and now there were not even daffodils. With the baby, Anna resolved, she would go out into the garden and make it bloom like this one. She saw a rug on sunny grass, a parasol, a basket of trowels and dibbers and bright seed packets. She did not see Kit. She was not thinking about Kit, not yet.

'Dar-ling!' called Pamela's voice. 'Are you out there? Brekkie! Derek, pop out and look for her.'

Anna sighed and heaved herself up from the bench as her father approached.

'Hi, Dad. I've had breakfast.'

'Your mother's cooked for you.'

'I had toast. Please God no egg and bacon, I still get queasy.'

'Oh, Poppet remembered about that. She used to get terribly sick. She's done you scrambled egg with no butter and slivers of smoked salmon in it. From the PP Cookbook.'

'Oh God.' Anna winced, but walked back at her father's side. He offered her his arm, smiling down at her and saying, 'I always like this. Reminds me of your wedding day.'

Anna ate the breakfast – which indeed turned out to be perfectly digestible – and when she had finished clattering plates and warming rolls her mother said, 'There's a PP convention this afternoon. Would you like to come?'

'Oh, Mum, I don't know.'

'The thing is, we've got a speaker. On pregnancy, would you believe. Positively Plump is doing a preggy fitness book, and this wonderful girl is writing it. You might pick up tips. It's all down to *stretching*.'

Anna wished her mother was quieter and wiser and more of a listener. A mother, of all people, might have been able to help her confront what she had to confront. But not this mother.

A father was, of course, impossible to confide in. About this, anyway. A father would see it as his duty to be angry with Kit.

Anna had thought during the drive from Kent that she might be able to unload this problem somehow; to phrase it in such a way that whoever she did confide in would not be shocked. Maybe they would not need to know exactly what the terrible and unspeakable thing was that afflicted Kit. She had not yet devised a way. She had not even been able to tell Pamela and Derek about Marianne Denver's charge and its withdrawal. In fact, she had not admitted that she was on a week's compassionate leave. Now she merely said:

'I'll remember about the stretching, and I'd love to see the book if it's out in time. But if you don't mind, I'll rest quietly here this afternoon. I have to set off early tomorrow to get back.'

'You rest, my duckling,' said Derek. 'Let your mother's fab fatties do the stretching.'

'Fab fatties?' said Anna, and her father thought that she gave a better smile than he had seen all weekend. 'What?'

'It's one of the new catch lines, isn't it, Poppet? *"Modern Mrs Melville with her fab fatties and chunky charmers."* Didn't you see the *Sunday Times*?'

'Don't be *silly*, Derek,' said Pamela, clattering plates. 'That was just the journalist's nonsense. Chunky charmers, indeed!'

Anna sipped her coffee and smiled. These were her parents. Their lives were tranquil and cheerful. They must be left that way. She would go and see Mary.

It was Monday evening, dark and wet, when she arrived at Mary's house high on the outskirts of Sheffield. Below her the city twinkled, and she remembered Don's descriptions of how it was when he was a boy and the steel foundries flared and glowed all day and night. Mary came out to greet her.

'Hey! How are you! You don't look nearly as ill and scrawny as Mum said on the phone not ten minutes ago. It's all right, I didn't let on you were coming here, because she didn't seem to know.'

'I have been force-fed for two days. I am virtually a Strasbourg goose.'

'Well, come in and eat some more. The kids are all lined up waiting for their long-lost auntie.'

Typically, Mary asked nothing about Kit or school until the children were in bed and Don had gone out to an evening class. Then she said, 'Your local newspaper is avidly read by a miserable cow at the library who used to live in Gravesend. She was solicitous enough to pass me a small item about someone who she reckoned had the same name as my nice sister-in-law.'

'Oh,' said Anna. '"Teacher Suspended In School Trip 'Sex Romp' Allegations"?'

'The same.'

'I don't suppose she passed you the rather smaller "Teacher Cleared" headline from this Wednesday?'

'Of course not. What do you take her for?'

Anna cradled her one permitted glass of wine, now nearly empty, and sighed. 'Well, he is cleared. It was rubbish, fantasy – a little girl who was in love with him and who flipped under the influence of Venice.'

'Was that the school trip you were meant to go on?'

'Yes.'

'Oh, what a piece of bad luck,' said Mary. 'The little hoyden would never have tried it on if the dreaded wife had been there.'

'I thought that,' said Anna. 'I felt guilty. But the trouble is, it isn't over. It sort of stirred some other things up.'

'What?' asked Mary. Her cool, intelligent, friendly eye almost lured Anna into a full disclosure, but as she was about to speak she caught sight of a picture on the radiator shelf.

In it, Martin was wearing flowered trunks, showing off an eight-year-old physique and a huge fishing net. Lee stood stark naked, back to the camera, gesturing furiously up at his brother. They were beautiful, unselfconscious, but laden now to Anna with dark and horrible meaning. How could she tell Mary? Nobody with children should have to bear the burden of knowing what Kit had told her.

Two more murderous abductions had been in the news all week. One case was in Yorkshire. The man had befriended the little boy, taken him to a caravan, raped and strangled him then raped the dead body. Anna had read about it in a service station on the M1, and wept openly at her plastic table. It took all the steadiness she could muster to repeat her constant mantra, the one she had written out privately on the evening she asked Kit the questions. She had memorized it and torn the paper up. It went: *'Kit's done nothing, I believe that. Kit would never hurt or harm a child, Kit would rather die himself. All normal men are not murderous rapists. Everybody knows that. The same thing has to be true about deviant desires. Wanting is not doing.'*

When she said it to herself, she never varied the words or the emphasis. It had become a kind of charm: a charm against the horrors in the papers. Only sometimes another line added itself, unwritten and unwelcome: *'But if Kit has the desires, and they are getting worse, who knows what he might do in the future?'*

Now she looked at Mary and said, 'Oh, you know. Marriage things. Men.'

'Don had an affair,' said Mary, matter-of-factly. 'The year after Janie was born. I said I'd leave him but I changed my mind when he cried.'

Anna stared at her sister in astonishment. 'I never knew,' she said slowly. 'You never said.'

'I wish I had,' said Mary. 'I'd have got over it quicker. So if Kit's had an affair, baby sister, spit it out.'

'No,' said Anna. 'He hasn't. It isn't that.'

'Hmmph,' said Mary, who thought she recognized all the signs, every single classic one of them, in her sister's bearing. She looked at Anna and said slowly, 'Well done him, then. But truly, telling someone is best. Several of my best mates here have told me about their straying chaps. What happens is that you curse and spit and hiss together for a while, make plots, utter threats of vengeance, then totter gently hand in hand back up the slope of sensibleness. You patch it up.'

'Does everyone?' asked Anna. 'Haven't any of your mates just walked right out?'

'Yep. One whose husband wouldn't stop, and one who is extremely vain and silly,' said Mary. 'Both regretted it. Even the one with the bastard husband. She still thinks she could have won if she'd hung on. Stand by your man. Not a moral precept, just a surprisingly good stratagem for survival.'

Anna laughed a little, and wished with all her burdened heart that Kit had simply admitted an affair. Mary regarded her sardonically, finished her wine and suggested an early night. She would try the next most likely hunch – a gay affair – when poor little Anna had had some sleep. Not that Kit ever gave any sign of being effete, but he was certainly oddly relaxed about wandering about half-dressed in front of his sister-in-law.

Kit took a taxi to the hospital on Monday morning with the card Dr Ransom had dropped in for him. 'You're bloody lucky getting a date so quickly,' he said with some severity. 'If you don't keep the appointment my name will be mud.'

Kit took the cardboard slip and promised to go. Tired as he was, enough life stirred in him to make him sniff the mild spring air and feel almost boyishly ready for a change of scene. He walked the short distance to the shopping street and hailed a taxi, then watched through its window as the rapidly greening countryside unrolled between the small town and the general hospital.

Shut in the hot waiting room, though, he grew bored and restless, throwing aside magazine after magazine in the quest for something whose prose style and values did not make him feel sick. At last he was called through, underwent uncomfortable jabbings of needles, and was returned to the waiting room with injunctions to stay put for the next phase. This time he found a copy of *Great Expectations* in paperback, jammed on a radiator cover next to some dog-eared cowboy fiction. When he was called again he was halfway through Pip's second interview with Jaggers. Taking the book with him, he walked down a long corridor lit by sickly neon, following a nurse whose shoes squeaked officiously on the lino.

The oddest feeling came over him as he moved through the bowels of the hospital, away from the outpatients' entrance. It was as if – blindly, without points of reference – he was being taken to another continent. There were trolleys in motion with people on them apparently unconscious, and signposts to wards. There were, once or twice, figures in dressing-gowns led by nurses. His own escort finally turned right and whisked him through a door whose label he could not quite see —COLOGY or —DOLOGY caught the corner of his eye.

A white-coated consultant sat behind a desk, writing. He looked up, and Kit caught an unfamiliar expression on his face. Was this, perhaps, how doctors looked when you had something properly wrong with you?

'We want,' said the doctor, 'to do a CT scan today. It may mean waiting a bit longer. There are a few things I have to explain.'

And he did.

'The weird thing is, there's nothing unusual these days about

bisexuality,' began Mary, casually on Monday evening, brandishing the newspaper as if the topic of bisexuality had been
dominating it. 'You hear of so many people now. Women as
well as men. I suppose there were always people who looked
both ways, only in the old days when most people spent most
of their lives bottling up some kind of sex drive or other, born
bisexuals just bottled up half of theirs. Now it all hangs out.
Everyone's got to express everything.'

Anna looked across at her. Don was in the kitchen washing
up. The day had been peaceful, made up of mindless strolls round
the shopping centre, a couple of hours reading *Middlemarch* in the
civic library near Mary's desk, and playing with the children after
school. She was relaxed enough to feel a flicker of amusement at
Mary's artful probing.

'I've read that *Daily Mail*,' she said. 'There's nothing whatsoever in it about bisexuals. Are you trying to confide to me that
you're in love with Miss Head Librarian? Sapphic romps along
the bookshelves? You can tell me. I'm your sister. Unless by any
awful chance you fancy me.'

Mary grinned, rolled up the paper and made swatting motions
towards her sister's head. 'All right. So it isn't that, then.'

'No,' said Anna. 'Not that.' She remembered Kit saying 'not
a flicker', and winced. 'But tell me, what would you do if it
happened to you? If Don fancied men?'

'I would ask him to choose,' said Mary. 'Me and the children
and a calm decent old age in return for a bit of frustration; or
out into the jungle with nothing guaranteed.'

'It sounds perfectly sensible, the way you put it. But what
about personal fulfilment? What about Oscar Wilde, and "releasing the city from its long siege" and "going the way that your life
takes you"?'

'Didn't do Oscar much good, did it?'

'So you think one should always opt for virtuous frustration?'

'Every time,' said Mary robustly. 'Gosh, can't you just tell that
I'm nearer forty than thirty these days?'

'Two months nearer,' objected Anna. 'Anyway, forty's nothing.'

'Bollocks,' said Mary. 'That theory is put about by a load of
media creeps and film stars stuffed with mares' hormones. Up

here in Yorkshire, when we turn forty we know what to do. We cram on a hairnet and fluffy slippers and get our thrills trying to catch the ear of Alan Bennett with our carefully-crafted fatalistic remarks.'

'What about the men?' demanded Anna, amused.

'Haven't you seen *The Full Monty*? They rip their kit off and make one last desperate attempt to catch our interest. It fails. They go back thankfully to their gnomes and football.'

Don came into the room with three chipped mugs of instant coffee. 'All right, girls?' he said.

'Yes,' said Mary. 'We'll do. Thanks for finishing off. You'll make someone a lovely little wife.'

Don grinned, and bent to kiss her smooth dark head. 'More than you will, y'owld slut,' he said fondly. 'Wish I'd had the brains to marry your baby sister.'

'She's booked,' said Mary. 'Lifetime contract, from what I hear.' She slid her eyes sideways to look for Anna's reaction.

'That's right,' said Anna, and curled her hands round the warm comfort of the coffee.

'It is, in one sense, a life sentence,' said the doctor carefully. 'In another sense, not a death sentence. If we're right about this then the bottom line is that you'll always need the monitoring, and probably need the medication for quite a time. That may be boring and irritating for an active man like yourself. But you should have a good many years to be bored and irritated by it.'

'I thought lymphomas usually killed you,' said Kit. 'Fast.'

'Not this kind. We are almost certain that you are Hodgkins, not non-Hodgkins. There is a good clear-up rate, especially when you catch it this early. You have a very sharp GP, which is your good luck.'

Kit looked down at his hands, and was surprised to see them shaking. 'So now?' he said. 'I mean, today?'

'We have bullied the radiographers and got you an appointment for a CT scan. Want to see how many internal glands are up as well as the ones we can see. I think we can find an overnight bed; if so, I would like to confirm some aspects of it all with another little test. A biopsy. Not too uncomfortable.'

'OK,' said Kit, as a response seemed to be expected.

'Anyone you need to phone? Expected at home?'

'No,' said Kit. 'My wife's away.'

'No cat or dog to feed? Children to pick up?'

'Nothing,' said Kit. 'I'm signed off work for a week or so anyway.'

'Excellent!' said the consultant heartily. Kit noticed him glance sideways at the small clock on the desk. 'And don't you worry. As I say, Dr Ransom has helped us catch whatever this is at a very early stage.'

The nurse took him along the corridor, and he sat for a while in a chair while a very old, very thin man with sunken eyes was discharged from the ward into the care of a weary-looking daughter. When the bed was remade he was given hospital pyjamas and ushered into it. He felt young and frightened, and was very glad indeed that he had kept the copy of *Great Expectations*.

The surfaces of life, Anna decided, were too beautiful to spoil. The weekend with her contentedly absurd parents, and two days with Don and Mary and their exuberant affectionate children, had been balm to her wounds. How kind people were, how spirited and humorous and busy and benevolent! How warm and down-to-earth was family life! She wished she could stay forever in this green garden, and never turn over any stones to see the corruption of worms and nightmare insects beneath. On Tuesday night Don and Mary had piled on the sofa with their three eldest children and Anna had sat in the chair with Lee on her lap to watch a video of *A Hundred and One Dalmatians*.

She had needed this relief. Abandoning *Middlemarch*, her time in the library that day was spent well away from Mary's eye, surreptitiously exploring in the Psychology and Criminology sections for information about paedophilia. Nothing that she read was of any use to her; the most common picture that emerged was of hesitant, socially inept loners, damaged and retarded by childhood disasters, inhabiting fantasy worlds fed by secret pornography, their reason and moral sense crippled by layers of idiot denial. One book expressed empathy with the paedophile searching for a stolen childhood through appalling intimacies, and this frightened her even more because it seemed – to her hypersensitive perception – that the author, a psychologist with a string of letters to his name, was enjoying his exposition far too much. Another was a level, painstaking account of the routes offenders had been taken through in therapy: the breaking down of illusions, the enforcement of remorse, the acknowledgement of the pain and injury they had caused to children who they kidded themselves were 'willing'. Another, unreadable by Anna on that day, dealt with the steps by which desire turned to resentment and then to violence.

Through tears of fear and indignation she eventually concluded that there was no way through this jungle which could lead her to the Kit she knew. Why did nobody write about non-offenders? Why was there no literature about the contained, the reluctant, the horrified paedophile? What the modern age needed, she thought savagely as she put the last book back, was a really good textbook on 'How to be repressed'. For a while, sitting with her chin on her hands waiting for the end of Mary's shift, she forced herself to wonder whether Kit had really been telling the truth when he said he had never yet given way, even to fantasy or pornography.

After ten dreadful minutes of deliberately thinking the worst, she decided that she believed him. They had hardly ever been apart in ten years, after all. She thought she would know if he were lying. But it was a dry, hard, cold decision which brought her little comfort. *It's getting worse. Who knows what he might do in the future?*

All things considered, the hundred and one dalmatians were a blessed relief.

22

Of all the Year 7 children who had not been on the Venice trip, Thomas Cox was the most volcanically resentful. It was plain to his clear childish perception how the fifteen had been chosen: they were all reasonably well-behaved – except Josh Bannerman, and he was an 'improver'. An 'improver' was anybody who was less bad than the term before; this, for some unaccountable teacherish reason, always seemed to convey higher status than you got if you behaved properly all along. Thomas had never been impressed by the parable of the Prodigal Son, feeling that the elder brother never got a fair answer to his protest. The other obvious thing was that none of them belonged to the 'special needs' group, who worked with support teachers and had trouble reading and writing.

By this reckoning, Thomas considered that he should have been chosen. He might be crippled but he was not a special-needs. He *would* have been chosen, he thought resentfully, if it were not for his leg. All right, crutches might be difficult in a trip with lots of walking. Leanne had said so, scornfully, when he complained. But all the same, he was good at English and behaved well and it was not his *fucking* fault that the *fucking* car ran into him when he was little, was it? He had now heard so much about the bat suits and the cloaks and the feather masks and the living statues and the fireworks and the gondola that he almost felt he had been there. But he hadn't. He should have been chosen.

And now because of Marianne Denver's nonsense, they didn't even have a proper English teacher, only rubbish like Mr Parker – who had now left – and his successor, a dull old lady with a grey face and a grey bun who made them write imaginary letters to cousins about the weather.

Thomas had signed the petition with the others, and after the return of Darren and the others from Mr Merck's office, he said, 'You give it me. My mum's got a photocopy machine in her office and we can make copies.'

'It's too big.'

'S'not. It's called A3. She's got a button does A3 to ordinary paper size. I did my picture on it once, it sort of shrinks it.'

'What'll we do with the copy?'

'Posters,' said Thomas. 'An' my mum's in the governors. She oughter see it. They come over Mr Merck.'

'Yeah!' said the others.

Anna left Mary's on Wednesday morning, pretending she was bound for home. For the first time since she was a student she set out in the morning without the faintest idea where she would sleep that night. She felt curiously light-headed, and remembered the Bedouin drive through the desert which had brought her to Manta Bay and to Kit. Since then, she reflected, she had led a quite unnaturally simple, cheerful, purposeful, companionable, amusing life with hardly a shadow across it. Unless you counted the two or three years of intensifying worry about why she was not pregnant. Now she *was* pregnant, and everything should be perfect. But it wasn't.

Maybe it never could be. Maybe every happy family surface hid some horror, even if it was a long-ago horror. She had sometimes wondered about her own mother's obsession with healthy rotundity and well-fed flesh; perhaps long ago some oddity in her own home had driven Pamela to take refuge in beaming, powdered plumpness and stretching exercises and recipes. Maybe Don's affair had marked Mary more deeply than she pretended. Maybe Kit—

Luckily the road was empty as Anna braked sharply. She fell back into the slowest lane of the motorway, crawling along at thirty miles an hour while she absorbed a new thought. She had known Kit's mother Marion very little; she remembered only a sweet, tired face and a vague benevolence, and the way that on her wedding day Marion had come up to her, pale and pretty with her cloud of white hair and draggled lace jacket to say, 'I'm so glad you'll look after him. One's son is very precious. You'll find that one day.' Anna had always thought Marion was a little afraid of her husband Eamon, a forbiddingly senatorial figure with his cold ascetic face and headmasterly, sniffing sarcasm. 'If you're *quite* ready,' he would say to his wife whenever they left anywhere together, and, 'If my *wife* can manage to get organized,' when an invitation was tendered.

Anna, in love and slightly dazzled by the erudition and patrician confidence of Kit's relatives, dutifully stifled her instinctive dislike of Eamon Milcourt. She told herself that she was simply not used to the type, that he was just an old-fashioned prep-school headmaster with the mannerisms of his class. Later, after Marion's death, it became increasingly apparent to her that Kit disliked his father's company even more than she did. She put that, too, down to the idiosyncrasies of a class she did not know. Eamon's health failed soon after his wife's death, and he left Priory Shore to enter a nearby retirement and nursing home at sixty. Kit said at the time, 'Best place for him. He's never cooked a meal and all his life there's been Matron or Mum to iron his shirts and find his socks. He needs an institution.'

What Eamon disliked, though, was the new sensation of having no power whatever in the institution, and Anna dreaded the snappish, morose visits they paid him twice a year. At Christmas, the matron of the home had asked to speak privately to Kit, and Kit had sent Anna into the cold garden for half an hour. Afterwards, driving home, he had not said anything about it but an air of suppressed anger hung around him. It had haunted him, she now remembered with a pang, right through to the desperate half-sleeping embraces in the dawn which had conceived the child she now bore.

Eamon Milcourt. Kit's father. The father who made him angry, but who he said had never abused him. The father who was frail now, but still cold-faced and wheezingly sarcastic and capable of disturbing his son's peace. Anna slowed down still further, to the irritation of a car behind her. It swerved out to overtake with its horn blaring. She had never been any good at simultaneously driving fast and thinking hard.

She had four days in hand and nowhere to go. In those four

days, she now saw, some kind of decision had to be made about where she and Kit would go next: whether she could forgive him this thing he could not help, whether she and he and the coming child could live together and, if so, what she must ask of him. None of these things could be clear to her when all she had inside her was an aching, useless black well of love and loss and pity. She was a teacher, committed to accuracy and research and knowledge and a logical quest for reasons and solutions. She must go and see Eamon Milcourt.

Lying in the tunnel of the CT scanner like a knight on a cathedral tomb, breathing in and holding his breath at the order of a robotic voice, Kit felt a curious sense of wonder. He was not ready for this new passive status. He wondered where Anna was, whether at her powder-puff mother's or at Mary's. He wondered how he would tell her about the doctor's revelations. He wondered what new revelations this astonishing, all-seeing monster of a machine would offer to the doctor. He thought of the clean white sheets of the ward, the narrow iron bed, the thin old man leaving with his pale daughter, and the way that a hospital narrowed your life down to white-and-iron simplicities before releasing you back to life, or onward to eternity.

He thought of eternity, and the thought was not unpleasant to him. The radiographer, glancing through the lead-glass screen at the patient as the scan completed its cycle, saw a smile form unexpectedly on the pale, ascetic face.

Mrs Cox was touched by the petition that Thomas brought home.

'Did you show it to Mr Merck?' she said. 'What did he say?'

'Nuffing,' said the boy. 'He's creepy.'

Mrs Cox, junior as she was among the governors, felt rather the same way but did not express this to her son.

'Well,' she said, 'after things like this, teachers sometimes prefer to change schools. I'm sorry, but it's just one of those things.'

'We were going to do a project. Not just the Venice people, but all of us. We were going to do stuff and make a carnival play and things. Natalie said Mr Milcourt promised that on the train coming back. Now we've got stinky Mrs Darley, and Miss Miles's worksheets. I hate English.'

Anita Cox sighed. She had been excited and grateful to see the change in her son last term and his new bold expressions of feeling about the old accident. She put it all down to the teaching of Kit Milcourt. Now it really seemed that she would have to discard her principled decision to stick with the state system for Thomas, and find him a private school. She would leave the governors anyway. They seemed set on the lazy, *faute de mieux* course of making Merck headmaster and Molly his deputy. To hell with Sandmarsh. But she just said, 'We'll see. You do your homework.'

'So will you copy the petition?'

'Yes. All right. Twenty times enough?'

'Yup. Josh and Leanne say we oughter send one to Mr Milcourt so he knows we want him to come back.'

Kit came home on Thursday to sour milk, dead flowers on the kitchen windowsill, and three days' newspapers. He saw the headlines about the dead boy in Yorkshire, surmised accurately that Anna would have read them too, and shook his head in weary pity.

When he had stuffed the newspapers and dead daffodils into the bin and chased the lumpy milk down the sink with hot water, he turned his attention to a number of bulky brown envelopes on the mat. They were from the police; the rest of his papers and the children's Venice diaries.

It was only mid-morning, but Kit had very much missed his whisky in the hospital; he poured himself two fingers of Laphroaig before settling down in the warmth of the kitchen to read the diaries. An hour later he was still sitting there entranced, his glass and half the bottle empty, smiling idiotically at a story by Sally Addams – dull, doughy child she had always seemed! It was about himself, and entitled 'BIG BAT'.

Big Bat, it said, led little bats through a magic city, keeping them safe from lions and moving statues. 'Big Bat,' it concluded, 'is a friend of little bats, because he is a little bats himself.'

Kit was thrilled by the neatness of the joke but even more by the cheek, coming as it did from this worried, dutiful child obsessed with the fear of spelling things wrong. The diaries, all fifteen of them, uplifted him. He saw through the warm fog of the whisky that he had indeed done good to children in his time, not harm. They could put that on his tombstone. He had thought a lot about his tombstone in the hospital. It had come reassuringly closer. Rising a little unsteadily from the littered table, he walked back to the front door and picked up the rest of the post. One flat white envelope intrigued him. When he opened it, he found himself unfolding a photocopied sheet with, preternaturally small and dense and neat, the miniature signatures of sixty-eight children he knew well. The headline read: 'WE WANT OUR ENGLISH TEACHER BACK (MR MILCOURT)'.

Kit smiled at it, but shook his head. 'Sorry, kids,' he said aloud. 'You're on your own now. But I will come and say goodbye.'

It was Thursday afternoon before Anna reached Trethavic, her back aching and her head spinning. She had spent Wednesday night in a motel near Newbury, anonymous and cheap, and had woken in panic from dreams of the baby. It had been born, and Marion Milcourt had been alive again and by her side, saying, 'One's son is very precious, very precious, you'll find that when you lose one.' A number of tall people, taller than Kit even, had entered the room and said, 'Ah, it's a boy. He can come with us. Better safe than sorry.' Anna had screamed that no, it was not a boy but a girl, and safer with her. Marion had smiled and said, 'No, they're always boys. And they always have the stain. It's just bad luck, runs in the family.' Anna in the dream looked down and saw a great spreading black birthmark across her new child's face. It grew as she watched.

Anna woke in the darkness and lay awake till dawn rather than risk the dream beginning again. In her belly the baby lay safe. If she was very, very quiet she thought that she could hear its fast little heart, as she had done once before through Dr Ransom's stethoscope. But maybe it was her own heart.

She drove on, south and west, finally reaching empty winding roads in the spring dusk. As she neared Trethavic village she could see along the coast the dark turrets of Priory Shore, and wondered how it must have been to grow up here, first a pupil at the little school and then a returning old boy. She imagined

being the headmaster's son, growing taller every year while –
caught in a time warp – you saw repeated in the corridors and
cloisters of the Priory small images of your old self, scuttling
round in the shorts and blazers of your childhood. Kit never
spoke of it, and only sometimes of the loftier Gothic cloisters
of his public school.

She stopped at the outskirts of the village, not far from the
nursing home, and knocked on the first of the many holiday
bed and breakfast homes. There was no answer. At the second, a sluttish blonde woman said, 'Not open yet, darlin'.
Try Crab Shells two doors down.' At Crab Shells a man with
a cigarette in his mouth looked doubtful but turned to call
his wife.

'Are you open? Is there any chance of a bed tonight? I would
have rung, but I didn't have any numbers.'

From behind the smoking husband appeared a neat little dark
woman with pink cheeks, who ran her eyes up and down Anna's
body and smiled conspiratorially.

'Is he telling you there's no room at the inn, my robin? Oh,
he'd be King Herod if he got half a chance, never mind the
innkeeper. You come in now. The guest rooms ain't ready till
Easter, but there's Billy's room aired. It got no en-suite, but you
won't mind that?'

Gratefully, Anna followed her, paid two nights in advance for
Billy's room, and accepted the offer of 'pot luck supper, whatever
we're having, three pounds on top'. The room was pleasanter
than her motel, and she sank onto the bed and kicked off her
shoes for an hour's sleep before the landlady roused her to eat
lamb stew.

She was served alone at a wobbly small table in the front
room, and her hostess seemed disposed to hang around and
chat. Anna, tearing her bread up, asked with apparent idleness,
'Do you know the little school up the coast?'

'Oh, that's Priory Shore. Ooh, yes. New headmistress, nice
lady, brings the little boys down to swim in the summer.'

'A headmistress? Not a man?'

'No, they wun't have no more headmasters these days, would
they? People do say wicked things, but I say that's just more
natural with little kiddies, to have a woman, like.'

'What wicked things?' Anna prickled with alertness. 'About the old head? Dr Milcourt?'

'Well, there warn't nothing in it, else the police would've come, I should say. But he did leave sudden like. And two, three times there was parents staying here, and along at Lobster Lea, coming to pick up little kiddies an' saying how they warn't coming back.'

'When?' asked Anna.

'I'd say twelve years back. I know, 'cos my Billy was the same age, 'bout ten years old. And he's twenty-two now, off with the fishing.'

Anna dipped her bread carefully in the gravy on her plate, for her hand was shaking.

'Why, d'you know that school?' asked the landlady from the doorway, uneasy at her silence and feeling she might have said too much. 'D'you have a little boy there?'

'I did,' said Anna. 'Years ago. When the headmaster was there. A little boy who was there then.'

'Fancy!' said the woman. 'I'd never have thought you was old enough!'

23

On Thursday evening, while Anna lay sleeping peacefully in west Cornwall, Dr Ransom called round to find Kit three parts drunk. He was not overly surprised. It often took men this way. The consultant had rung him with the results of the biopsy and scan, and incidentally with warm congratulations on his guess about the lymphoma.

'I don't think we'll have to lose this one,' he had said. 'He's young and he has clearly been very fit very recently. And thanks to you, we've caught it early. I want to start the chemo next week, but thought we'd better send him home to talk to his wife and settle down with the idea. Personal life OK, I take it? Baby expected, he said.'

Dr Ransom decided not to share the patient's recent personal history with the consultant, whom he knew to be heavily protective of three sultry teenage daughters. Nobody knew better than a provincial GP how hard it was for a man ever to be really cleared of such allegations. In the Milcourts' position, he would move somewhere else pretty soon. Poor Anna. But Kit must stay put for a few months at least, during his initial course of treatment. The district hospital had taken him on now and would waste no time; besides, for his own satisfaction the doctor wanted to see this lymphoma run well and truly out of town before he lost touch with the family.

He was surprised to find Anna not there, but the bottle of whisky was par for the course among the newly diagnosed.

'Bit of a shock, I daresay,' he began, when Kit had let him in and led him to the kitchen.

'Iss – theonly warm room,' Kit said, slurring a little. 'Shorry.'

'The diagnosis. A bit of a shock. Could be worse, though,' said Ransom.

'It'll do,' said Kit. 'Do very nishely, by the sound of it.'

'We don't always talk about complete *cure*,' said Ransom. 'But we absolutely can contain it, probably with drugs only. Rather than radiotherapy or anything too debilitating. And then we've still got radiotherapy up our sleeve.'

'I don' talk about any *drugs*,' said Kit pleasantly. 'I talk about nature taking her glorioush course.'

The doctor looked at him hard, suddenly alert. 'Are you suggesting you don't want treatment?'

'Not shuggesting,' said Kit. 'Shaying. Firmly. Let God'sh will be done. 'Sh all here.'

From the litter of diaries on the kitchen table he plucked a dark, bound book which the doctor saw was a combined Prayerbook and Testament, printed on thin filmy paper with gilt edges. As Kit fumbled, Ransom saw that on the title page in careful childish italics was written: 'Christopher Eamon Milcourt, Priory Shore School 1967.'

Kit gave an exclamation of annoyance at having lost his place. Riffling distractedly he said, 'If thine eye offend thee, pluck it out, and cast it from thee . . . if thy life offend thee, ditto. Better that a millstone were hanged about his neck and that he be drowned in the midst of the sea. It would have to be the midst. Wouldn't work in the surf, would it? No point paddling with your millstone on, only get a headache.' He threw the book down. 'Find the place later. Shorry. I get the headaches already, musht be the millstone.'

'You'd better go to bed,' said Ransom heartily. 'I'll come round tomorrow, see how you are, and we can arrange the timing of the treatment. I work quite closely with the oncology bods. Sooner we start the better.'

'No,' said Kit. 'I'm not taking anything. Bugger to medicine. Nature takesh its course. There's a reason for this, you know. Ask the chaplain. No, better. Ask Oscar.' He picked up another book, a limp morocco edition of Oscar Wilde's poems. This time it fell open directly at the page he wanted, and taking the floor Kit began to declaim from *The Ballad of Reading Gaol*.

> *The wild regrets, and the bloody sweats*
> *None knew so well as I;*
> *For he that lives more lives than one*
> *More deaths than one must die.*

'You see, doctor? Might as well make a start on the first one.'

And as Kit's eye met the doctor's, Ransom felt a firm and terrifying conviction that he was not nearly as drunk as he made out.

When Anna woke, the morning was so beautiful and the West Country birds so sweet outside her window that she thought for a moment to avoid the visit to Eamon Milcourt altogether. Life could be good: blue skies, gardens, birds, babies, some kind of agreement with Kit to forget every word spoken in past days. Why turn over stones whose upper sides lay smooth and pleasant among the spring flowers? Maybe they could get jobs somewhere like this: far from bleak marshes, bypasses and blighted docks, far from bloody Sandmarsh and bloody Merck. They were young, they had a baby coming and it was spring. She would just go home and conspire with Kit to pretend nothing had happened. To hell with Eamon Milcourt. Cold, he was, thin-lipped, nothing like his golden son. He had jibed and sulked his way through the whole of lunch on their Christmas visit, spitting enough petulance and poison to blunt even Anna's compassion for his invalid state. He was a nasty old irrelevance.

She pretended to herself all through breakfast that this line of argument would prevail, and only when she crumpled her napkin and put it on the table did she accept that she was still on her way to the Trethavic Nursing and Retirement Home, formerly, in a more ecclesiastically spacious age, known as Trethavic Rectory.

When she arrived there she stood in its echoing tiled hallway and looked around at the hunting prints with a shudder. Visits here were never easy. Without Kit she felt positively threatened. Nine other old men and women lived in this house with the small staff, but it seemed to her that the building was given its sinister personality only by the chilly presence of her father-in-law.

The matron was surprised to see her. 'Oh,' she said. 'You've hardly had time to get my letter. Is Mr Milcourt here?'

'No,' said Anna. 'What letter?'

The matron looked uncomfortable. 'It was all explained in a letter,' she said. 'But as you're here, come into the office, if you would.'

Mystified, Anna followed her. The office was claustrophobically small and cosy, with too many cushions on too many chairs, and more dusty hunting prints. Matron sat down and motioned Anna to do the same.

'It's just that we aren't sure this is the place for your father – sorry, your father-in-law – for much longer. Obviously, we wouldn't dream of asking for a move until you've had time to get suited, but we can't deal with his kind of case.'

'But you do full nursing care?' said Anna, still puzzled. 'I mean, you've people in wheelchairs, and bedridden.'

'Easier if he *was* in a wheelchair, dear,' said the little woman. She wore nurse's uniform, dark blue with some sort of ornate gilt badge of rank on her bosom. 'We could put him away from the path. But we aren't really geared up for certain kinds of dementia, and that's the truth.'

'What? What dementia?' said Anna. She was appalled to be here, discussing this without Kit, when she had braced herself to come and speak to an undemented, difficult, scornful Dr Milcourt.

'In a way it's easier to tell you, dear,' said the matron. 'It's the blood relatives who take these things worst. But none of us can help how our dementia takes us, can we? My Auntie Agnes, now, thinks she's the Queen Mother, and she's easy as a lamb to handle if you just show her enough deference. But Dr Milcourt, oh dear. I'm really quite glad it's you and not your poor husband.'

'What are you talking about?' said Anna, fearing that she knew.

'The school. Complaints. The little boys come down to bathe, and pick up shells in the winter – you see how nice our beach is under the rocks there – and he's spry enough, God knows, to manage the steps. Not to put too fine a point on it, he frightens them.'

'How?' It was not Anna's voice but another one, from far away in regions of shock.

'Needn't go into it, need we? In a way, one could control it better if it was just the obvious. We've had chaps here before who did that kind of caper at young ladies on the rocks, and our Norah's got quite used to rigging them up special trousers to stop them doing it. But your father-in-law, dear, he *says* things. Quite explicit things. Pretty loud. Sometimes it's more of a *reminiscence* than a threat, but you can imagine.'

Anna thought to herself that the matron was enjoying this at some unspeakable, Matronly level. Perhaps if you lived all the time with the sordid side of geriatric care you started to take fierce pleasure in rubbing the noses of cowardly relatives in it when you got the chance.

'And the school's been on to us. The headmistress says flatly that she's going to go to the police unless we stop him well before summer. It's got worse, you see, in the warm days this year. When you came at Christmas it had hardly begun. I did have a teeny word to your husband then.'

Anna sat still, stunned.

'So, as I say, a wheelchair would be quite a convenience. Keep him pinned down where we can have an eye on him. But as long as he's tottering around freely, with his poor old mind gone, and reminiscing rather coarsely about school and dormitories – well, you see our position . . .'

'And this is all in the letter?' Anna murmured, thinking of Kit at home and the post on the mat.

'Well, yes. But we can give you a month or two to find somewhere with a bit more security. Or,' she added as an afterthought, 'a nice home that's nowhere near a school. He can't walk *that* far.'

Anna did not go through to see Dr Milcourt, although the matron breezily suggested it ('It's not as if you're a little boy, dear, he'll be quite his usual self'). Instead she walked for a long time along the cliffs, remembering for the first time the way that Kit had answered her last questions before he stepped away into a night of silence.

'Were you interfered with as a child?'

'No, I wasn't. Not that I know of.'

'You've never got on with your father, have you?'

'No. But no, he didn't touch me up either. He never touched me.'

Anna could hear both their voices again, see the glow of the electric fire and feel the desolation of that evening. But in memory she heard more clearly an intonation which had escaped her in the shock and grief of the moment.

'He didn't touch me up either. He never touched *me*.'

'Never touched *me*.' It was childish, petulant. A small echo of boyish grief reached her. In the dim, sniggering dormitory world, Kit would always have known about the others, about the boy subjects in those 'reminiscences' of which the matron had lasciviously spoken. But his father the headmaster never gave *him* such special attentions. Not his son. Probably he would not dare, not with a mother close at hand. So Kit had been left out. Apart from the odd caning.

Much later, in the moonlight, Anna knelt alone on the clifftop and wept for father and son and for whatever blighted descendant of the line was growing, helpless, in her womb.

24

On Friday morning Graham Merck had a visitor. He was expecting a brisk new mother who wanted to start a parents' association (the last had folded for lack of support five years ago). But the school secretary, whose hatred for her new master grew every day, spitefully refrained from telling him the identity of his visitor until the newcomer was almost upon him. So Merck was entirely unprepared for Kit's appearance in the doorway, thin and pale and – the acting head thought in disgust – badly in need of a haircut.

'Morning, Graham,' said Kit. 'Thought I'd better come in and sort out our arrangements.' He stepped forward, quite at ease, and sat down on the other side of the desk with a faint crooked smile on his face.

'There are still things to be considered,' said Merck, wishing that Molly Miles, for all her treacherous malevolence, was at his side. 'The matter of the Dewar expedition and certain complaints which have reached me. From, among others, Miss Miles.'

'The Dewar expedition,' said Kit, 'was a howling success, and contained more education than Molly Miles provides in a year. And I bet you a fiver you can't name anybody else who's complained. Except Mrs Denver,' he added as an afterthought. 'And that doesn't count now, does it?'

There was a silence. The two men looked at one another across a gulf which neither particularly wanted to bridge. It was not a gulf of understanding; they knew one another's value perfectly well. Merck was not stupid. He had read the OFSTED inspectors' praise of Kit, listened to Anita Cox's encomium of him at the governors' meeting, and held the children's petition in his hands. On the other side Kit knew that Graham Merck, while not brilliant, inspiring or generous of spirit, was an organizer and a disciplinarian and probably the only reason that this school had not declined to levels of anarchy in which even he could not have taught effectively. He had liked Ron Harding but knew his weakness and the degree of his dependence on the unprepossessing deputy.

So they valued one another more or less correctly, but liking could never grow between them. The gulf was emotional. Kit reflected how strange it was that emotion, routinely disregarded by those who analyzed institutions and their ways, should in the end be the only important thing.

He ended the silence by saying, 'All right, we don't have to argue about it. The point is, Graham, that I have to resign my job here, as of today. Ill health.'

Merck knew where he was now. Ill health had been suggested to him by the chairman of governors as 'an excellent solution' as soon as the Denver girl's allegations were first made.

'It's often the most sensible thing,' he said with enthusiasm. 'Saves talk, and leaves you clear to start again at something else. Teaching is acknowledgedly stressful. I'm glad you see it that way.'

'You're a buffoon,' said Kit, quite tranquilly. 'I really *am* ill. I have a lymph gland cancer. Probably untreatable.' Childish, he crossed his fingers behind his back. 'I don't have much time. The time I do have, I need.'

Merck stared at him for a moment, looking for signs of debility and finding enough to convince him that this was probably not a Milcourt joke. He dropped his eyes and muttered, 'Oh, I am sorry. I really am sorry.' He was, too. The shadow of death closed the emotional gap for a brief moment and let the pallor of one man's face touch the other man's heart directly and uncomfortably.

Kit saw this, and allowed Merck a moment to compose himself before he added, 'But there is one thing I want to ask.'

'Er, 'fcourse. Anything,' muttered the acting head.

'I want to say goodbye to my Year 7s. The Dewar group and all the others. I want to take a special double period with the whole year to read the Venetian diaries and talk about *carnevale*. Just before the Easter break would be best. The Thursday morning, ten thirty to eleven fifty.'

Merck had a moment's panic. He did not want to be seen to hesitate, but this man was an accused sex offender, by his own account dying and therefore with nothing to lose. He opened his mouth, but his jaw trembled and he closed it again. Finally he said, as levelly as he could, 'Yes, of course. Perhaps since you aren't well, Mrs Milcourt could come and take the class alongside you? Just as back-up?'

Kit stood up and looked down from his full height at Graham Merck. This time his smile was unmistakable, broad and mocking.

'It's all right, Graham,' he said. 'I'm not going to open fire on them with a machine-gun, you know.' And he left, the door swinging behind him.

Merck was left gasping in outrage at the tastelessness, the callousness, the cheek, the sheer bloody blasted unprofessional *nerve* of the man. The gulf between them yawned once more, wider than ever. Merck felt the better for it.

He still had Molly Miles to square, but she would be so pleased about Kit's impending and permanent departure that she would put up with the prospect of a triumphant farewell class.

There was not much doubt that it would be triumphant. Merck thought of the sixty-eight signatures on the petition (which was now duplicated on every noticeboard, often on top of his own neatly printed strictures). He thought about the hum of interest it had aroused higher up the school, and the signatures which had appeared on top of the photocopy, from far older children formerly taught by Kit. Merck resigned himself to a day's beargarden on the Thursday before Easter.

Anna left Trethavic after an early cup of coffee, dry-eyed, composed and determined. She had promised the matron that they would get to work on finding another home for Eamon, so she stopped in Truro to pick up a list of nursing homes and some prospectuses at the information centre. It suited her to have a practical problem to consider. Before she left the town she sat over another cup of coffee and sorted out the brochures which specifically mentioned willingness to cope with accelerating dementia. They all looked pretty grim to her, but she was in no mood to worry any longer about Eamon Milcourt's comforts. Kit could make the final decision.

Her focus on Kit was now more intense than ever. She felt that she had been given the rest of him, the part which had been missing through the years when she knew only his adult strength and love. It was a sorrowful enough gift at the moment, but in an unsuspected part of herself she rejoiced to have it. It was horrible but real. It forced her at last to grow up, for she saw that until the past week she had inhabited a sheltered nursery all her life, a Pamela Melville paradise in which all that was required of a girl was to be polite, and sweet, delicious and kind and Pleasantly Plump, briskly busy and always well-meaning. She had lived in a place where all these easy sweetnesses were duly rewarded with enough to live on, plenty of laughter and lots of cuddles.

Of course, she was a socially concerned person, a teacher and co-ordinator of charitable doings. She would always have paid lip-service to the truth that of course this was not the way things were at all. Officially Anna had always known that the world is full of innocents for whom innocence is no shield, of refugees and victims, of unregarded playthings of repulsive cruelty, pawns of fate's and mankind's nastiest games. She knew these things, but never before believed them in her heart.

But in last night's storm of grief, she had become at last an adult. She remembered some gruff American film character saying: 'Shit happens. You clean up the mess.' Nothing is ever quite so delicious and new and clean again, but what the hell? You carry on. There was extraordinary comfort in the thought. 'Shit happens,' she said to herself, briskly discarding nursing homes in residential streets which might have primary schools. 'You clean up. You carry on.'

The baby deep within her, she thought with an oddly light heart, was all the safer for her new understanding of the horribleness of life.

She drove on, reaching the cold lights of the M25 motorway at dusk, and wondered briefly whether to spend one last night with her parents in Richmond. It was tempting: one last evening, she thought, in the world of deliciousness and cuddly paternal adoration, one more cosy bedtime surrounded by the illusion that if you do enough stretching exercises and eat properly, the world will stay sweet. In the end, though, she forged on eastwards towards the chill flatlands where her home and husband lay.

Kit, returning from school, was also oddly light of heart. He felt less tired after the days in hospital because they had given him injections to lessen his anaemia, and knocked him into long dreamless sleeps with neat little pills. He gathered together the fifteen Venetian diaries and made a parcel to drop into school on Monday, tidied up the papers that the police had sent back, and went through his computer files, idly rearranging the desktop and folders where his work lay.

He hesitated over some items: the painstaking schemes on which his playground grammar games were based could be worth publishing, and so could some of the research he had done in his student years into Elizabethan journals. He swept these things into a new folder on the glimmering screen and marked it *Resch. 2 Pub?* Then he tidied the drawer where Anna's early letters were kept, the ones she wrote during the year before their wedding. He spent a long time over these, but at last snapped a rubber band round the bundle and dropped them back into the darkness of the drawer. When everything was tidy, he watched the television news, made himself cocoa and a sandwich and took them up to bed.

Anna found him there, asleep with half the sandwich still in his fist. She removed it carefully before climbing in beside him and curling up, close to his warmth but not touching. There was a bottle of pills on the side table which she recognized as sleeping pills. It had a hospital dispensary label rather than the chemist's, but she was too tired from the journey to think of that as odd.

She woke hours later when the telephone rang, distant and insistent. Incredibly, it was morning. She stumbled from the bed where Kit still slept and pulled on the nearest dressing-gown, which was his. It was Dr Ransom calling from the surgery, surprised to hear her.

'Oh, your husband said you weren't back till Sunday night,' he said. 'Have you had a chance to talk yet?'

'About the glandular fever? No, not since his hospital tests,' said Anna. 'I was out of phone reach and he was asleep when I got in. I thought he looked better. Less white.'

'The anaemia's under control,' said Ransom. He wished he had not rung; Anna Milcourt plainly knew nothing yet about the diagnosis. 'How are you and Baby?' he asked, to divert her.

'Fine,' said Anna. 'No more sickness. Blooming, I think, is the usual word.'

'Splendid. Look, I've got surgery starting. No rest for the wicked. Could you give your husband a message? It's just a reminder. Tuesday at the clinic. Nine thirty. He'll explain it all to you, but it's a little something we have to knock on the head sooner rather than later.'

When he rang off, Anna stood frowning at the telephone for a moment. Very evasive! Sounded like a kindly family doctor trying to spare the little woman news of something embarrassing. Syphilis? Herpes? She padded to the kitchen to put the kettle on, made Kit tea and took it up.

Sitting on the bed, she regarded him with new eyes and found that the old love was intact, even stronger now that it would always contain an element of pity. Pity, she thought, was an underrated feeling. Why did people think it was demeaning to be pitied? Pity was only a more complete form of love, she thought, a love that accepted the humiliations and sadnesses of the loved one's life. A song, one of her favourites, floated through her head: *I'm holding out for a hero . . . he's gotta be strong and he's gotta be brave and he's gotta be fresh from the fight.* Kit had been her hero since the moment she saw him. She had watched him battle seas and colleagues, hard climbs and hard classrooms, and never known him weaken. Now, sick and flawed and damaged, he lay there and seemed to her better than ever.

Better than heroic, because she knew more about the fight.

25

His tea went cold long before he woke. During that time Anna focused properly on the pill bottle by his bed, felt a moment's chill of terror and then saw with relief that it was nearly full. The hospital dispensary label bothered her a little: why would a clinic give him sleeping pills for a complaint already involving endless sleeping? And why from the hospital dispensary?

Her moment of loving euphoria evaporated, and all the troubles of their situation rolled back and nearly overwhelmed her. But not quite. She tidied the bedroom, as noisily as possible but without effect, then went down to the corner shop for the makings of breakfast. In the depressing sweaty freezer cabinet at the shop she found some liver and some stiff bacon, and brought them back to defrost and create an iron-rich casserole for his lunch. It would be lunch by the time he woke, she thought, and again went upstairs to check the fullness of the pill bottle and make sure there were no others.

His desk was tidier than when she left, and a large brown Jiffy bag lay on it marked 'ATTN. YEAR 7 ENGLISH. RETURN TO CHILDREN'. It was not sealed, so she pulled out some of the notebooks and began reading. Kit found her there, the books once more scattered on the desk, entranced and laughing over Sally Addams' 'Big Bat' story. She had no trouble in identifying the big bat himself from Kit's account of the costumes. Come to think of it, there was a bat headdress still hanging out of the pocket of his terrible black coat. She looked up at him and stretched out a hand, holding the little book open with her other hand.

'I like this,' she said. 'Big Bat is a little bats himself.'

Kit came over, took her hand and kissed it.

'Dr Ransom rang,' she said. 'Not to forget Tuesday morning. Very insistent. Wants you at the clinic.'

'Ah,' said Kit, letting go of her hand. 'I hoped to come round to all that slowly.'

'What happened?' demanded Anna. 'I wanted to ring that night, but you told me not to.'

'Better not,' said Kit. 'It wasn't good news. Except for me, and that's in a way you aren't going to like.'

This banal exchange, incredibly to Anna, began a conversation in which Kit told his wife that he had a treatable form of lymphoma which he had no intention whatsoever of having treated.

Later, much later, he wondered how he could have been so callous towards her. Perhaps the sleeping pills had a more deadening effect than anybody understood, and he spoke to her so brutally from some half-trance. Perhaps he was a little mad. Whatever the reason, the result was that minutes later, everything else forgotten and the diaries tumbled to the floor, Anna stood in the middle of the room trembling from head to foot, breathing fast, whiter than he was.

'That is appalling! How can you say that? It's treatable. They said so. Dr Ransom wants you to go in there quick, for whatever thing they do.'

'Chemotherapy. And I don't want it. You know what I have to face if I go on living. It can only get worse. I read the Prayerbook last night: better to die clean than live as an abomination. Pluck out thine eye. Millstone round the neck rather than harm the little ones. And now, by gentle fate, I'm being offered a lifeline.'

'Deathline you mean! How can you? It's as bad as suicide!'

'No it isn't,' said Kit.

'What about me? And your child?'

'You really think,' said Kit with that alarming, trance-like coldness, 'that I ought to stick around and risk having a *child*? Of my *own*? A child who might be a poor bloody boy?'

Anna sank into a chair as if he had struck her. But behind the shock and the inward shrieking, a small cool part of her maintained that she was not defeated yet, nor could afford to be.

*　　*　　*

There was no question of finishing the liver-and-bacon casserole. Anna threw the ingredients to the elderly dog next door, and walked out of the house with a slam of the door, a sound which had never before marred their wedded life. Kit gathered up the diaries again and found the Sellotape to finish his parcel for Sandmarsh High. Anna half ran through the outskirts of the town and down to the surgery, where she sat waiting in a line of coughing patients until the appointment slot which Dr Ransom always kept for last-minute emergencies. Luckily, there were none, and she slipped into the consulting room and began, 'Kit has told me he has lymph cancer.'

'Hodgkins, we think,' said the doctor, seeing that her first need was for information. 'And spotted very early. Nasty business, but treatable. I would say, given his physique and age, better than an eighty-five per cent chance of a very successful outcome.'

'If he agrees to be treated,' said Anna, bitterly.

'Ah,' said Dr Ransom. 'I wondered. I looked in the other night and he said something to that effect. He was drinking quite heavily, so I put it down to that.'

'He's cold sober now, and he says he wants to die. He thinks it's a godsend, this illness, and says we can just quietly pretend it wasn't treatable. No scandal.'

'Depression,' said Ransom, 'takes some curious forms when people have this kind of shock. And people have a great fear that cancer therapies will be violent. But we must try and get him to start the treatment on Tuesday as booked. The faster the better. They would have started last week, but he said he had to talk to you.'

'It isn't depression,' said Anna. 'And he's not frightened of treatment. It's because he's got what he thinks is a very sensible reason to die.'

'Marriage problems?'

'No,' said Anna. She tilted her chin. 'There is nothing wrong with our marriage.'

'Money? He should know that life insurance companies are not sympathetic about this kind of thing. I had a religious chap die refusing a transfusion two years back, and his family did not win their case against the insurers.'

'Not money. Sod money! It's a personal idea he's got hold of.'

The doctor looked at her carefully over his half-glasses, and said with gentle emphasis, 'Then you had better tell him to let go of it, quick. Or he might not have as much choice as he has right now. He should have got a letter from the clinic—'

To his surprise, Anna's careful calm seemed to crumple at the innocuous word 'letter'. She started from her chair.

'Oh my god, the letter. It could have come this morning. Shit!' Then, recovering herself, she said, 'I have to go. The post will have come. He'll get to that clinic, I swear it.' She moved to the door.

'Careful of the baby,' said Ransom in alarm. 'Keep things as calm as you can.' He heard his own voice and cringed. He would have liked to run out after beautiful, distraught Anna Milcourt, drive her home to her brilliant eccentric husband, and help them bring this thing to some right conclusion. But he was a dutiful man and there were other, albeit less intriguing, patients waiting for his call. Mrs Milcourt was on her own. Everybody was, in the end, he thought glumly.

Kit was at the kitchen table reading his black prayerbook. He raised his eyes when she came in from the hall holding a bundle of envelopes. He said, '". . . and there is no health in us." It's wonderful, the way it's all here.'

Anna reached out and closed the book with a snap. 'I won't have it, Kit,' she said. 'I went to Cornwall. I know all about everything. All about your father.'

Kit sprang to his feet, steadying himself on the chair. 'How *dare* you! My father is old—'

'I never saw him,' said Anna flatly. 'Didn't need to. The matron told me because they want him out of the home. It's all come back, you see. The stuff with little boys. But because he *is* old, he's lost the ability to disguise it.'

Kit stared at her, wordless.

'But,' she continued, 'I *would* have talked to him. I was going to ask him if any other teachers or boys might have done something to you years ago. I wanted to understand.'

'And?'

'Now I do understand. I know that it's the opposite. You were left out, weren't you?'

Kit sat down, and put his head in his hands. 'No health in any of us,' he said. 'No health.'

'So now,' said Anna, 'tell me.' She was gentle now, and pulled a chair next to his to sit close, her arm round his thin shoulders. 'Tell me.'

After a while, he did.

'It's incredible to think about it,' his voice was slow, wondering, 'but he was only coming up to forty when I started at Priory Shore. My age now. He always seemed a hundred. It must have been going on ever since he'd been there, I reckon. I always knew. The other boys used to giggle about what he did. He came into the dormitories and if people were talking after lights out there were punishments. Sometimes they had to stand out in pyjamas in the cold corridor. With him "supervising". Then he'd forgive them and the stuff started. We were what? Seven, eight years old. Small.'

Anna shifted her position slightly for comfort, but did not take her arm from his shoulders.

'You probably can't have any idea of how it used to be with prep school boys in the sixties. Not like any school today. You were a sort of primitive tribe, and you'd no sooner tell things to adults than backwoods tribesmen would tell their tribal mysteries to the District High Commissioner. It seemed quite normal to have your showers supervised by a grown man, and open-plan bathrooms where you weren't allowed even to cover yourself with a flannel. Nobody even questioned the famous bare-handed spankings. He used to say they were for lesser offences – less painful than the cane – and that he was a very merciful man. Wheeze, wheeze, ha, ha, bend over, boy, trousers down, aren't you a lucky boy, just the flat palm for you. Obviously, it was always the cane for me. Every time.'

Anna kept silent, and kept her arm on him.

'Anyway,' he said bleakly, 'I knew about the finger games and the willie games. All of it. Boys talked about it when they came back into the dorm from the corridor. Oh God, I don't suppose he was as bad as lots of other bastard teachers were back in those days. He wasn't brutal. But you're right, I was left out of the loop. I could talk after lights out every night and I still wouldn't be the one he picked out for the corridor. My thrashings were all at the far end of a cane. He never even kissed me goodnight, even when I was small. He kept away.'

'Did your mother know anything?'

'I think she had an idea. Christ, she knew him all his life; she was a housemaster's daughter at the school where his father – my grandad that I never knew – hanged himself in the thirties.'

'I never knew,' said Anna, distressed.

'No. Why should you? Anyway, my mother must have had an idea. But wives didn't interfere with eminent men's professions in her day, did they?'

'Maybe,' said Anna, 'she warned him off you. Maybe he never dared even show you ordinary affection.'

'Maybe,' said Kit bleakly. 'Maybe not. But actually he didn't like me much. When I was older I couldn't do anything right. Even my First wasn't good enough because it wasn't a Classical First. All I ever knew was that I wasn't good enough. And he was fun in those days, Anna. You won't believe it, but he was a bloody good teacher, and most of the boys really liked him. In spite of the dormitory stuff.'

'Were any of them damaged by what he did?' said Anna. 'Any that you know of?'

Kit frowned. 'I was at public school with three of them. Two turned into big-league bullies. One was a bit of a school tart. So I suppose, yes.'

'Why didn't you ever tell? Any of you?'

'Oh, Anna,' said Kit sadly. 'You're nearly ten years younger than me, and Priory Shore was twenty years out of date even then. That's thirty years. A generation apart. You can't understand.'

'What I *do* understand,' said Anna with an edge of anger, 'is that children always think the bad things that happen are their fault. Divorce, anger, sex, everything. Part of growing up is admitting that it wasn't your fault. Your father was just a bent old man. If he hadn't been, he would have been proud of you. You can turn your back on him now. It's over. The circle is broken.' She stood up, still keeping her hand on his shoulder.

Kit had turned aside again and was fiddling with his Testament. He spoke softly. ' *"For I the Lord thy God am a jealous God, and visit the sins of the fathers upon the children unto the third and fourth generation."* '

'No,' said Anna. 'No! It withers away. People get better. Look at you: as soon as you knew what you felt, you stopped yourself. You've kept away from small boys and from boarding schools. You wouldn't teach primary. You tried not to teach Year 7, even. You've done nothing to any child. Have you?' It was a hard, flat challenge. All her hours of doubt were in it.

Kit looked her in the eye. 'No,' he said. 'Truly never. But who knows? All this explaining, Anna, all this amateur analysis, it's fine as far as it goes. What you don't understand is that it doesn't change anything. I have this thing within me. It may get out.' His eyes fell, and for the first time caught the new roundness of her silhouette as she stood close by him. 'You of all people should understand. You look down at yourself and know that what you're carrying is just an innocent baby. But if you knew for certain that you were gestating a demon, a devil that would prey on children, wouldn't you be grateful for a quick way out?'

'You are not a demon!' said Anna, but there were the beginnings of hopelessness in her voice.

'No, I'm not,' agreed Kit. 'But I am a home and hostel of demons. And by great good luck, my foundations are crumbling into the sea.'

'And you'll do nothing to stop yourself dying?'

'Nothing.'

Anna's voice seemed to her to come from a long way away, suddenly thin and childish.

'So don't you love me?' it asked.

She did not hear the answer. Kit caught her in his arms as she fell.

She swam up from cold, dark depths to find sunlight on the sea surface. The blanket surface. She found that she could breathe now, but she was still in despair because in the dream the bubbles from the dark swimming shape beneath her had ceased altogether and she knew he must be dead. But his voice was still in her ears, and somebody's hands warm on her shoulders.

'Anna,' said the voice. 'Anna, can you hear? Anna. I love you. I always loved you.'

'You can breathe, then?' she said. 'You've still got air? The bubbles stopped.' She would not open her eyes. She knew there was a reason it was best to stay asleep.

'I can breathe,' he said. 'Were you dreaming of diving?' He knew this nightmare.

'I swam over you,' she said, a whining edge on her voice, her eyes still shut. 'You were moving, but the bubbles stopped.'

'Look again,' said the voice. 'Shining bubbles. Big ones. All around you. Swim through them. Gently.'

'I can see them,' said Anna more happily. 'Big ones and little ones. Perhaps you were just too deep before.'

'Far too deep,' said Kit's voice. 'Feel the bubbles. I'm breathing up to you.'

'Gone inside,' said Anna indistinctly. 'Prickling. Like a fizzy drink. Inside. I can feel them in my tummy.'

'That'll be the baby,' said a woman's voice, amused. 'The first kicks feel just like bubbles bursting.'

Anna was asleep again.

'She'll be all right,' said Dr Ransom. 'Breathing fine now. I'd like her in for observation, though. Gave us a fright. Has she ever been out this long before? Does she faint much?'

'No,' said Kit. 'But there's never been much cause before, has there?'

'So,' said the doctor, whose supply of professional patience was exhausted by the tension of the last half-hour, 'are you now planning to co-operate with your own treatment? Or do I have to watch you die to indulge your own whims, while poor Anna faints with grief?'

The woman paramedic who had come upstairs from the waiting ambulance was shocked. This was not the way she had been taught to address relatives of stretcher cases. GPs, she thought, employed at times a strangely unprofessional tone. But the husband seemed to take it very meekly.

'I'll come,' he said. 'I'll take the pills. I suppose there's always the chance they won't work.'

The paramedic could stand this no longer. 'If we're taking her in, let's get on with it,' she said. 'Mr Milcourt, will you come in the ambulance?'

'Yes,' said Kit.

Anna was in hospital under observation for three days. Doctors spoke vaguely but reassuringly of hyperventilation, of stress and low blood sugar and the unwisdom of living on nothing but coffee for thirty hours when pregnant. When she was discharged, the baby now moving strongly enough to reassure even her, she went straight down the corridor to the oncology clinic to meet Kit. He was waiting for her, holding a large dispensary paper bag.

'They say I'll feel a bloody lot worse for a week or two,' he said. 'The chemotherapy drugs hit you quite hard.'

'Serve you right,' said Anna. Her heart was too full and still too fearful to be anything but flippant with him within these hospital walls.

He had sat by her bed for some hours of each day, stroking her hand and shushing her fears. When she asked if it was true that he was going for his treatment he only said, 'I thought you were dying. It made me understand how bad it would be for you if *I* was dying. So I can't, yet, can I? I'll have to think of something else.'

The house looked strange when they got home: grimy and oddly diminished. The Boyhood of Raleigh on the dining-room ceiling was perceptibly fading and cracking when they saw it under the merciless spring sunlight; the windows were streaked, and the kitchen at the old house's heart was neat and dead and boring. Almost together they said, 'I'm sick of this house' and 'It's time we moved on.'

Then Kit told Anna about his resignation, and Anna said it was a good thing too, and that she would hand her own in straightaway so they could move at the end of the summer term, well before the baby.

'Where?' asked Kit.

'Don't know,' said Anna. 'We'll try and sell the house, shall we, and rent somewhere?'

'I'll try and get back into the City, shall I?' said Kit. 'I rang some guys I used to know at the bank and they say the insurance companies are getting very keen on people with a background in adventure sports. Setting out conditions, assessing risk, all that stuff.'

'Boring for you,' said Anna. They were talking politely, almost like acquaintances.

'Well, it's only while I think what to do, isn't it? Keep the baby supplied with bootees or whatever the hell they wear. Six-month contracts are all you get these days, anyway.'

Anna wandered to the window and looked out at the sunlit marshes. In a softer, more intimate tone she said, 'I don't know what's going to happen, do you? I'm wiped out.'

'That's right,' said Kit, wonderingly. 'No idea. No more maps.'

'I don't even know if we'll ever make love again,' said Anna, to the marsh. 'I don't know whether I care. I don't know how I feel about any of that stuff. I don't know if I'm going to be permanently afraid of what your demon might do.'

'I've been afraid of him for years, on and off,' said Kit. 'Especially this last year. But that might be the illness. When I was fit it was easier to ignore him.'

'But you'll go on feeling ill for quite a while, the doctor said.'

'So I'll go on being afraid and careful. Every day, all the time. The prospect doesn't thrill me either.'

'But you decided to live.'

'I decided not to leave you, that's all. Not until I have to.'

'It's a start,' said Anna. 'It's a good start. I decided not to leave you, either. Ever.' She turned to him. 'Got to keep an eye on the bubbles, you see. So it's decided, then. We move?'

He took her hands. 'We move. On the road again. *Beyond that last blue mountain barred with snow, across that angry or that glimmering sea.* When we've said a few goodbyes.'

26

Graham Merck was right about the bear-garden. Thank goodness, he thought morosely as he reached his office, that it was the last day of term. A banner hung over the corridor that led to the Year 7 classrooms, saying 'WELCOME BACK BIG BAT'.

Worse, the same slogan was decoratively inscribed on six large sheets of art paper pinned to wooden boards and propped against the outside of the school gates. He knew for a fact that the expensive paper – of a type reserved for GCSE coursework – and the boards had been purloined from the art room without any attempt at prevention by Nellie Armstrong.

There was also evidence, in the form of widely circulated computer graphics of a bat made up of Ms, that the information technology room had been invaded by quite skilled, and there-fore quite senior, pupils. And if any other proof were required of the disruptive influence of Kit Milcourt, he had received a message from his acting deputy head that regrettably she had to take a day's leave of absence for medical reasons.

Medical reasons, my foot! thought Merck in exasperation. Molly just wanted to dissociate herself from anything that might happen. Not, of course, that anything would. It was simply a farewell visit from a well-liked member of staff, suffering from a serious illness (although, naturally, the children did not know the terrible prognosis). Tolerating disruptions of routine was proof of a school's strength, not its weakness. Ronald Harding used to say that. Merck had thought a lot about Ron Harding these past weeks, and for the first time allowed himself to dwell on the man's strengths as well as his inadequacies. A difficult, unwelcome sense was growing within him that things might not be entirely as he had imagined and designed them. Over the past weeks he had suffered queer dreams, of barricades in the streets and lines of battle where he was required to choose a side for some irrevocable eternity of conflict. Always on one side of the barricades were Harding, brighter-faced and more energetic than he was in life, and Kit and Anna Milcourt, and his late mother. On the other side were darker figures, but with a comfortable familiarity about them. He would wake from the dream with an obscure, whimpering, fearful, childish longing to change sides.

Which was, of course, nonsense. There were no sides. He composed himself to work through some papers over the remaining hour and a half before Kit's arrival. Everything would be all right.

After ten minutes the first bell went and he could bear it no longer. He left his office to walk the corridors as Harding once had, between classes, and watch the children. Many of those he saw were wearing the computer images of bats pinned to their jumpers, and one or two had curious bag-like masks on their heads, with pointed black ears. They were laughing, and threw him sly glances. In the Year 7 classrooms, children were opening the dividers – Merck, in his restless confusion, mentally called them *barricades* – between the rooms to make a long open space. Desks were being pushed back to the walls. Merck had no clear idea why, but the children seemed to know exactly what they were doing and he hesitated to question or prevent them.

Suddenly, idiotically, the acting head found himself smiling. He wished Molly Miles was here. Not for his sake, but for hers. Molly, he thought to himself in an unaccustomed idiom that popped unbidden into his mind, really ought to *loosen up*.

'Are you *sure* you're all right?' asked Anna, for the third time.

Kit looked terrible, to her anxious eye; the medication was making him sick and causing his hair visibly to grow thinner and, she imagined, greyer. But Dr Ransom, almost a daily visitor, strongly assured her that the signs were good and that these early weeks of treatment were by far the worst. In any case, Kit's spirits were now high and calm and optimistic. He still took the sleeping pills every night, and woke smiling and saying, 'No dreams. Anna, no dreams. It's years since I didn't have dreams.

If they can stop me dreaming, I can hack anything.' She had found herself able to curl in his arms again as they slept, and feel the baby's tiny bubbling kicks between them.

'Fine,' he said now. And, 'Don't fuss.' Despite the physical weakness, some of his old breezy competence had returned; he had spent his waking hours showing prospective buyers round the house, telephoning old friends about jobs, and negotiating to rent a two-bedroomed flat in Wapping from a former City friend who was abroad for a year. Anna privately thought that a year would be enough: a new baby did not need a garden, but a growing child, in her view, certainly would.

'Will you come into school with me at nine?' she asked. 'Or on your own at break?'

'On my own,' said Kit. So she left him, and at break went straight to the staff room to wait for him.

He never came to the staff room, though. At ten fifteen an expectant crowd of children was gathered by the main gate, and a ragged cheer made Anna and Ian Atkins rush to the window to look out over the comfortless tarmac of the playground. A tall figure in a flapping black coat was advancing towards the children, masked as a bat with prominent pointed cotton ears, its raglan arms outspread into wings.

'Oh, look at that,' said Caroline Chang, joining them more slowly with her stick and short plaster. 'I have now seen everything.' Banners lurched uncertainly on sticks rising from the crowd: WELCOME BACK BIG BAT. The tall figure, followed by a stream of children, was moving towards the classroom block. Anna could see in the front rank of running, skipping, bubbling followers the long tousled hair of Marianne Denver. Kit was pausing now, looking around him; momentarily a space seemed to clear around him and Marianne so Anna could see him look down at the child and hold out his hand, gravely. The two shook hands with formality, and as the throng pressed onward round their leader, Ian Atkins said, 'Now *I've* seen everything.'

Anna watched the black figure moving far beneath her like the diver in the dream. Distant laughter frothed up to her in bubbles of sound from the children who swirled around him. She watched until they were all gone, following the tall flapping figure into the building and along the corridors towards the Year

7 classrooms. Even with the screens open, those rooms, surely, could not contain the mob.

'Half the school? No, maybe a third? Well over a hundred of them, anyway,' said Caroline. 'Is there any point the rest of us even trying to teach?'

'No,' said Ian. 'Not the juniors, anyway. Shall we go along and press our faces to the glass and see what's going on?'

'No,' said Anna. 'Leave him alone with them. He has to say goodbye. It's his last class.'

She turned away from the window and the empty playground, and made herself smile, rather than weeping.

THAT WAS THEN

SARAH HARRISON

Newly single, safe and sorted . . .

Eve's separation from Ian is amicable, her daughter Mel is a high-flier, and her son Ben, the apple of her eye, is the local charmer. She has a congenial job, good friends, and all the time in the world to improve her tennis. But passion is no respecter of plans, and Eve's chaste tranquility, like Ben's boyhood teddy, is about to go out of the window with a vengeance. Because when sons grow up, mothers must too . . .

Praise for Sarah Harrison:

'believable and touching . . . Harrison's writing is lively, crisp [and] full of humour.' *The Times*

'moving and funny' *YOU Magazine*

Sarah Harrison lives with her family in Cambridgeshire. Her previous novels, LIFE AFTER LUNCH and FLOWERS WON'T FAX (Shortlisted for the 1997 RNA Award) are available from Hodder & Stoughton.

The author of twelve novels, she has written several children's books, short stories, articles and scripts and is also a regular broadcaster on Radio 4.

HODDER AND STOUGHTON PAPERBACKS

A selection of bestsellers from Hodder and Stoughton

Home Leave	Libby Purves	0 340 68041 5	£6.99	☐
That was Then	Sarah Harrison	0 340 70731 3	£6.99	☐
In the Heart of the Garden	Helene Wiggin	0 340 69571 4	£6.99	☐
The Trespassers	Pam Rhodes	0 340 71236 8	£5.99	☐
Kinvara	Christine Marion Fraser	0 340 70714 3	£5.99	☐
Defrosting Edmund	Nina Dufort	0 340 71682 7	£6.99	☐
The Bobbin Girls	Freda Lightfoot	0 340 67438 5	£5.99	☐
A Promise Given	Meg Hutchinson	0 340 69684 2	£5.99	☐

All Hodder & Stoughton books are available at your local bookshop or newsagent, or can be ordered direct from the publisher. Just tick the titles you want and fill in the form below. Prices and availability subject to change without notice.

Hodder & Stoughton Books, Cash Sales Department, Bookpoint, 39 Milton Park, Abingdon, OXON, OX14 4TD, UK. E-mail address: order@bookpoint.co.uk. If you have a credit card you may order by telephone – (01235) 400414.

Please enclose a cheque or postal order made payable to Bookpoint Ltd to the value of the cover price and allow the following for postage and packing:
UK & BFPO – £1.00 for the first book, 50p for the second book, and 30p for each additional book ordered up to a maximum charge of £3.00.
OVERSEAS & EIRE – £2.00 for the first book, £1.00 for the second book, and 50p for each additional book.

Name _____

Address_____

_____

_____

If you would prefer to pay by credit card, please complete:
Please debit my Visa/Access/Diner's Card/American Express (delete as applicable) card no:

Signature _____

Expiry Date_____

If you would NOT like to receive further information on our products please tick the box. ☐